THE
SKIDS

FIRST EDITION

The Skids © 2016 by Ian Donald Keeling
Cover artwork © 2016 by Erik Mohr
Cover and interior design by © 2016 by Samantha Beiko

Distributed in Canada by
PGC Raincoast Books
300-76 Stafford Street
Toronto, ON M6J 2S1
Phone: (416) 934-9900
e-mail: info@pgcbooks.ca

Distributed in the U.S. by
Consortium Book Sales & Distribution
34 Thirteenth Avenue, NE, Suite 101
Minneapolis, MN 55413
Phone: (612) 746-2600
e-mail: sales.orders@cbsd.com

Library and Archives Cataloguing Data

Keeling, Ian Donald, author

   The skids / Ian Donald Keeling.

Issued in print and electronic formats.

ISBN 978-1-77148-385-8 (paperback).--ISBN 978-1-77148-386-5 (pdf)

   I. Title.

PS8621.E35S55 2016   jC813'.6   C2016-904212-X

                                          C2016-904213-8

CHITEEN
An imprint of ChiZine Publications
Peterborough, Canada
www.chizinepub.com
info@chizinepub.com

Edited by Samantha Beiko
Proofread by Leigh Teetzel

Shelfie

A free eBook edition is available
with the purchase of this print book.

CLEARLY PRINT YOUR NAME ABOVE IN UPPER CASE

Instructions to claim your free eBook edition:
1. Download the Shelfie app for Android or iOS
2. Write your name in **UPPER CASE** above
3. Use the Shelfie app to submit a photo
4. Download your eBook to any device

Canada Council   Conseil des arts
for the Arts   du Canada

We acknowledge the support of the Canada Council for the Arts which last year invested $20.1 million in writing and publishing throughout Canada.

ONTARIO ARTS COUNCIL
CONSEIL DES ARTS DE L'ONTARIO
an Ontario government agency
un organisme du gouvernement de l'Ontario

Published with the generous assistance of the Ontario Arts Council.

Printed in Canada

IAN DONALD KEELING

THE SKIDS

CHI·TEEN

For my Grandfather, Donald Keeling, for teaching me how to dream, and to my nephew Bruce, for showing me how to smile.

CHAPTER ONE

Johnny almost died when he missed a popper on the Slope.

Crisp Betty, he thought, clamping a Hasty-Arm to a ledge just below the popper. *Gotta catch that. Stupid way to lose a game.* His entire body—an electric blue ball with tank treads and white racing stripes—quivered with disgust. He swung one of his three eyes around: where was Albert?

Right there: a silver ball of hate dropping out of the sky for the kill.

"Snakes," Johnny swore, retracting the eyeball and hurling himself off the ledge. He had to launch with the Hasty-Arm so he didn't have much speed, but fortunately he caught another skid on the way down. Stealing the skid's kinetic energy, Johnny greased his treads flat and rebounded like a rocket in the opposite direction. Albert passed through the space that Johnny and the surprised skid just vacated, scorching dust and swearing like a sailor. Johnny absorbed the Hasty-Arm back into his body and swung his eyes around.

One hundred metres below, nuzzled against the sixty-five-degree Slope, Johnny spotted a flat-top. Lousy points, but right now he needed to regain control more than he needed the points. He created a windshear with the left side of his body, dug in with the right side of his treads, bounced off a tree and angled onto the flat-top with a satisfying thud.

Johnny peered up all two hundred kilometers of the Slope, one of the twelve games the skids lived to play. Scanning for action, he examined each rock, ledge and tree. Not a lot going on. *Strange.* He checked his internal speedometer for his last speed. Two hundred and eighty kilometers an hour. At least he'd hit the flat-top at a decent gas; that would count for a bit. He remembered a magenta-gold flash and realised the other skid he'd hit might have been Torg.

Wonder if I popped him?

A faint grinding sound. *Learn to stealth your treads, squid,* Johnny thought contemptuously, digging in. A wave of dust and a sudden elastic jolt, followed by a popping sound, cursing, and an orange-yellow blur, fading into the ether. No doubt about that one.

Someone just got evaporated.

Technically, the Slope was a race—with a start and a finish—but the real way to win was to pop other skids. Collide with another skid the right way and *Pop!*—away they went, sailing off into the ether, falling until they hit the killing sea far below. Johnny wouldn't really have died if he'd been popped—they didn't waste Level Eights; only the Level Ones and Twos who'd yet to learn full control of their molecules. But getting vaped still sucked. It usually took Johnny a couple of hours to pull his body back together, during which time he might miss a game.

Plus, dying on the Slope meant losing and Johnny did not lose on the Slope. Not on any day if he could help it, but especially not today.

Today, he was chasing immortality.

Razor thin transparencies—shimmering like flames and knocked from the skid Johnny just vaped—drifted down and settled in the dust. "Somebody's gonna need to buy new tatts," he chuckled. Swinging an eye, he spotted Danica on a rounder, locked in and launched.

A fantail of dust billowed out in Johnny's wake. How GameCorps got the dust to stick to the Slope no one knew, but it looked good when the skids skid. And that meant ratings. And ratings meant that someone, somewhere . . . was *watching*.

Johnny popped Danica—a Level Four—then scanned the Slope. He spotted a magenta-gold ball, covered in skins and tatts, resting on a pebble one hundred and fifty metres down and to the right. *Didn't think so*, Johnny thought with a grin. You weren't going to pop Torg on a clearslope, even in freeskid. Torg was a Level Nine, one of only five.

There were no Level Tens. Hadn't been in fifty years, not since Betty Crisp. Ten lifetimes since the only skid to hold two names.

Since a skid had been *remembered*.

Torg was balling in his direction. He winked when Johnny made eye contact. "Come get me, squid." A *squid* was a Level Two skid. Torg was in a playful mood.

"On a pebble?" Johnny laughed. "Not on your tread, you old panzer." A *panzer* was a Level One.

Torg was bluffing, one of the oldest Slope tricks. Attempting to pop any remotely experienced skid resting on a pebble was suicidal. Sure, pebbles were the smallest outcropping on the Slope and offered the most tenuous hold. Landing on one at any speed was tricky and worth huge points. Theoretically, popping a skid off a pebble should've been easy.

Theoretically.

Johnny had seen Torg kill legions of skids simply by getting out of the way. A sly grin would cross the older skid's ball as the inexperienced panzer or squid popped off the tiny outcropping into the ether. As Torg was fond of saying, "Even Betty Crisp couldn't latch a pebble at dropspeed."

"That was some nice moves up there, son," Torg drawled.

"I was lucky," Johnny admitted. "Never should have had to do it in the first place. I missed a popper." A popper was the most common outcropping on the Slope: medium size, average friction. Most of the action took place on poppers; that's where they got the name.

Torg laughed. "Too much sugar at the bar, Johnny?" He extended a Hasty-Arm and waved it in the general direction of the sky. "Careful. All Out There's probably watching today."

No skid really knew who watched the games they played. Whoever they were, they came from . . . Out There. No one knew how long the Skidsphere had existed. A few hundred years, maybe more. Maybe a lot more. And no one knew who'd created the skids, or why they'd been created this way, or why they lived for exactly five years . . . and then died. Perhaps if they lived longer, they could've asked more questions. Perhaps they could've found some answers.

Perhaps that's why they all died at five.

Laughter drifted up the Slope. Johnny swung an eyeball down—keeping one on Torg and the third looking upslope—to find Albert resting on a popper a hundred metres below Torg.

"Nearly popped you, Johnny." Albert's grin split his silver skin, stretching out to his eight razor-thin racing stripes. "Would have been a while."

"Keep dreaming, squinty." Johnny smiled as he watched Albert's chronically damaged third eye flinch. The grin on what had once been his best friend's face faded.

All most skids could do was play the games, eat some sugar, run a race, have some fun. *Live fast, die fast*, the saying went. After all, you couldn't live forever. If you were lucky and good, maybe—*maybe*—you'd make it to Level Nine before you died.

Except that fifty years ago, there'd been a skid named Betty. A skid who'd set records in every single game: who'd owned the Slope and the Rainbow Road. Who'd done the Leap. The only skid who, when she died, had made Level Ten and been given a second name.

The only skid with two: Betty Crisp.

That name was still talked about by skids—in the games or in-between—at the sugarbars where the skids came down and got high; on the highlight hollas that ran every day and everywhere. And if the skids still talked about Betty Crisp, and the hollas *still* talked about Betty Crisp, then maybe . . . somewhere . . . Out There. . . .

Sometime in their third year, not long after they'd each made Level Six—months younger than any skid in memory—Albert and Johnny began to realize that while they were both special . . . Johnny might be more than that.

Albert could've supported his friend. Instead, months later, on the night Johnny made Eight, Albert had loudly declared that Johnny was going to die the only Level Nine-Point-Nine in history.

It took a lot to damage a skid permanently without killing them. On the night Albert coined the concept of Nine-Point-Nine—a phrase that for some reason hurt and terrified Johnny more than anything he'd seen or heard or felt before—Johnny had done a lot to Albert.

The amazing thing, most skids agreed, was that it wasn't the only reason they hated each other.

Dust settled onto Albert's third eye, which blinked rapidly several times. Then the silver and white grin swung into place again.

"You don't need to die today, Johnny," Albert said. "Slope's clear and I got three hundred metres on you. Betty Crisp's record is going to see another year." He waved a Hasty-Arm at the sky. "Do you think they'll really care?"

"More about me than . . ." Johnny stopped. "Wait— *what did you say?*"

"Squid's right, Johnny," Torg drawled. "Think I'm sitting on my treads for a bleach? Slope's clear. Danica was the last one. 'Fraid it's just us three."

"Impossible." Johnny scanned the entire slope. Nothing moving. But that wasn't possible. They still had more than thirty kilometers left in the run. Johnny couldn't even hear the sea yet.

"While you were slipping off rocks, Torg and I were busy cleaning house," Albert purred.

Johnny checked his inner tally. You could win the Slope without hitting the finish line first—it happened all the time, even though most skids couldn't seem to grasp that pivotal truth. First place got full points, but top fifty got partials. It was popping skids that mattered.

Unless, of course, it was close.

Johnny had done well on the upper slope, popped more than his share. He did the math. *Way too close to tell*. Especially with only three of them left and Torg and Albert cleaning house. If Albert hit the finish line first, he'd probably win. And all he had to do was hold a two hundred and fifty metre lead on a clear slope. Which meant . . .

"Later, Johnny," Albert said, and began the Drop.

It was very rare. But if the upper slope cleared, leaving only a couple of skids near the bottom—a couple of *high level* skids who were too canny to be popped—then strategy evaporated and there would be a freeskid to the sea.

The Drop.

This is bad, Johnny thought, even as he hurled himself downwards. He'd never heard of a Drop starting this high on the Slope. Not that it mattered, after a certain point height became irrelevant. No matter how hard you launched, once everyone hit terminal velocity the race was basically over. And Albert had two hundred and fifty metres on Johnny. Which meant Johnny was going to lose.

Had it been on the Skates, Johnny might have stomached a loss to Albert. Albert was murder on the Skates. But Johnny couldn't lose on the Slope. He couldn't.

Of all the records Betty Crisp set, her greatest was on the Slope, by far the highest rated game. Two hundred and seventeen straight races, more than an entire season. That was the astounding thing about the record—you only got one shot at it.

Most skids spent their first two years dinking around as Ones and Twos, learning to hold it together, happy to survive. Occasionally, they might get a top ten in something—Johnny had, several times—but for the most part, they were happy with not dying.

Somewhere around the end of year two—at Level Three or Four when dying mercifully became more metaphorical—a skid might start winning games. Streaks rarely came before Level Five and up. So by the time a skid could put together a real streak on the Slope, they were into their fifth year, with no time to start again.

Johnny's current consecutive win streak on the Slope stood at two hundred and sixteen. If he won today, he'd tie Betty Crisp's unassailable record. If he lost . . .

There were nineteen Slope races left in the season. Next year, his fifth, a full season of one hundred and twenty.

There would be no sixth year.

Dust-tails from Torg and Albert threw up a cloud, bringing a second layer of protective thinlids down over Johnny's eyes. He was dropping nearly blind now, but it didn't matter. He'd telescoped in the milliseconds before he'd launched and had a clear line to the finish. He threw everything into his treads, desperate to gain on Albert and Torg. And he was gaining. He could sense it, metre by metre; he was stronger on his treads, he'd had the best launch. Maybe . . .

He felt an unmistakable shift in his equilibrium. Terminal velocity, with Torg and Albert still ahead. Which meant he'd lost. You couldn't go any faster.

Unless . . .

The truly terrifying thing for Johnny, the thought that had haunted him for months, was that he could win today, he could match Betty Crisp's most impressive record . . . and it still wouldn't matter. Because the records were important, but they weren't why Betty Crisp was remembered.

In the end, Betty Crisp was remembered for the Leap.

She'd done it on the Rainbow Road, a five hundred kilometer long, twisting, looping, multi-coloured track, hanging in empty space. Her record on the line. Caught in the pack, kilometers behind the lead. Three-quarters done.

Screwed.

And then, in the most shocking move a skid had ever seen, Betty Crisp had committed suicide. She'd swerved violently to the left, off the track and into empty space. Half the skids got knocked out of the race this way: falling for seconds, sometimes minutes, into the eviscerating void.

Betty Crisp had done it deliberately.

To fall, not into the void, not to her death, but down about four hundred metres . . . onto another section of the winding, looping, multi-coloured, *multi-level* track.

Four kilometers from the finish line.

There wasn't a skid alive who hadn't told that story a hundred times. And the Out There had noticed: first, when a new game called the Leap had been added by GameCorps; and, finally, when Betty Crisp had died with a second name.

Johnny needed to do more than break one of Betty Crisp's records. He needed to do something that they'd talk about forever.

This is such a bad idea, Johnny thought, even as he did something no skid had done before. He created a miniature windshear, shifting trajectory ever-so-slightly, and caromed into a tree at terminal velocity.

Skids moved by stealing energy. Their treads might get them moving, might be good for a stroll, but they moved by stealing energy. Most often, kinetic energy from moving objects like other skids. But they were also engineered to steal *potential* energy. Which meant they could hit even stationary objects to increase their speed. Theoretically, without limit.

Though there were other limitations besides energy.

His third and last set of thinlids snapped into place as he caromed off another tree and—for the first time in his life—Johnny felt some serious pain from impact. His vision dimmed and blurred, which was going to be a problem. He had to see, because if he hit anything smaller than a tree it would pop him at these speeds. Johnny knew the Slope like the back of his treads, but everything was slashing at him with a quickness almost impossible to anticipate. He was trying to manoeuver during a Drop, praying he didn't kill himself before the finish.

His speedometer crept towards a thousand kilometers per hour. He was pretty sure he was now moving faster than any skid had ever moved before.

A magenta-gold blur flashed by on his left—what might have been a call of surprise. Then silver and white, dangerously close. This time there was a definite curse.

Johnny was in the lead. He was also in serious trouble.

An ugly burning came from his treads, even though he'd moulded them near frictionless. He didn't know what kind of shape he was in, but it sure the *hole* wasn't round anymore. No longer able to see, not even pretending he was still in control, Johnny banged off another tree and increased speed again, plummeting towards the finish line less than a kilometer away.

The finish line was going to be a major problem.

Two hundred metres above the killing sea, a thick red line marked the end of the Slope. One hundred and fifty metres below that—a mere fifty metres above the waves that would eviscerate a skid's skin—were a series of wide, flat ledges. If a Slope was finished at speed, any skids that survived used the ledges as a final safety barrier. Even after a fast race, landing on a ledge was relatively easy. A panzer could do it. During a Drop, it was trickier. There was a reason why only experienced skids did the Drop. Even Torg had died once. As he often said: "Hitting anything at terminal velocity is just wrong, son."

Johnny hit the finish line a few kilometers per hour shy of the sound barrier.

A millisecond later he plowed into a ledge and was instantly crushed flat. Agony ripped through his body; he struggled to hold onto consciousness. Onto his molecules. If he evaporated from impacting with a ledge—which he was certain had never been done—then it was the same as dying: he'd lose and it would all mean nothing.

It was close. The first thing that told Johnny he was still alive was a strange wafting sensation. He realised it was his third eyeball, pounded flat: hanging over the ledge and flapping in the wind. *Eewww*, he thought, and wondered how long before he had the strength to pull himself back into a ball.

The second thing that told Johnny he was still alive was the sound of cheering. All around him, thousands upon thousands of skids he didn't know, losing their freaking minds. The sound of cheering, so loud it reached into the sky and maybe—just maybe—into somewhere beyond the sky.

Out There.

Johnny's flattened teeth worked themselves into a grin. He was thinking about his second name.

CHAPTER TWO

"No more!" Johnny cried, as another skid approached with a tray of swizz. "If I have any more sugar, I'm gonna hurl."

The Level Three flashed a grin and deposited the tray at Johnny's tongue. "I said the same thing when I got my name and it didn't stop you from getting me vaped. Suffer, squid."

In fact, it'd been only a few weeks since Johnny and a couple of the older skids had taken the two new Threes— Tosh and Shi—pit-hopping and left them absolutely twisted. It was a tradition he and Albert had started when they were Fours. Now it was coming back to haunt Johnny.

The Slope pit was packed. Slide Rock thrummed through the room, pulsing in time with the morass of colour on the dance floor. Johnny's booth overflowed with skids whose only intention was to leave the newest Nine choking on his own tongue.

Which he might have done even if he wasn't so twisted.

Only a few hours had passed since the Slope and Johnny's body still ached. They'd had to carry him to the podium after the race, as he slowly rounded back into something resembling normal. Then he was carried straight from the podium to the bar by an entourage that seemed to number every skid with a name. He was already half-vaped when a holla from GameCorps flashed to inform the vibrating pit that the hero of the day had been upgraded to Level Nine for his historic performance. And that wasn't all GameCorps had announced.

"So the squid got another stripe." Torg's voice cut through the din and a space was made. "What does flat feel like, Johnny?" The booth roared its approval.

"Like your mother on a good day, you old panzer. Tongue some of this, for the love of Crisp." Johnny bobbed an eye towards the massive pile of sugar. "Any more and I'm going to evaporate."

"And here I thought the squid could hold his sweet." The older skid stuck out his tongue and took a taste. "Now this is fine," he said appreciatively.

"Refined," Johnny intoned. "Leticia brought out the good stuff."

"Crisp, nobody treated me like this when I made Nine."

"That's because they didn't have sugar back then. And you're full of grease, because I remember leaving you singing war songs on the Spike."

"Yeah, between Albert and then you, I'd say I got treated right that night."

On cue, a voice said, "I'm glad you think so. It cost me a few points."

The crowd parted and Albert tread up to the table. The group tensed as Johnny's eyes stopped drifting and narrowed into slits, but Albert was grinning and had two eyes on Torg. "I thought skids who tongued that much sugar ended up in rehab."

"I wish," Torg snorted. "I could've used the publicity."

Albert swung an eye towards the hero of the hour. "Johnny."

"Albert," Johnny said coolly.

Albert caught the tone, hesitated, then said, "That was a pretty stupid stunt you pulled today, panzer."

Johnny looked directly into Albert's damaged eye. "Glad you were there to see it, Albert."

That definitely brought a hush to the table.

Torg broke it with a bark of laughter. "Crisp Betty," the older skid swore, "why don't you two just snug and get on with it."

The corner of Albert's mouth twitched. "I don't think that's going to happen anytime soon." His damaged eye remained centred on Johnny. "I just came by to congratulate the newest Nine. I'd buy you some sugar, but I can see you've had enough." He turned and bobbed an eye. "Torg." Then he disappeared back into the throng.

"Come back soon," Johnny muttered, sniffing sugar.

"He did offer congratulations, Johnny," Torg said softly.

"Only 'cause he'd look like a jackhole if he didn't."

"Well," Torg drawled, "we wouldn't want to do that now, would we?"

The music shifted and the crowd at Johnny's table poured onto the dance floor. Bian, a Level Seven, drifted by the booth before following the crowd.

"You've got an admirer," Torg growled, watching the blood-red skid glide away. She had glit all over her seven yellow stripes and sparkles trailed in her wake. "Funny, I thought she was with Albert."

"She's a Level jumper," Johnny sniffed. "And that Eight just got jumped."

"That is true," Torg agreed.

"Hold up," Johnny said, leaning forward. "They're running the 'lights."

At the far side of the bar, a massive holla showed scenes from the Slope. The more spectacular moments flashed by—Albert had popped three skids in one shot; even Johnny had to admit that was sweet. The number of competitors dwindled; a shot of Torg, Albert and Johnny hanging out . . . and then the Drop.

He'd already seen it twice, but Johnny wasn't watching the race. He was waiting for the announcement at the end.

"Say it," he whispered, his stripes pulsing once.

The rest of the bar had gone silent. Which never happened. Skids scanned their own highlights, but rarely paid attention to even the most extraordinary events more than once. Too little time between games, too much sugar to inhale. Living fast. . . .

In the holla, Johnny crossed the finish line. He watched as his body was crushed flat, unaware that he winced a little at the impact.

"Say it," he whispered.

The frantic play-by-play faded out, replaced by the formal GameCorps announcement that the winner of that day's Slope—who had tied Betty Crisp's record for consecutive wins—was now the youngest Nine in the history of the Skidsphere. And the name of that skid . . .

"Say it."

. . . was Johnny Drop.

"TWO NAMES!" Johnny screamed, and the entire bar, save one, screamed with him. "MY NAME IS JOHNNY DROP!" All three of his eyes swung towards Albert.

"That's right, you panzer-squid! How many names you got?"

The cheering began to die as the bar stared at him in shock. To his side, someone murmured, "Snakes, Johnny. . . ."

Johnny's stripes flared, filling half his body as they pulsed hot-white. Up on his treads, two Hasty-Arms popped out as if to envelope the pit.

"How many names, *Albert*?" he sneered, spitting Albert's name like it was rotten. "How's Level Eight feel, you grease sucking squid!"

Across the bar, the silver-white skid looked back, his eyes flat. Very slowly, he extended his own Hasty-Arms—hands spread except for a single tucked thumb—and deliberately tapped the air twice.

Nine, nine.

"*Vape me!*" Johnny screamed, lunging forward. "You think anyone's going to remember you, you—"

"*And . . . that's enough.*"

A hand snapped forward and wrapped around all three of Johnny's eye-stalks. Which *hurt.* "Hey!" Johnny cried. He tried to shake free, but froze when a spike shot through his eyes like the pain he'd felt on the Slope.

"Come with me, champ," Torg said calmly, twisting out of the booth. Skids cleared out of the way, staring. All three of Johnny's eyes teared up. He tried to bring down a thinlid but it got stuck halfway.

"Snakes," Johnny swore. "Leggo, Torg, that kills."

"Once we're outside."

His fellow Nine dragged him out the back door and hurled him by the eye-stalks—*Crisp Betty, that hurt*—into a pile of sugar.

"Oww, oww, oww," Johnny spat, waving his eyes apart and blinking furiously. "Don't ever do that again, Torg."

"Don't earn it," Torg growled. "Honestly, what the hole was that? You just got a second name, squid. How about a little magnanimous joy?"

"That was joy," Johnny muttered, massaging his eye-stalks.

"Really? 'Cause that looked a lot like rage to me, Johnny."

"He deserves it."

"Does he?"

Torg's second eye swung in Johnny's direction. That wasn't something a skid could ignore for long. "What?" Johnny said sullenly.

"You know what I saw in there? I saw a skid that hates your treads but came over to congratulate you anyway. And then I saw you treat him like tread-grease in front of the whole bar."

"Don't care," Johnny mumbled, although his second eye dropped away, unable to hold Torg's gaze.

Torg looked up into the night sky. "You know, Johnny, you're the one who's always talking about getting remembered. We all think about it from time to time, but you . . . you're obsessed. And now that you got yourself a second name . . ."—the older skid's eyes widened as he said it—"I'd say you have a pretty good shot." His gaze fell back from the sky. Held Johnny's for a beat. "You might want to think about what kind of skid you want them to remember, son."

Johnny felt like he was deflating. His stripes dimmed. After a moment, he whispered, "He killed her, Torg."

"Aww, snakes," Torg sighed. "Johnny, I think you're great, and I know for some reason this is hard for you, but you don't know that. Hole, even if you did, you gotta let it go."

"I can't." Johnny's voice grew hard, his stripes pulsing.

"You have to. No skid—"

"*I can't!*" Johnny screamed. "What do you think happened, Torg? You believe his story? She just disappeared? Is that it? You think she just vaped herself—poof—and that's it?"

Torg sat on his treads like he was embedded in the ground. His first and second eyes closed a little. "And just what do you think Albert could have done to her?" he said gently.

There was a great hole in Johnny's heart. He'd won his second name today. He'd come from behind during a Drop. From this moment on, he was probably immortal.

Why didn't it feel like it mattered?

"I don't know," he whispered, and this time he did deflate, his body visibly shrinking. "But he . . . she couldn't just . . ."

Torg rolled forward and nudged Johnny's tread. "Hey, I get it. I liked her too. Not like you, but Peg was grand. But you got to let it . . ." He stopped. "You feel that?"

All three of Johnny's eyes had already swung outwards, his whole body on alert. "Yeah."

Almost imperceptibly, the ground beneath their treads was trembling.

Four eyes swung and met. "Corpsquake," Torg and Johnny said together.

No skid knew why GameCorps sent them corpsquakes; most assumed it was to mix up the highlight shows every once in a while. Most quakes were harmless, causing the ground to tremble a bit every few months. Quakes that did any real damage were rare.

But they weren't unknown.

"Probably just a shaker," Torg said. "Nothing to . . ."

The ground beneath their feet pulsed once, like a

speaker cranked to full. A tearing sound filled the air.

"Or not," Torg sighed.

Behind them, the sugarbar was pulsing to its own vibe, the music pounding. No way anyone would sense the quake until it was too late.

Johnny and Torg gunned their treads. Bursting through the doors, they screamed: "CORPSQUAKE!"

Too late.

The tearing sound accelerated into a roar and the entire bar shifted to the left. Hard.

"Get out!" Johnny yelled, grabbing the first skid he saw—it was Bian—and hurling her through the door. The ceiling cracked and part of it collapsed. Johnny pushed a Five out from under the falling debris, flattening out to avoid getting squashed himself.

On the dance floor, Albert gathered skids, one of the few helping out; most raced for the doors without a second thought for anyone else. Albert had been the first inside to react to the quake, which Johnny had to concede wasn't that surprising. Albert was a gearbox, but no one said he was slow.

A pillar behind Albert began to topple, but the silver skid had all three eyes pointed front. Johnny saw it and for a split second didn't move. Then his conscience kicked in—*Oh what the hole*—and he dived for the Level Eight, pushing him away before the pillar crashed to the floor.

An eye swung back, looked at the pillar, then looked at Johnny. "Thanks," Albert said. "Now stop wasting time and protect the Ones and Twos."

Johnny felt like slapping himself in the eye. The panzers and squids were the only ones in any real danger. Dumb, dumb, dumb. That Albert had realized it first made Johnny cringe.

Swinging around, he spotted a squid about to get crushed by a speaker. Gearing up, he shoved the Two out of harm's way.

"Outside, people," he heard Torg yell. "Looks like this one's going to—"

As suddenly as it had begun, the trembling stopped.

". . . last," Torg finished. He hesitated, then swung a sloppy grin towards Johnny. "You know, sometimes I take great pleasure in being mistaken."

"Anyone hurt bad?" Johnny asked, scanning the room.

"Panzer got vaped," a Six said, standing next to a jagged crack in the ground. "Floor just opened and shut. Yellow-maroon kid."

"Oh," Johnny said, his eyes dipping. Squids and panzers got vaped all the time. But to have it happen outside a game . . . "Anyone . . . anyone know his name?"

A silence.

"Uh, Johnny?" Torg said. "He was a panzer. He didn't have a name."

The silence hovered for a moment, then everyone began to move. Sure it was sad, but skids died all the time. Across the room, Albert wore an expression that matched how Johnny felt: like he'd been the one permanently vaped. The silver skid caught Johnny's gaze, held it, then left the bar without saying anything.

Johnny stayed and began cleaning up the mess, even though GameCorps would have the pit rebuilt by morning. As he hauled rubble, Johnny found his gaze kept wandering towards the crack in the dance floor.

He'd earned his second name today. Some skids never got the time to earn one.

CHAPTER THREE

The next day, Johnny went to visit Peg.

On the way, he passed the SlopeMart. Skids of every level—mostly Ones and Twos—poured in and out, beneath a blazing marquee that could be seen for kilometers.

The Marts were where skids spent most of their points. A few points might get spent in the sugarbars, but the pits weren't really that expensive. After all, too much swizz might get you twisted, but every skid needed a little daily sugar to survive, especially the panzers who didn't have any points to spend yet.

The merch inside the Marts wasn't vital, but skids blew mass points on it anyway. Skids couldn't change their basic colours or the number of their stripes, but they could glam them up with skins and tattgrams, glit and shim. Coloured thinlids of every shade and hue under the sphere, signature prints for your treads, bubbles or lightning or fire to trail in your wake. Skids bought the newest Slide Rock tunes to accompany their entrance at the start of a game and custom fireworks to go off at the finish. Johnny knew of a Seven who looked like a rug, and a Five who owned a soundbyte that cried *Boo-yah!* every time she popped someone. Every skid shopped at the Mart.

Except two.

Peering through the garish window displays, Johnny remembered the first and only time he'd stepped into a Mart. Barely a month old, a single stripe on his side. He and Albert had just won their first serious points: Johnny with a top thirty on the Slope, Albert with one on the Skates. Both *way* too young to have finished that high; cocky and looking to trumpet their score. They'd gone Mart-surfing, searching for hours to find just the right thing to make them stand out. Fittingly, they'd been in this very Mart when Johnny had abruptly pulled up, surrounded by glit, shims, and sheens.

"It's all meaningless," he'd whispered, shocked. "There isn't a single thing here that would help you in a game."

He remembered catching Albert's gaze. He remembered exactly—*Snakes, it was vivid*—how quick Al had got it.

They weren't going to buy anything. That's how they'd stand out.

Even though years had passed and the friendship was dust, Johnny and Albert were still the only two skids with more than one stripe who played without any fanfare, any fireworks, any glam.

Amazing how clear that showed on the 'lights.

A spark popped in front of Johnny's eyes and he blinked. He shook himself, blinking again. *Fond memories of Albert*, he thought with a smirk. *Torg's right, I gotta cut back on the sugar.* He stared through the window a moment longer, then he grunted and rolled away.

As he rounded the corner of the Mart, he saw a smudge of black near the bottom of the wall and shuddered.

Skids called it 'black moss.' It came and went, mostly near the Spike. Sometimes in a race there'd be a spot on the course. Johnny hated the stuff. He didn't know why, he just knew it made him nervous. The one time he'd seen it on the Rainbow Road he'd been so rattled he almost sailed off the edge.

Never seen it on a Mart, he thought, glaring at the black blotch. His stripes twitched. Sometimes GameCorps had a gear jammed up their stripes.

Leaving the Mart behind, he headed for the Spike.

The Spike sat near the edge of the Skidsphere, beyond the other games. If a skid tread out past Tag Box and the Slope, past the Combine where the panzers and squids tried to figure it out, down a long tree-lined path, eventually they'd come to a clearing. And in the centre of that clearing . . . sat the Spike. Twenty-one metres tall, a metre wide at the base. Tapering ever-so-slightly as it rose from a circular clearing fifty metres in diameter.

It was the biggest mystery the skids had.

Some thought it was a communications tower. Many believed that this was where the Skidsphere began—that the Spike was part of an ancient game, created by the Out There, long since abandoned. Indeed, even though it sat at the edge of the Skidsphere, most skids considered the Spike its heart.

Of course, a lot of skids thought GameCorps created it just so skids would have a place to make-out.

Johnny tread down the path towards the Spike, the leaves in the oak trees to either side rustling in the wind. *They look better that way*, he mused.

He was in a very strange mood.

Yesterday, he'd been given a second name. Only the

second skid ever to have one. Unless there was some forgotten skid somewhere in the bowels of time.

"*See*," he muttered, grinding his teeth. "Where the hole did that thought come from?"

He should have been filled with joy. Transcendent. He was Johnny Drop, now and for the rest of time. He would be remembered. So few skids could say that.

He didn't feel transcendent.

Stopping a few metres inside the clearing, he looked up. He'd always found the Spike comforting, ever since he'd discovered it alongside Albert in their first year, not long after they'd sworn off the Mart. Almost a lifetime ago. There was something about its permanence that settled Johnny. When he looked up at it, it was like he could hear it whispering to him: *It's all right kid, some things last.*

"Not all things," he murmured, turning away from the Spike. There were dozens of nooks and crannies tucked into the woods where skids might come to fool around. Johnny tread for one. He knew it would be empty.

At the back of the clearing, with the glade's entrance blocked by the Spike to lend the illusion of privacy, there was a hollow, smaller than the rest. And inside that space, there was a stone.

New things appeared from time-to-time on the Skidsphere, the odd touch here and there to splash things up for the viewers. The black moss was only one example. So when a new stone had appeared six months ago—about one third of a skid's size, polished on one side and rough on the other—it wasn't that surprising.

That it had appeared a few days after a skid had gone missing struck some as peculiar. That the stone had her name, clear and distinct, etched in its surface. . . .

"Hey, Peg," Johnny said, rolling up to the stone.

Every skid knew the story. It was etched into the current skidlore like some mythic tragedy. Half a year ago, a Level Six named Peg was seen rolling into the glade near the relic called the Spike. A few minutes later, a Seven named Albert had been seen doing the same.

Peg was never seen again.

The incident occurred in a blindspot. Holla coverage was spotty at best near the Spike; that was why so many skids used it to get a little privacy. So no one saw what happened.

Had Peg been a One or a Two, it might have been an easy call; at least then she could've somehow been vaped. But Peg had been a Six—bordering on Seven—she knew how to control her molecules.

Still . . . getting vaped was more plausible than what Albert had claimed.

Albert never told anyone why he was out there with Peg, who was seeing Johnny at the time. Most made the self-evident guess—skids were notorious for jumping from skid to skid. Johnny and Albert's feud was already old news: Albert had thrown the first 'Nine-Nine' at Johnny's treads a couple of months before, getting a damaged eye in return. Trying to score time with Johnny's girl was an obvious play.

Whatever the reason, Albert claimed they hadn't been there long when the ground opened up and swallowed Peg whole.

Even skids sympathetic to Albert found that a stretch. There'd been no corpsquake that day, and a couple of Fives who'd been making a little time on the other side of the Spike claimed they'd heard and seen nothing: no ripping sounds, no flashes of light. Granted, they might have been distracted.

At a sugarbar a few days after Peg died, Johnny went

a step beyond skepticism: he accused Albert of murder. Most skids had already moved on. Skids died everyday— yeah, it was weird she was a Six, but who had time, there were games to play. . . .

Johnny had screamed the accusation across a shocked sugarbar. That no one could even begin to imagine how a single Seven could have wiped a Six off the board permanently didn't stop Johnny.

And when a stone with her name had appeared out of nowhere the next day, near the spot where she'd apparently disappeared, Johnny took it as a sign that the Out There was confirming his hate.

"So . . ." Johnny said to the stone. "I got a second name. Johnny Drop." His third eye swung around until all three pointed at the stone. Abruptly, they filled with tears, his stripes growing jagged at the edges.

"You should've been there." His voice broke. "You should've seen all those skids, you . . . you should've been there." He and the stone remained silent for a while, then he sniffed and blinked away the tears. His stripes reformed.

"I think this is what Torg was talking about," he chuckled, sniffing again. "Me, talking to a rock. Pretty sure that counts as holding on. Everyone thinks I slipped a tread." He sighed and swung an eye to the sky. "Wonder what they think?"

He stared into the blue, then his whole body twitched. "There," he complained to the stone. "That's what I'm talking about. *'Wonder what they think?'* What the hole does that mean? We both know what they think. I got a second name. Made Nine. That didn't happen by accident. They think I'm the best." He wasn't boasting, there wasn't a skid alive who'd dispute it now: Albert might hate him for it, but he wouldn't deny the claim.

"So why do I keep thinking stuff like that? I should be happy, I shouldn't be . . ." He stopped, staring at the stone. "Torg said something last night. He said if I want be remembered, I might want to think about what kind of skid I want them to remember. So . . . I've been thinking about that . . . and I've been doing that *a lot* lately. Thinking. I guess since you died, but lately . . ." He bit his lip. "Lately more. I—"

Johnny. . . .

His whole body went still. Then all three eyes swung up, focused on the woods. *What the hole?*

The crunch of treads behind him. Normally, his third eye would have been looking that way; every skid over Level Three trailed an eye. But with Peg, in the privacy of the moment . . . two of his eyes swung, a deep part of his stripes expecting to see . . .

It was Bian, the Level Seven. Her stripes muted beneath her glam, eyes hung out of respect. "Johnny, I'm . . . I'm really sorry to intrude."

What was she doing here? Johnny timed his moments with Peg when most skids would be at another game, during one he wasn't scheduled to play. Today, it was the Skates.

Bian rolled to a stop. "I could wait, if you want," she said. Her eyes swung, taking in the area as if embarrassed.

"No, that's . . . that's fine," he said reflexively. It wasn't, he wanted his privacy, but . . . "Did you just call my name?"

The Seven blinked. "No," she stammered. "Should I've done that? I wasn't sure how . . ."

"Don't worry about it." He popped a hand and waved it dismissively. "What are you doing here, Bian? I would have thought you'd be at the Skates."

Her stripes brightened and diffused a little. "I . . . I skipped it."

"You skipped it? *You were scheduled to play?*"

"Yeah."

Johnny stared at her. Most skids spent their down time attending games; they were their own live crowd, gambling like lunatics. He'd opted out from sitting in the stands, watching Albert in his best event, dealing with the hundreds of skids who would've wanted a piece of the newest Nine. It wasn't unheard of for Eights and Nines to do this, he'd done it before . . . so he'd opted out of the crowd.

Bian had opted out of a game.

Johnny couldn't remember the last time a skid had done that. Certainly, he never had. In addition to gaining nothing in the game they should've played, they were penalized points on the season. They could be suspended, which was worse than dying for a skid. Theoretically, Bian might even be demoted a level.

"Why would you do that?" Johnny said.

Her stripes flushed an even deeper shade of yellow. "I . . . I wanted to talk about Albert."

Johnny's third eye twitched in her direction before settling back on the woods. "You want to talk about . . ." He glanced at Peg's stone. "I don't think that's going to happen, Bian. You can go."

"Johnny, wait," she begged, treading forward. "I skipped a game to come out here."

"Yeah, that was silly."

"Johnny. . . ."

"Don't Johnny me!" he snarled. "This is my time. This is Peg's time. How dare you interrupt me, here, in this place. And . . . for *Albert?*"

"I had to." Her eyes hung so low they almost dragged the ground. "You're hurting him."

She kept saying stupid things. "Good! Tell me exactly what I'm doing so the jackhole can—"

Suddenly, an image of Torg, last night, outside the pit. Saying the words he'd just repeated to Peg: *You might want to think about what kind of skid you want them to remember.*

He bit his lip, hard, and glanced upwards.

Bian sat there, treads trembling, her stripes and sparks a mess, eyes dragging. She'd skipped a game to come talk to him. In this place. He knew she knew about Peg. Every skid knew about Peg. They might think he was weird for holding on, but they knew he did. And he was Johnny—Johnny Drop now. Nobody would waltz in here without a good reason.

Johnny sucked air. Exhaled. "All right," he said. "You want to talk about Albert. Fine. Talk." He tried to keep the anger out of his voice.

An eye came up and her stripes straightened out a little. "I know you don't like him, maybe even hate him . . ." She glanced at the stone behind him. "And I respect that. Everyone does. It's not really any of my business, but . . ."

But you like him, Johnny thought. He didn't get it: Bian was known to get around. A lot, even for a skid. He sighed again. "All right, Bian. I'm sorry if I was rude earlier. I've been a little edgy recently." If the other skid thought this was strange behaviour out of the most celebrated skid since Betty Crisp, she gave no sign. "Any mention of Albert doesn't help. But you came out here, so . . . say your piece."

After she hesitated, he softened his stripes. "Really, Bian, it's okay. I'm sorry if I was rude. Albert?"

"When you attack him . . . in public like you did the other day . . . it's tearing him up."

"I think Albert's a little tougher than that."

Bian's second eye came up. "You don't have any idea how he feels about you, do you?"

"I know he hates my guts." He might have added—*As much as I hate his*—but he was trying to be nice.

"No, he doesn't."

Johnny rolled an eye. "Bian. . . ."

"Okay, maybe he does, but he doesn't just hate you. He also . . . I mean . . ." Her stripes shrank abruptly. "I shouldn't be saying this—it isn't fair to him. I should go." She spun and started back the way she came.

"Hey!" Johnny spun after her, then geared it and zipped in front. "Hey, you can't just come out here like that and then take off."

Her treads ground to a halt. She stared at him. Then: "He thinks you're the greatest skid that ever lived."

What about Betty Crisp? The thought came so fast it didn't have time to register before he was rolling both his eyes and his treads. "That's nuts. You don't know what you're talking about."

"Really?" Her stripes flared, as now she zipped in front of him. "Because you spent more time with him this year than me, Johnny?"

"I think I know . . ."

He stopped.

She had a point.

For the first three years of their lives, no one knew Albert better than Johnny. But in the last year? Johnny's stripes twitched. Last night's fight might have been the longest conversation they'd had outside a game in months.

Bian slid forward. "He's jealous of you. Fine, who

36

isn't? But he's stupid about it and I've told him that. And the main reason it's stupid is because he still loves you. I've never seen a skid care that much in any way about another skid. Every time you attack him it's like you're vaping his soul."

From behind the Spike, a couple of skids rolled into view, looking to get a snug on before the next game. They took one look at Bian and Johnny and rolled to the far side.

"What do you want me to do?" Johnny said, sighing.

"Ease off a little. I know you're going to talk during a game, whatever, just, in the bar, after the game . . . maybe go a little easier on him."

Behind them, Peg's stone sat in the shade at the edge of the woods. Looking into the trees, he wondered how far back they really went. His stripes twitched. Crisp Betty, he was having weird thoughts.

"Just what do you think he did to her, anyway?"

His gaze snapped back to hers. Almost the same question Torg had asked the night before, word-for-word.

"I'll do what I can," he said abruptly. "No promises, but I'll try to . . . play a little nicer. Just remember this isn't a one-way lane. Albert's as bad as I am." *Worse*, but he kept the thought to himself.

"I know. Thank you." She started to leave.

"You really like him, don't you?"

Her treads paused. "I like a lot of people." Then her trailing eye dipped and she rolled away.

Now, what the hole does that mean?

Checking his clock, he sighed. The Skates would be ending soon. In a few hours, he'd have to begin gearing up for Tilt. In two days, he'd race the next Slope. Which, if he won, would break Betty Crisp's record. Weird how that seemed like an afterthought. It was all he'd focused on for more than a year, nearly one-quarter of his life. He had his second name. Over a year to get to Level Ten. What else was there for him to accomplish?

"Be nice to Albert," he murmured, chuckling. "That's a nice challenge."

He rolled towards the Spike. The other two skids had disappeared into an alcove somewhere, burning time. Another pair was coming up the path. Living fast. . . .

Behind him, a stone sat sheltered in the shade. It wasn't until Johnny disappeared up the path that black moss appeared on the stone's surface and began to grow.

CHAPTER FOUR

Johnny wandered aimlessly for a while, lost in thought. Eventually, he ended up in front of the Combine, staring at the ramp that led inside.

Though squids and panzers spent a lot of time at the Marts gawking at merch they couldn't afford, they passed most of their waking hours at the Combine. Here, Ones and Twos honed their skills in a non-lethal environment without fear of getting vaped. The huge training facility extended towards the sky and deep into the earth; dozens of levels with hundreds of stations working every skill a skid might need. Including the most vital skill of all.

How to stay alive.

Johnny watched a squid zip by without giving him a second glance. Every skid pouring in and out of the Combine was like that, lost in their own little world. Squinting down the ramp, Johnny frowned.

Now what was he doing here?

There was no official rule that skids over Two couldn't

enter the Combine. But why would they? Skids played
enough games to get better by playing, especially once
they didn't have the fear of death hanging over them.
And no skid was going to help another skid get better,
especially a panzer. Until the Ones and Twos got their
molecules together, no one cared.

Nonetheless, after a minute Johnny's stripes abruptly
tilted and he tread down the ramp, trying not to draw
any attention. Not that it mattered; no one looked his
way. A rust-coloured Two actually bumped him and kept
rolling. *Amazing,* he thought with a grin.

He wondered if the hollas would notice him.
Remarkably, not only was the Combine recorded, its
ratings were off the chart. Why anyone would want to
watch someone doing speed runs, especially a squid, was
beyond Johnny.

The ramp led to a huge bowl that filled the Combine.
Far above, the sky could be seen through an opening
in the clear ceiling. Dozens of tunnels ran off from the
field, leading to massive underground facilities.

Settling into a nook near the entrance, Johnny looked
around. He'd never seen so many panzers and squids; or
at least, not where he'd pay attention to them. In a game
he focused on skids who might actually be dangerous. In
the stands, he hung with skids like Torg, if he hung with
anyone at all.

Hundreds of Ones and Twos worked in sight: some
on strength, some on speed, some on specific skills.
Nearby, about twenty squids were hurling themselves
into a wall, trying to learn how to absorb energy. Most
didn't come close to the speeds Johnny tended to collide
with things, although one aqua-black panzer was at least
putting a little effort into it. The wall would soften if a
skid approached vaping speed, but Johnny didn't see any

danger of that happening any time soon. *They might as well be tickling it.* He grinned as his attention continued to wander, settling on a white squid with two red stripes on the far side.

Now what's she doing?

The Two would accelerate down a short track, begin to turn, flip over, then start again. Unconsciously, Johnny rolled forward a tread. The squid flipped once more, right where the track changed colour. *Ohhh. . . .* A smile cracked Johnny's face. *I forgot about practicing that.*

He wasn't sure why he moved. One moment he was watching the squid sprint, turn and flip . . . the next he was crossing the field.

It blew his mind that he could cross the entire span without a single skid looking his way. He was the most famous skid alive. Hole, there was a holla of him running above one of the strength benches.

Nevertheless, he reached the other skid unnoticed. "Hey," he said conversationally. "Whacha working on?"

"Who wants to . . . ?" the skid started to say. Then she stopped, stunned, as one of her eyeballs focused on Johnny. Then a second. Then slowly, as if the squid knew it was going to be rude but she couldn't help herself, the third.

"You're Johnny Drop," she whispered, her eyes widening until you could barely see the lids.

Johnny's stripes tilted. "It's nice to be recognized," he said casually. "That's a grease-pad. You're working on greasin' your treads, right?"

Blink . . . blink . . . blink went the squid's eyes. A tattgram of a dragon popped off her stripes. "You're Johnny Drop."

Johnny chuckled. He tried to put himself in the Two's place, although it was hard. Sure, most young skids looked up to the Eights and Nines, but even as a One Johnny had been a cocky little spare, unimpressed by anyone but Johnny.

Still, he thought, *I suppose if Betty Crisp had rolled up to me in the Combine I might have vaped myself a little.* Reaching down, he picked up the tattgram and held it out. "Careful, these are expensive. You're a Level Two, right?"

"You're . . ."

"I know my name," he said gently but firmly. "You're working on greasing your treads, right? Going frictionless?"

But the Two was back to staring at Johnny like he'd just turned into a tree. "What are you doing here?"

"I was watching you from that nook over there," Johnny said, pointing.

"*What were you doing over there?*" the Two protested, all three eyes swinging towards the ramp. If Johnny didn't do something, the poor squid was going to vape herself on the spot.

"Hey," Johnny said, fighting a twinge of frustration. Squid needed a name—how was he supposed to get her to focus? "You're thinking too much."

The Two blinked. One of her eyes swung back to Johnny. "What?"

"When you're greasing the treads. You're thinking too much."

"Oh." The Two stared at the track where she'd been practicing. "I don't get it."

"You're trying to figure out exactly how to do it, right?"

"Uh . . . sure. What else am I supposed to do?"

Johnny took a deep breath and sighed. *Squids.* "For one thing, stop trying so hard. You're not supposed to think it all the way through. Here—ask me the exact right way to grease your treads."

"What's the exact right way to grease your treads?"

"No idea." He laughed when the Two gaped at him. "No one knows exactly how to do it, squid. There is no exactly. You just . . . feel it out."

"Feel it out?" the Two said skeptically.

"Yeah. Don't think it happening . . . *feel* it happening."

"Uh-huh," said the Two. "And how am I supposed to know what it *feels* like if I've never done it before?"

Johnny opened his mouth to speak, then stopped and looked around. Maybe there was a reason why they left the panzers and squids to figure things out for themselves. "Well," Johnny said, pretty sure the lesson would take better if the Two made her own connections, "what do you think it would feel like?"

"I don't—" she started to protest, then stopped. "I guess it would feel slick."

Johnny beamed. That was exactly how he thought about it. "It probably would."

"Yeah, but what does that feel like?" the Two murmured, her eyes dropping away from Johnny, lost in thought.

Now it was Johnny's turn to stare. *Slick* always seemed to do the trick for him. "I don't know that you need . . ."

"I guess it's a little like grease." She glanced at him. "That's why they call it that, right? Greasing your treads."

Johnny looked back at her, bemused. He'd never needed to get that specific with his imagery, but if it worked for the squid. . . . "I imagine that's where the phrase came from, yeah. Wanna try it?"

A grin split her face. "All right."

"Remember," Johnny said, "don't think—*feel*."

"Right," the squid said. She crouched into position. Remained that way. "Uh . . . would you mind turning around? You're . . . you're kinda making me nervous."

"Sure," he said with a smirk. He swung his eyes away, although he kept watching with the edge of his peripheral vision. *Bet she hasn't figured out how to do that, either.* He stifled a laugh. *Seriously, how do any of them survive?*

Revving up, the squid fired down the pad, twisted where it changed texture . . . slid a bit . . . then spun out and flipped.

Johnny barked a laugh as he tread over. "No one gets it on the first try," he said. "But it was better, right? You felt it?"

The Two had a faraway look. "I think . . . yeah . . . there was a moment . . . yeah, I think I got it." She grinned sheepishly. "Kind of."

"That's a start. If it helps, most stuff works that way. Including getting vaped."

"Really?" the squid said, three eyes swinging Johnny's way. If there was one thing a Two was desperate to figure out, it was avoiding permanent evaporation.

"Sure," Johnny said. "Most squids think *way* too much about it. Hole, a lot of them think you have to keep track of every molecule in your body." He held back a smile as the squid's stripes flushed.

"Oh," she said. "So, ummm . . . so you don't do that?"

"How many molecules do you think you have in your body, panzer?"

"I'm not a pan . . . oh, I get it. A lot?"

"Yeah, *a lot*. Way too many to worry about when you're getting sliced to shreds. Trust me, don't try to math your body back together, just . . . make it happen."

"Oh. All right." The Two didn't sound too sure of herself, but given that her death was on the line, Johnny could understand the doubt. He laughed. "Don't worry, squid. You'll figure it out. If it helps, I usually focus on my colours first—body and stripes—along with my name."

"I don't have a name," the Two whispered, her eyes dropping.

"Keeping working at stuff like this . . ." Johnny said firmly, "and you'll get one."

"Oh." Her eyes came up and her stripes flushed with pleasure. "Okay. Um . . . thanks." She frowned, as if remembering how surreal this was.

"No problem." Johnny said, starting to roll. "One last thing. Learn to trail an eye. It'll feel weird at first, but what's the point in having three if you use them all together?"

"Right," the Two said, and swung one of her eyes self-consciously. She watched with the other two the entire time Johnny tread back to the ramp.

No one gave him a second look. Who would—it's not like a Level Nine with two names was suddenly going to drop in.

As Johnny emerged from the Combine, a One glanced his way. All three eyes went wide, then his body shook in disbelief and he hurried inside. Stopping, Johnny watched the panzer disappear down the ramp. Around him, skids of every level came and went, ignoring the Combine. After all, why wouldn't they?

Why hadn't he?

Johnny stared down the ramp for quite some time. The squid probably wouldn't survive the week. Johnny knew the numbers, most Ones and Twos never made it. Hole, Johnny might be the skid who finished her off.

Still . . .

Whether the Two survived or not, one thing was true. For the first time since winning the Slope . . . Johnny felt good.

CHAPTER FIVE

Three days later, Johnny sat at the top of the Pipe. He wasn't feeling good anymore.

They fixed it! The thought had been hammering inside his head for half a day. *They fixed it! The panzers!*

Twelve hours before, Johnny had competed in the Slope for the first time since tying Betty Crisp's record. A win and the record was his alone.

If there was a skid anywhere in the Skidsphere other than the Slope, then they were either vaped and recovering, or just plain vaped. They all wanted a part of history. Thousands lined the Slope. The noise was enormous, threatening to crack the sky.

He was half-way down before he realized something wasn't sliding right. For one thing, he'd led the entire race. Easily. Despite not popping a skid the entire way. In fact, he hadn't seen any skids getting popped.

That's when his trail-eye picked up the pile behind him. The entire pack, four hundred skids strong, were trailing fifty metres back. Even Albert was there, scowling as if he hated all of them for doing this. At the front, Torg grinned like a madman.

It wasn't a race: it was a coronation. Which Torg confirmed when Johnny confronted him after the contest.

"*Are you out of your mind!*" he screamed in the winner's circle. "You fixed the Slope? You can't fix a game!"

Torg just laughed. "Do you really think anyone was going to pop Johnny Drop in his first race after getting his second name? Get vaped, squid. And for Crisp's sake, cheer up."

He had a point. Twelve hours later, even Johnny had to admit this. Hole, had Johnny been among that pile, he wouldn't have wanted to crush history. He was surprised Albert had played along; but then again, anyone beating Johnny in that race would've been a villain forever. And Johnny never thought Albert was dumb.

It still infuriated him. It was the Slope, for Crisp's sake! It was Crisp's record—you couldn't just give it away. Technically, he was pretty sure he shouldn't have gotten his second name until after breaking the record—maybe until he *died*. He had no idea why GameCorps did it so quickly. The whole thing just made him so . . .

Stop it, he thought, blinking rapidly. Snakes, all he'd done since getting his life's dream was scream at people or act half-vaped. Torg was right: he had to cheer up. He glanced towards the Out There. He doubted if they were impressed.

"So go impress them," he growled, looking down the Pipe.

In many ways, the Pipe resembled the Slope, except where it was completely different. For instance, both games were on a hill, but the Pipe was a practically gentle forty-five degrees, compared to the Slope's ridiculous sixty-five. Whereas the Slope was covered in dust, the Pipe was covered in snow.

No obstacles peppered the Pipe's blazing white surface, which curled up to form a fifty-kilometer long half-pipe. Above each edge, hundreds of rings, bumpers and grab-bars; a maze of contraptions to make each launch off the sides an aerial circus. The Slope was about speed and violence. The Pipe was all about style.

Though it had its moments.

Johnny waited in the gates, blind to the others that would start with him. Twenty skids were launched every thirty seconds. Contact with other skids was not allowed on the Pipe, the only game that had such a rule. Any contact and both contestants would be punished with point deductions.

Interference, however . . .

As the buzzer sounded and Johnny moved, a silver streak cut across his line. *They launched me with Albert?* He couldn't decide whether he was amused or outraged.

"No free rides today, squid!" Albert yelled.

"Like that was my call," Johnny muttered. Changing his line, he geared up for his first trick.

Swinging right, he did a quick calc on the other skids, aiming for a yellow ring a few degrees downslope. Dingo, a sea-green Five covered in tattgrams, was coming from a different angle and would hit the ring just in front of Johnny. It would be close, but close was fine. Contact was illegal. Close brought the Out There out of their seats.

Johnny hit the curve, picking up speed. Soaring off the edge, he dove through the yellow ring right behind Dingo, the Five squeaking in protest. *Check your math, squid, we're fine.* Johnny laughed as he popped a Hasty-Arm, leaning out to catch a handle-bar. Swinging around, he flattened for style, cork-screwed into a twist, calced the skids and slid between two others for a cross before landing in the Pipe.

Decent enough start. The trick with the Pipe that most Fives and under didn't get was you played for the slo-mo. More than any other game, little things mattered on the Pipe. Get close enough to shave the skid going through a ring before you? Sweet. Flatten out while spinning? That looks good on the hollas. Torg, who'd done some fine things on the Pipe over the years, once said: "The key to the Pipe? Relax, son. Make it look like you just don't care."

Of course, if you couldn't relax. . .

Johnny couldn't stop thinking about the Slope. And Peg. And Betty Crisp. And the fact that he was a Nine with over a year left to get to Ten and what if—*what if?*—Ten wasn't the end? Every skid assumed Ten was the top because only one skid had ever achieved it.

Get to Eleven and he could shove Albert's Nine-Nine right up his treads.

Speak of the devil. Albert screamed across the Pipe behind him, a streak of snow spraying into Johnny's trail-eye.

"You look tight, panzer."

"Better tight than slow."

"If you say so."

Jackhole. Too much a spare to defy Torg and give Johnny a real race yesterday.

He was half-way through a trick when he first noticed it. Downslope, a black spot on the white, too far down to be a skid this early in the game. Besides, skids might change their shape on the Pipe, but they didn't . . . grow.

What the hole?

A second later and the thought became even more appropriate as the black spot surged up the Pipe and spread. The ground trembled. He didn't think it was a corpsquake, not so soon on top of the other. Plus, GameCorps never sent a quake during a game.

In the stands, the screaming started.

Beneath Johnny, the entire right side of the Pipe was being consumed by darkness. *This isn't a quake.* He needed to get off the hill. Except . . .

If skids didn't help other skids at the best of times, they sure the hole didn't do it in a game. You didn't take care of the young—you *vaped* them. Another thing Torg was known to say: None of the letters in 'Team' appeared in the word 'Skid.'

But Johnny had been in a mood for days. He'd gone to the Combine, for Crisp's sake.

Vape it, he thought, gearing up and tearing down the hill.

Unlike the Slope, low level skids tended to finish the Pipe the fastest, not realizing that style slowed down sometimes. The best tricks occurred when a skid appeared to stop in mid-trick—*hang the edge, squid, hang the edge.*

The black clawed its way up the hill as dozens of Ones, Twos and Threes scrambled to turn and climb to safety. Flashes of colour began to disappear into the gaping maw. The Threes would survive . . .

You so sure of that? Johnny thought, reaching out to latch a Two. He spun and hurled it upslope. *Whatever that is, I don't think it's GameCorps.*

"Playing hero now?" Torg appeared on his left, treads gunning.

"That's not natural," Johnny said, spin-flinging another Two.

"What is?" Torg drawled. "Nice technique. Let me have a go." He caught a One and gave it a boost. "Beauty," he said, admiring his work. "But why are we saving panzers and not ourselves? 'Cause whatever that is, I'm not so sure it's going to let me pull myself together."

Down below, the first skid Johnny recognized—Kass, a lime-blue Level Four—was run down by the growing scar, his tattgrams and glam ripped from his skin. His scream followed him into the dark . . . then ended.

"The stands are back that way," Johnny said. "Anyway, that thing's fast, but we're faster." By his count, the black was climbing the Pipe at the speed of the average Five. Even uphill, Johnny and Torg could outrun it.

If it didn't speed up.

"Ah, hole," Torg sighed. "Live fast, die fast." Torg poured on the speed, then his treads hitched as his voice hushed with fear. "Crisp Betty, you don't think that's the Hole, do you?"

Maybe, Johnny conceded.

Many skids believed in the Hole, a black place were the skids without names weren't just vaped, they were vaped forever. Even if it existed, Johnny had always been pretty sure he wasn't going to end up there himself, so he tended not to think about it.

He was thinking about it now.

Taking an angle, Johnny aimed for a purple-orange One. Torg swung a Three upslope.

That's when the black tear below . . . *accelerated*.

"Vape me," Johnny breathed. He could hear it now. A ripping sound, like a hundred treads geared up to full, slashing up the Pipe, threatening to take the entire right side. If he didn't get off . . .

"Help me!" the panzer squealed in terror.

Ah snakes, at least I got my second name.

A black spike of emptiness stretched towards the terror-filled skid. The white beneath its treads began to crumble away. Johnny gunned it, creating a windshear as he accelerated into the turn and sailed into the black.

This is now the dumbest thing you have ever done.

Stretching out a Hasty-Arm as far as he ever had, Johnny snagged the One by its own arm. Beneath it, nothing but black.

No, not nothing.

Amazed, Johnny's eyes went wide. Deep inside the black, there were lights. Faint lines, distant pulses, all infinitesimally distant and dim. And broken. The lines ended, frayed and sparking into a black that seemed to eat the light. *The darkness was eating . . .*

"Don't drop me," the One screamed, glitter streaming from her eyes. Her only glam.

Workin' on it. The speed from his turn bled away. He flung out his second arm but there was nothing there. The Pipe beneath him was gone.

Really? Like this?

At the very end of his second arm, a hand clamped onto Johnny's own. He tore his eyes away from the horror below.

Up into the face of Albert.

"You are a grease-sucking spare," the silver skid said grimly, his arm stretched out to its limit. Above him, clutching a ring floating in space, Torg hung on for his life, creating a chain.

The panzer was screaming. Torg was trying to haul them up. There was a tearing sound . . .

Albert swung all three of his eyes towards Johnny. "I hate that the last thing I see is going to be your stupid stripes."

"Then why do it?" Johnny asked.

He didn't get an answer. The tearing sound reached up and tore the world to shreds.

CHAPTER SIX

This is not evaporation.

That was the last clear thought Johnny had for a while.

They fell into the black—faint lines of light flaring and dying far, far below—and then the black fell on them. The panzer's hand tore free. Albert was there for a flicker more, then his grip ripped away.

Johnny's cells began to cleave apart.

This is . . .

Here's how evaporation normally felt: cell-by-cell—too fast to realize it was sequential—the building blocks of a skid separated, connections sheared clean by millions of tiny scalpels, snapped each time in a single precise break. It sucked large, but it was clean. If you knew what you were doing, you could find the pieces, reconnect, and put the puzzle back together. Cell-by-cell. Provided there wasn't another step.

This is not . . .

Johnny hit the black. His cells began to cleave. And then . . . the darkness began to eat his cells.

. . . is not . . .

Nothing clean. No cuts, no breaks. Just tearing, tearing, tearing—the knives were serrated, they had teeth—the building blocks were ripped and shredded and then consumed.

Nothing ever hurt like this.

. . . not this . . .

Blind with panic, Johnny reached for colour.

He'd said it to that squid in the Combine: the final thing you learned at the end of Two, when you finally figured out how to hold it together after getting vaped. Colour. Every skid identified with it. Levels change, skids die, but the stripes stick. Abstract and clear. Something to grasp when your brain was being cleaved in two with a knife.

Or eaten by buzzsaws.

Johnny reached for blue. Then he reached for white: perfect, flawless white, the opposite of whatever the hole surrounded him now. White: perfect and flawless and clean.

Then he got mad.

Vape this. The thought came through like a beacon— emotion following colour, anger filling the blue and white as it always did. Being vaped sucked, it sucked tread hard. No skid, no *anything* should ever go through this: it wasn't natural, it wasn't right.

Johnny was still terrified—*notthisisnotisthisnot-thisnotisnotisnot*—so he rammed the fear into his rage and punched his consciousness into the black.

Mine. Over and over. *Mine.* Lashing out and tearing his torn cells back from the darkness, ripping the ripped building blocks away from whatever the hole was filling the world. *Mine.* He seized piece after piece until . . .

Johnny.

Inside the dark, Johnny's soul grinned. *Not Johnny. Johnny Drop.*

Mine.

He thought he heard screaming. A flash of magenta-gold.

Torg?

Inside his own terror, Johnny found a sliver of rage and hope and heaved it in the direction of the thought. *Colour!* he screamed into the darkness, flinging magenta and gold at the other scream.

And then Johnny did something he'd never done before. Something he'd never even heard of. Drenching his soul in blue and white, roaring his name like a shield—*DropJohnnyDropJohnnyDrop*—Johnny followed the magenta-gold flash, latched onto it and hurled the name *TORG!* into the colour.

Something reached out and caught it.

A red-yellow smear in the darkness. *Bian?* Dragging the spar of Torg with him, Johnny plunged after the Level Seven.

Again and again, Johnny caught flashes of colour and reached out. He lost most—he had Kass and then felt him shredded away—but he latched onto one . . . two . . . three and more. Too many to count—he still couldn't think straight—but he was pulling himself together even as he grabbed more and more—helping them pull together—finding more, pulling them . . .

Deep in the darkness a light flared, unbroken and white.

Count it, thought Johnny Drop, dropping towards the light like a blade, pulling dozens of shattered skids in his wake.

The light grew—*falling?*—and grew until the darkness peeled back and the colour white filled the world. And then they were *falling,* skid after skid falling through the light, away from the tearing dark . . .

Impact.

They landed hard, though it was nothing compared to the torture they'd just endured. Johnny felt his body flatten before snapping back into shape. *That's it?* he thought, surprised at his own clarity. He blinked, surrounded by hazy white light, and dropped a thinlid.

Beneath his treads, solid ground. The world was solid. The only question: which world?

A scraping sound came from his left. Swinging an eye, he found Torg in the haze a few metres away. The Nine looked like he'd been in a bar-fight. Which was pretty much how Johnny felt.

"That was unpleasant," Torg coughed, shaking his eyes. His body had been completely stripped of any skins or glam.

"Yeah," Johnny agreed, trying to adjust to the light. The diffuse white seemed to saturate everything.

"Thanks," Torg said. "Whatever that was, I wasn't coming back until I heard you scream my name."

"Don't worry about it," Johnny said. The haze was peeling back. Either that or his eyes were adjusting. He did a three-axis sweep . . .

His upper eye froze, staring up. "Crisp Betty," he heard Torg whisper.

Far above them—maybe a few hundred metres or maybe a few thousand—a black scar stretched across the white.

"We came out of that?" Torg said, his voice hushed with awe.

"Think so," Johnny murmured.

"Think it will . . . attack us again? Like it did on the Pipe?"

Johnny stared at the scar in silence before he replied. "I don't think it's moving."

"Uh-huh. Maybe let's not trust it to stay that way."

A sound came from their right. Johnny's eyes adjusted a little more and he made out a red-yellow skid. Like Torg, she had no skins or glam.

"Bian?" he said, treading in her direction.

Her eyes came up, wide and full. "Johnny?"

"Yeah. You okay?"

"I think so." She paused, eyes wide. "You saved me."

He didn't want to keep saying don't worry about it. Suddenly self-conscious, he said, "I'm glad you're okay." Nearby, other shapes began to appear.

"You saved me," Bian whispered again, as if to herself.

He'd saved a few more than he'd thought. He recognized a brown-red here, a blue-green . . .

A silver-white ball emerged from the haze.

Huh, Johnny thought as a few hundred emotions washed over him.

Albert rolled up. Stopped five metres away. Completely unable to think of anything intelligent to say, Johnny settled on the obvious: "You're alive."

A familiar smirk worked its way over Albert's face, although he looked shaken. "Apparently."

"I didn't help you out," Johnny said, amazed.

Albert's eyes swept over the other skids. "Surprise, surprise. Why? You keep this lot together?"

"He saved my skin," Gort, a green-white Five said.

"Me too."

"Me too."

"He saved everybody," Bian said. Her eyes were like satellite dishes.

"Not everybody," Albert murmured, two eyes swinging back to Johnny.

"Yeah," another voice suddenly spoke. A purple-orange skid rolled up.

The panzer from the Pipe.

"Albert saved me," the Level One said. Her stripe was quivering. "I thought I was dying, it was horrible, then I heard him screaming my colours at me and he helped me find my pieces. It was awesome."

Johnny kept one eye on the panzer and one eye on Albert. "Sounds pretty awesome."

"Should have been more," Albert said. "There were hundreds of skids on that side of the stands."

"Yeah," Johnny said, thinking of all the flashes of colour he'd failed to save. "Yeah, it should."

Keeping the eye on Albert, Johnny tried to remember if he'd seen a silver-white flash anywhere in the black. It was hard to remember anything, he wasn't even sure how long they'd been in there. *Did I see him and ignore it? Did he do that with me?* So much had happened so quickly; he'd lost far more skids than he'd saved . . .

Albert was still eyeing him. Johnny considered making a joke about the numbers they'd each saved—something about Johnny beating him again—but Bian continued to stare and he'd said he would try to be nice.

"Glad you made it out," he tried. He thought the words weren't very convincing.

"Right." The white stripes twitched. "You too."

"Anybody know where we are?" Shabaz, a grey-aqua skid asked.

"Not a clue," Johnny said, relieved to be able to take an eye off Albert.

"Wherever we are, can we get out from under that?" Shabaz said, nervously scanning the scar above their heads.

"That is a fine idea," Torg agreed. "Only one problem, squid."

"What's that? And I'm a Six," Shabaz added sullenly.

"My mistake." The eye pointing in Johnny's direction rolled. "Which way are we going to go? All I see is a lot of white."

Which pretty much summed it up. Except for the scar, every point on the compass was white; the colour so uniform it was impossible to grasp any scale. They had solid ground beneath their treads, but where it ended and the scarred sky began was uncertain. The scar above them seemed very large and very high and stretched out in one direction, but they couldn't tell the vectors without anything else to . . .

"What's that?" Albert said abruptly, two of his eyes swinging up and off to Johnny's left.

Johnny swung an eye and followed the angle. "I don't see . . . oh."

At the very edge of the scar, small black shapes were falling from the darkness towards the white floor below. Against the white backdrop they almost looked pretty, like black raindrops falling in slo-mo. Watching them, Johnny realized the space they were in was far larger than they'd thought. Scoping his eye, the shapes grew slightly.

Crisp Betty, those are far off.

"Whatever they are," he heard Torg murmur, "they aren't large."

"They're large enough," Albert replied.

"What's large enough?" the One said nervously. She wouldn't learn to scope her eyes until at least Level Four.

The first of the shapes touched down. "Crap," Albert said.

Johnny felt a warm tension sink through his body as he tried to see what Albert saw. Johnny had better reflexes, probably better peripherals, but nobody scoped like Albert. Swallowing his pride, he said, "What do you see?"

"Whatever they are, they're moving."

"Which way?"

Albert gave him a look that pretty much said everything.

Johnny sighed. "How long till they get here?"

"Not long enough. They're farther away than I thought possible when we landed, but they're moving fast."

"How fast?"

Albert apparently decided this question wasn't stupid. "Hard to tell at this distance straight on." His stripes twitched. "But I think they're moving fast enough."

"Sounds like a good time to move," Torg said.

"Which way?" Shabaz said. "I don't see anywhere to go."

So that's why Albert gave me the look. Johnny popped an arm and pointed in the direction of the black shapes. "How about away from them?"

"Oh," Shabaz said, her eye widening with fear. "Right."

"Okay, skids, let's tread." Johnny pitched his voice to carry, and they rolled away from the shapes behind them.

"Johnny," Torg said as they picked up speed, "we should do a count."

He hadn't even thought about that. "Good idea. Could you?"

"On it."

The count wasn't going to be easy; already, they were spread out. Some Fives and Sixes had rolled the second the black shapes hit the ground. Some took different angles from the group.

Johnny sighed. Skids just didn't do team.

Behind them, the black shapes grew. He wasn't sure, but he thought . . . "Albert, you see any light inside those things?"

"Like the hole up there? No, I don't think they're the same stuff."

"Wonder if that's a good thing?"

"Why don't you slow down and find out?"

Johnny bit his tongue. He hated relying on Albert.

"They're moving a lot faster than we are," Albert added.

Behind them, the Ones and Twos were struggling to

keep up. Whatever he'd done to save them wasn't going to matter unless he did something. "Torg," he said, turning on his com, "drop the count, just get the group in line."

"I'll help," Bian said.

"Great. Get them moving fast, but don't out-tread me. I'm going to grab the Ones and Twos."

Cutting his speed, he swung around in a wide arc, dropping back to grab the stragglers. The black shapes began to grow in size a little faster.

Albert dropped back with him. "What are you doing?" Johnny snapped.

"Helping them," he said, pointing towards the skids falling behind. "Or did you want to do that alone, Johnny Drop?" He spat the last two words.

"Vape me," Johnny replied, his anger rising. Then he realized going solo was stupid. Gritting his teeth, he said, "Come on."

The spread at least made it clear how many low levels survived. A couple of Ones, including the purple-orange panzer Albert had saved, three Twos, and one Three named Olli. Johnny was pretty sure he'd seen a few other Threes in the pack, but the emerald-bronze skid was struggling.

"Gear it, Olli," Johnny said, spinning and matching speed. "The bad guys are gaining."

"I'm trying," the skid growled. "Speed isn't my thing."

Johnny eyed the shapes. "Better make it your thing. I can't stay with you, I need to grab the squids."

"Screw the squids."

Johnny couldn't hold it against him. Johnny was fighting the instinct himself. "Keep moving," he said, then dropped back some more.

Torg's voice came over the com. "Johnny, we got skids

breaking off from the group. Alva, Jad, Peralta, some Fours and Fives I didn't recognize. I can't get them all."

"They're trying to clear away from the target," Albert said.

"I know what they're doing," Johnny snapped. It wasn't even that stupid on an individual basis. "But where the hole do they think they're going to go?" To Torg he added, "Get who you can while staying on the line. We go straight until we find something to reference."

"And if we don't find that?" Torg said. He didn't sound scared, just asking the question.

Hole if I know. "Worry about that later. Just keep them in line."

Albert matched the fastest squid and coached some more speed out of him. Johnny aimed for one of other Twos.

Skids rarely used pure speed on level ground. In a game, dozens of factors beyond speed came into play, even in races like the Slope or the Rainbow Road. So the difference between the absolute strengths of the bottom and top levels blurred a little, particularly because there were talented Ones and Twos along with uninspired Fives and Sixes.

But here, in this flat empty space, the Ones and Twos moved at half the speed that Johnny, Albert, and Torg could hit. Johnny knew they weren't dogging it, they were desperately trying to keep up with the pack.

They simply couldn't.

"Hey," Johnny said, pulling in beside a pink-yellow skid. The Two's stripes quivered and her eyes were wide with fear. At least she'd learned to trail one. "You need to relax a little," he said gently.

"Yeah?" the Two snapped. "How relaxed are you right now?"

"Good point," Johnny conceded. The black shapes had closed enough for details to emerge. They each looked like a black ball of fangs. "You have to try. Suck oxygen, deep breaths. Then—and this is real important—stop thinking about your treads."

The Two flicked a guilty glance his way.

"Don't worry," Johnny said, keeping his voice cool. "Everybody does it when they start. But you're straining." He tapped an eye in the direction of the pack. "Instead, concentrate on where you're going. Use two eyes." The Two's upper eye came forward and focused in the same direction as her forward eye. "Good," Johnny said. "Now get there. *Hard.*"

He saw her eyes narrow. *Got some fire in there.* She took a breath.

And began to pick up speed.

"Nice," Johnny said. "Now stay focused. The pack's matching speeds so it's not going flat out. Once you get there, get a little inside, hold there. I'll catch up."

"Thanks," the Two gasped. Her upper eye twitched his way. "About up there . . ."

"Not now. I gotta help the Ones." He winked. "Keep moving, squid." He was rewarded with a smile as he dropped back again.

Albert was treading beside the purple-orange One, so Johnny fell in beside the other panzer, a maroon skid with a bronze stripe. *We're going to have to name these guys,* he thought with a grim grin.

"They're catching up, aren't they?" the panzer whined. Two eyes looked back in terror.

"Relax," Johnny said. "Get one of those eyes forward, that's where you need the depth perception."

"Then how will I know if they're getting close?"

Johnny almost laughed. "They'll get bigger."

Talking him through the same advice he'd given the Two, Johnny coached some more speed out of the One. It wasn't much, but they'd catch the pack. Eventually.

"We're going to die, aren't we?" the One protested. Despite Johnny's advice, his second eye kept twitching back to look at the dark shapes. "They're going to eat us."

If we don't find a way out of here, Johnny thought. Aloud, he said, "You're still alive, right?"

"Yeah."

"Well, unless I'm wrong, half-an-hour ago you got vaped. And yet here you are. Which means you're now one of only two Level One's to survive evaporation." He nudged the bronze stripe. "The other one's over there talking to Albert."

"I only survived because of you," the One said, although an uncertain pride snuck into his voice.

"I helped you pull it together, but *you* did the pulling." Johnny wasn't certain that this was completely true—who knew exactly what had happened in the black—but it felt at least partially true.

"Stay focused on the pack," Johnny said, projecting as much confidence as he could. "We'll get out of this."

That's when Bian swore over the com: "*Oh, Crisp Betty, guys, look up!*"

Johnny swung an eye.

Remarkably, they were still under an edge of the black scar, after gunning at speed for almost twenty minutes. The corner from which the shapes had originally dropped was far, far behind.

From the corner above their heads, however . . . more dark shapes were beginning to fall.

CHAPTER SEVEN

The urge to burn the panzer was almost impossible to fight.

Johnny had no idea how many Ones and Twos had been vaped in his lifetime. Thousands. Maybe *tens* of thousands—all in less than five years. Panzers and squids were the cannon-fodder of the games; they made each contest exciting and deadly, which meant ratings from the Out There.

It also meant getting left behind to die.

"Sport, you have *got* to speed up," Johnny said evenly, eyeing the dark shapes falling from above. They came in on a direct line, making them brutal to read for distance.

"I'm trying."

"Try harder. Torg, Bian, what's going on up there?"

"I managed to convey to some the benefits of coming home," Torg drawled, "but others have decided to follow their own counsel. Alva told me to vape myself."

"Figures." Alva was a cocky little Five who treated the skids above him as summits to be climbed. Usually, Johnny admired that. Once, he'd been the same—but that was back in the Skidsphere.

"Alva," Johnny barked into the com, "where do you think you're going?"

"Where do you think *you're* going, old man?"

Fair enough. "We have to stay together."

"Really? Last time I checked, you were getting chased from behind and bombed from above. I'm getting clear. Seems Jad and Peralta think the same."

Johnny tried playing the only card he had. "Vape it, Alva, I saved your life!"

"Yeah, thanks for that."

Gearbox, Johnny thought, though it was hard not to admire the moxy. "Look, Alva—"

"Hold up, flat-tread," Alva said. "Jad, what the hole is that?"

What the hole is what? Johnny thought.

"Not sure, but it looks . . ."

"Crisp Betty!"

"Alva?!" Johnny barked. "Alva?"

"It killed Peralta, it killed Peralta!"

"Jad, get out—"

The com went dead. Johnny scoped, but he didn't know the bearing they'd taken. Dots of colour splashed the plain; he could see Torg returning to the pack, but so many were still spread out.

I'm starting to get a serious hate-on for this place.

"Pay attention!" Albert barked. "We have incoming."

"I'm trying." It was ridiculous. He had three eyes. Probably the best peripherals of any skid in years. Yet things kept surprising him.

The trailing shapes finally became clear. They reminded him . . .

Oh snakes.

They looked like the black moss.

Each dark shape was slightly larger than a skid, not quite round. Pitch black. Chewing through the white landscape like a shifting ball of razor blades, the black surfaces seethed: random spikes popping up, covered in fangs. And the fangs were covered in spikes, which were covered in fangs, which were covered in . . .

"Sport—" Johnny started to say.

That's when the first dark shape hit from above.

It landed near the back of the pack, plunging into the pink-yellow squid Johnny had just coached up to speed. The Two screamed, a howl of terror that Johnny had never heard in a game. Black splotches like spores blistered over her skin—jagged and raw—spreading out to shred the yellow stripes and pink skin until nothing remained.

The scream cut off as suddenly as it had begun.

What the hole did I save them for? Johnny thought, despair crushing his heart as more dark spores struck the pack.

Anger followed the despair. "Torg! Get us something to hide in, now!"

"Johnny, there isn't—"

"There is or we die." He eyed the One beside him. "You need speed. Arms front. Now."

To his credit, the One didn't ask questions. He flung both Hasty-Arms forward as Johnny raced out front. Popping his own arms, Johnny reached back and grabbed the One. *I hope this works.*

"Now hold on." He gunned it. They accelerated, but not enough. "Grease your treads," he growled, straining for speed.

"I don't know how!"

Of course you don't. The spores behind them were about

thirty metres away. "Fine, go neutral. Let 'em spin."

"I don't—"

Oh for Crisp's sake. "Think about your treads, then—"

"I thought you told me not to think about my treads?"

"*Do you want to die?*" All over his com, skids were screaming. The pack was getting bombed. Something had killed Peralta . . .

"Feel the part that feels stronger than the rest? Don't force it, just feel it out." He didn't have time to sympathize with a skid trying to absorb levels of experience into a few hole-filled seconds.

"I think so."

"Pop it."

"Pop it? I don't—*oh.*"

Johnny felt it even as the One did. He surged forward. "Nice. That's where your gears are. Pop it out, you're in freeskid. Pop it back in, you're pushing."

The lesson ended as a black spore landed in front of them.

"Snakes!" Johnny swore, swerving hard and retracting his arms. "Hold on, squid!" *I've got to give him a name.*

They sheared around the black shape and it turned to pursue. *Now what?* Johnny thought. The original pack of black spores trailed fifty metres back. The core of skids ahead was getting eaten alive. All around them, nothing but empty white space, peppered with skids trying to flee.

Johnny could probably outrun the spores, even dragging the One. But that meant abandoning everyone, except maybe Torg, Albert—where the hole was Albert?—a couple of the Sevens . . . *And where am I going to go?* Frustration seethed beneath his stripes. What the hole had he saved them for?

"Johnny!" Bian yelled. He couldn't see her, she was on the other side of the pack. "I've got something. Fifteen degrees off the line!"

Relief flooded through him even though he had no idea what she'd seen. "I'm on my—"

Three spores—one on either side and one in front—landed and turned his way. Twisting his body to keep the panzer clear, Johnny felt something cold and searing gash his left side.

Another spore landed in his path.

Really? he had time to think before he and the black spore plowed into each other.

Pain—almost exactly like he'd experienced in the black scar above. Almost. Something was different, but it was close enough. The black tore at his insides, ripping him apart, shredding its way between the cells of his skin. It happened so fast.

Then, like before, Johnny got mad. Rage bloomed like a bomb in his heart and, with it, an epiphany: this time it was Johnny who surrounded the black. *Let's see how you like it.* Focusing on his cells, he connected them and squeezed. Separating the darkness, tearing it apart piece-by-piece, then absorbing each piece until nothing remained.

The whole process took less than a second.

Woah, Johnny thought, veering a little. A wave of nausea swept over him, like the day after a sugar-binge. His trail-eye was messed up; he struggled to snap it back into focus. *Not sure how many times I could do that, so let's not . . .*

Another black shape landed in his path.

I really hate this place . . .

A flash of white-on-white came from his left and tore into the black spore. It blew apart without a sound.

"What was that?!" someone screamed. *Good question,*

Johnny thought as another white flash tore into the black shapes behind them. "How you doing back there, squid?"

"My arms hurt."

"Just hold on." Johnny gritted his teeth and tried to get around the pack. He could pick out the white shapes now. Whatever they were, they were shaped like knives. And they were attacking the black spores. *So they're on our side.*

He really wanted that to be true.

"Everyone get clear of the black things. Whoever's left, form on me." Coming around the pack, he gunned it. Ahead and to their left, a dark shape could be seen rearing out of the white. Whatever it was, it was huge.

Not the same dark, though, he thought, comparing the shape ahead to the rift in the sky.

Bian rolled up. "So we head for that?"

Johnny considered the riot going on behind them. The white knives were tearing into the black spores, the same way the spores had torn through the skids.

"What do you think they are?" Torg breathed, treading up.

"Don't know," Johnny murmured. Out of the corner of his damaged eye he saw Albert, taking a wide circle around the carnage, dragging the purple-orange One behind him the same way Johnny had dragged his.

"Until we do, perhaps we might want put a little space between us and that," Torg said, pointing back.

"I don't think the white things are after us," Johnny said.

"Don't be so sure," Albert said, pulling up. "Something got Alva and the others, and they weren't acting like it was the black things. They'd seen those already. Alva sounded like it was something else."

"Huh," Johnny said, unwilling to concede the point. He watched a white shape slice into a black, instantly shredding it apart. "Guess a little more distance couldn't hurt," he said, ignoring Albert's smirk. "Let's go see what Bian's found."

As they approached the new shape through the haze, Johnny saw further shapes emerge in the distance.

"New territory?" Torg said.

"Hole if I know," Johnny muttered. It took them several minutes to get near Bian's discovery. They stopped and stared. "Huh," Johnny said.

It was a thunderstorm, hitting a city. He didn't recognize the architecture of the buildings; they resembled nothing in the Skidsphere. Clouds piled across a sky like a bruise. Strange trees tilted under assault from the wind; their long broad leaves flung out as if pleading for help.

"Why isn't it moving?" Shabaz asked.

'Cause that was the thing. The whole scene was trapped in a giant box, frozen in place like a holla on pause.

"Where the hole are we?" someone breathed.

Bian glanced at Johnny. "What do you think?"

"What do you mean: 'What do you think?'" Shabaz protested. "You're not thinking of going in there?"

Johnny had to admit he wasn't sure the idea appealed to him either. There was something deeply creepy about the scene. He stared at raindrops—flat and driven at an angle—hanging in space.

"Maybe we'll skirt the outside, check around." For what, he didn't know. "See if we find something a little safer."

"That might not be an option," Albert said, looking back.

"Why?" Johnny asked, swinging an eye. "Oh. Just lovely."

The white knives had finished off the spores. Now they bundled together, each rotating like the needle of a compass.

They came to a stop, pointing at the skids.

Not on our side, then.

"Maybe they want to make friends," Torg drawled, already backing towards the frozen storm.

"We need a place to hide. Friends come later," Johnny said. Lifting his voice, he yelled: "We're going in, stay tight." He eyed the One still keeping a death-grip on his hands. "You all right, squid?"

"Sure as sugar." The bravado was false, but it was a good sign. Johnny was starting to like him.

The white knives crept closer. They sure the hole didn't look friendly. Jad's final cry of terror: *It killed Peralta! It killed Peralta!* echoed in Johnny's head. Gunning his treads, he raced into a storm that didn't move.

Two seconds later, he started to scream.

CHAPTER EIGHT

"Betty Crisp!" Johnny screamed as a thousand tiny scalpels ripped through his skin.

He'd expected the storm. Once inside, he'd anticipated getting drenched as it came to life. A stupid thought in hindsight, but then he wasn't running a race he knew.

Instead, as they accelerated, the skids hit a wall of rain suspended in space. A billion drops of water saturating the air. Frozen, mashed flat by the unmoving wind, each might as well have been a blade made of diamond.

They tore through Johnny—or rather, Johnny tore through them. For the third time that day, his body felt like it was getting vaped. Not as bad as the spores or the dark—that had felt almost evil—but it wasn't good.

I'm getting real tired being treated like a knife-rack. Instinctively, he swerved from side-to-side.

Which, sadly, was the worst thing to do.

As Johnny swerved, the One behind him slid out from his wake and into the frozen rain. The panzer barely had time to scream.

Then he evaporated.

"*No!*" Johnny cried, as the One's Hasty-Arms came apart in his hands. "No, no, no, no!" He swung around, rain tearing through his own skin, desperately reaching out—reaching out like he had in the darkness—reaching out to find the One. But it was too late.

The panzer was gone.

Screaming with rage, Johnny's eyes bulged as he roared at the sky.

"Get it together," Albert hissed, suddenly at his side. "There'll be time later. We need cover—from the rain and from those white things. Now."

Johnny almost swung at him. He was so angry and his hate of Albert ran deep. Then he saw the purple-orange panzer. Albert had reversed the curve of his back, forming a bowl, the sides further protecting the panzer from the rain. The combination of the One's obvious fear and the shame that Albert had sheltered his charge better than Johnny knocked away the most of the rage.

"Get behind me," Johnny said. "I'll cover." He deserved the pain.

"I'll help," Bian said, pulling up alongside.

"Three's a party," Torg added.

Forming a wedge in front of Albert, they made their way through the storm.

The city was so strange. Skids lived in towers, but here the buildings were only one or two stories tall. Like skid buildings, the walls were smooth. But the windows were rectangular; windows in the Skidsphere were round. Here, there were angles everywhere.

The broad-leafed trees bent by the unseen wind were also bizarre. The green was practically black under a slick sheen of water, with violent splashes of red crossing each leaf. Thorns the size of spikes covered the tree-trunks.

The thought of trying to pop off of one made Johnny shudder.

Running through different wavelengths of light, Johnny found one that cut through the rain. His trail-eye still wouldn't focus; he blinked it violently, trying to fix the problem. In the distance off to his right, he could see a gap between buildings and what might have been the sea, stretching out. Except the white hazy space they'd left behind should've been somewhere over there.

They tried several doors but couldn't get them to budge. They didn't even vibrate when Torg and Johnny rammed them together.

"Snakes!" Johnny swore. "Come on, you grease-sucking spare!" He slammed into the door over and over. "Why . . . won't . . . you . . . move!"

"You're not getting anywhere," Albert said.

Rage flared and Johnny swung all three eyes. "I don't see you helping."

Albert glared back at him, his eyes flat. "That's 'cause I'm busy keeping this One alive."

"What does that mean?" Johnny bumped Albert's tread.

"Uh, gentlemen . . ." Torg said.

"You think I wanted that panzer to die? You think you're better than me?"

"No," Albert said, cold and hard like the rain hanging in the air. "But I think charging in full speed didn't help."

"What was I supposed to do!?" Johnny snapped. "Those white things killed those black things. And those things destroyed us!" He backed up and bumped Albert again, harder than before. "Maybe you ought to try charging in full speed for once; you wouldn't keep finishing behind me all the time!"

"Johnny . . ." Torg said.

Albert stared at him. They were all staring. "Is that what this is, Johnny Drop?" Albert sneered. His trail-eye squinted. "Still just a game?"

"*Of course it's not!*" Johnny screamed. He moved to bump Albert again, but instead he turned and struck the unmoving door, pouring all his rage into its surface.

The door vanished. It didn't blow apart or shatter like glass. It just . . . vanished.

"What the hole?" Johnny said, shocked.

"Later," Torg said. "We need to hide before those things find us."

They piled into a sparsely furnished room. A narrow window shielded with partially drawn drapes; a large curved seat covered in some kind of yellow hide. A low glass table. What might have been a lamp.

"Leave the lamps off," Johnny snapped. "Stay away from the door and the window."

"I'll look out," Torg offered.

"Right."

Johnny rolled to the back of the room, shaking with anger. As he passed Albert and the panzer, he considered apologizing. Something deep inside told him that no matter what Albert had said, Johnny had gone too far. But promise to Bian or no, Albert was still Albert and the thought of apologizing made Johnny more nauseous than the black spore's attack. So he rolled by without apologizing and felt even worse.

Why did I rescue any of them? He wanted to puke.

"Hey, look at this," Shabaz said. The thought that, out of everybody, the whiney Six had survived, made Johnny smirk as he crossed the room. "Look," the grey-aqua skid said, eyeing the floor as Johnny rolled up.

A thin, dark carpet covered the floor. But not the *entire* floor. A triangle of carpet splayed out from the opening in the drapes, encompassing the space where the few pieces of furniture lay. Otherwise, bare, blank floor.

"Weird," Johnny said.

"Who decorates their apartment like this?" Shabaz asked.

Johnny examined the room. "There's carpet under the window, but not by the doorway."

"So?"

"So there was a door there until a few moments ago."

Shabaz rolled her eyes. "*So?*"

Johnny stared at the window. He stared at the door. Then back at the window. "Line of sight," he said finally.

"Line of sight?"

"Line of sight. Carpet's only where someone looking through the drapes could see. Furniture too."

"And what does that mean?"

Johnny smiled a grim smile back at the Six. "Don't know the answer to that one."

He tread over to Bian. "Sorry if I was a little harsh with Albert." That he could apologize to her and not to Albert made him grimace. He was beginning to feel like a serious jackhole, and the fact it was Albert making him feel like this made him angrier. Which made him feel more like a jackhole, which made him feel . . .

Bian gazed at him and said, "It's okay. What happened to your eye?"

"It's that noticeable?" He probably looked like Albert. Which was not acceptable. "Hold on a sec," he said, concentrating on the eye. He felt a tiny surge of nausea, then his vision cleared and stayed clear. Mostly. "How's that?" he said, moving the eye a bit and snapping his thinlids up and down.

"Better," she said. "It's still there, but you wouldn't

notice it unless you knew." Her eyes narrowed and unconsciously she inched a little closer. "Are you all right?"

"It's just the eye, everything else is good."

"Not the eye," she said softly. Another inch.

"Oh," Johnny said. "Yeah. The rest." He inhaled then blew it out, grimacing. "Been better?" The joke made him feel worse. "I mean—"

"Johnny, you want to look at this?" Torg said from his spot by the window.

"Hold that thought," Johnny said to Bian, sighing. She smiled as he rolled away. "What's up?" he said as he slid in beside Torg.

"Look," Torg whispered, tapping an eye through the part in the drapes.

Far down the street, Johnny could make out a white shape, clear as day. Moving slowly, its point swung from side-to-side.

Like it was hunting for something.

"Snakes," Johnny swore. "Do you think it will find us?"

"Johnny . . ." Torg said deliberately. "Look harder."

It took a moment before it hit him. A couple of blocks away, the white knife could be seen clearly despite the frozen rain that obscured buildings next door. And the reason why the white knife could be seen clearly: a path of rain-free space running down the street. A path created by a bunch of fleeing skids.

A path that lead straight up to their door.

"Snakes," Johnny said again.

A little too loudly. Down the street, the point of the knife swung in their direction. It picked up speed.

"Snakes, snakes, snakes," Johnny swore, very softly this time. Too late to lead the thing away. It would see any of them leave and if it checked the house or brought friends. . . .

Barely above a whisper, Johnny hissed, "Away from the door. Nobody makes a noise. Back of the room— behind the furniture if you can—then don't move. If you're sending anything, kill it. No com, no scans. Move."

Silently but quickly everyone but Johnny and Torg moved to the back of the room. All the Sixes and up got as small as possible, packing their molecules into dense clusters.

Slowly but purposely, the white knife made its way down the street. It no longer swung from side-to-side, cutting straight down the centre of the clear path.

It'll come right up and through the door. And no matter how small the skids could get, this thing wasn't going to miss a dozen of them trying to huddle behind a sofa.

Johnny considered his options. He'd survived whatever tore through the Pipe. Somehow brought a number of skids with him, even if most were dead now. He'd survived a hit from one of the black things that had fallen from the sky. *Yeah, except for the punk eye and needing to puke, I'm a beacon of health.* Still, he'd survived. Could he take the white thing on? What if Torg helped?

Or Albert. The silver skid had survived the black scar by himself. He'd even saved a skid.

The white knife reached the end of the front walkway. It rotated. *No hitch, no hesitation*, Johnny thought grimly. *Just slow and nasty.*

He should ask Albert for help. Not only did they need to take that thing out, they had to do it without it warning any of its friends—*What if it already had?*—or there was no point. They sure the hole weren't going to fight twenty of them.

The knife began moving up the walkway. Beside

Johnny, Torg was a statue, three eyes wide.

He couldn't ask Albert. He just couldn't. Besides, the silver-white skid was huddled around the panzer he'd saved like a mother protecting her cub. Maybe if Johnny failed . . .

The knife-point reached the doorway. Johnny tensed, ready to move. Fast and hard. He'd hit it before it hit them. *Yeah, that'll work,* he thought, wondering if he was going to die.

Johnny . . . a voice said out of the ether.

What the hole? The point crossed the threshold.

Outside, the world exploded into movement. Rain battered the window, the roof, the street, the trees. The wind roared: a hurricane throttled to full. The pungent smell of salt and moisture filled the air as debris ripped across the street.

The knife stopped, its tip inside the room but the rest outside, battered by the storm. Slowly, it turned, the point coming back around to face the street.

As instantly as it had begun, the storm froze again. The hollow silence was more deafening than the wind that had died away.

The knife held its position, floating a metre above the ground, pointing out from the house. As frozen as the rain drops once again hanging in the air, driven and flat like the knife itself.

Then the knife shot away: away from the house, across the lawn, down the street and out of sight. All in a few heartbeats.

"Crisp Betty," Torg breathed.

Got that right, Johnny thought.

CHAPTER NINE

"What made it stop?" Johnny whispered.

"I do not know," Torg breathed, staring down the road where the knife had disappeared.

"It focused on the black things first."

Both Torg and Johnny jumped. Albert had rolled up behind them, the One in his shadow. Johnny'd had all three eyes focused on the street. Not a good habit. "What do you mean?" he snapped. He didn't like things sneaking up on him, especially if it was Albert.

"It attacked all the black things before turning on us. It prioritizes."

Johnny squinted. "I don't know. It was probably one of those things that took out Peralta."

"When there weren't any black things around them. Or Peralta and the others just got in its way."

"Maybe," Johnny said, one eye peering through the window. "I'm not sure though. That felt . . . weird."

Albert's stripes tilted. "Whatever. It was just a theory."

"I said maybe, all right? It's not like you were standing here."

"Yes, you were very brave—"

"Do you think perhaps you two could kill each other later?" Torg said smoothly. "We finally have a quiet moment, why don't we use it?"

Johnny and Albert eyed each other, the panzer behind Albert glaring at Johnny. *Great, he's made a friend.* So much for Johnny's efforts on the Pipe.

"Whatever," Johnny said finally.

"Huh," Albert grunted.

Torg sighed. "Better than nothing." He swung an eye. "Shabaz, get over here."

"What do you want?" Shabaz grumbled as she rolled out from behind the couch.

"I need you to watch the window."

Shabaz scowled and glanced at Johnny. "I thought he was in charge. Why me?"

Torg sighed again, a little more air in it this time. "Because we need someone we can trust to watch the street, all right? If you see anything, let us know." He rolled away, muttering to himself.

Bian looked up as Albert and Johnny tread into the centre of the room. "There's nine of us," she said. She flicked a guilty glance at Albert, then centred on Johnny. "Everyone's Five and up, except for a Two and her." She pointed at the One with Albert.

Nine left. Out of how many he'd saved following the Pipe? Dozens? The black spores had absolutely destroyed them.

"Wait a minute," Johnny said, scanning the room. "Where's Olli?"

"Vaped."

"Are you serious?" He felt an emptiness right down to his stripes. What was the point? He remembered telling the emerald-bronze skid he'd better make speed his thing. Apparently, it hadn't been enough.

"Hey," Bian said, bumping his tread. "There are nine of us here. I'm here. You made that happen. You saved us."

"Not all of us," the One said, glaring at Johnny.

Yep, she's picked a side. Although he was surprised to find himself smiling.

Bian rolled an eye. "Listen, I didn't mean . . ."

"It's all right, Bian," Johnny said. "Why don't I take this one?" Focusing two eyes on the purple-orange skid, he gave the panzer his full attention. "You're right. It wasn't just me." He brought one of the eyes up to Albert. Took a deep breath. "You saved two skids. That's worth something."

Albert smirked, his damaged eye twitching. "Two vs. seven, huh? Johnny Drop wins again?"

"Oh, for Crisp's sake, jackhole, I'm trying to give you some credit!"

"How magnanimous—"

"Stop it!" Bian snapped, rolling between them. "Both of you. Crisp Betty, you're like a couple of squids."

"Say hey to that," Torg murmured with a grin.

"It's not my fault," Johnny protested. "I was trying—"

"Stuff it in your gearbox," Bian said. "We don't know where we are. We don't have any idea what happened to the Skidsphere. For all we know we might be the only ones left." Her eyes narrowed—one on Johnny, one on Albert. "We're lost and we're scared. And wherever we are, we're not getting out of here without both of you. Torg's right: you can kill each other later."

The tension hung, then Johnny said, "Fine."

"Fine," Albert said in return.

"Good," Bian said, looking anything but satisfied. "Now . . . someone should say something to the group."

Johnny eyed Albert. The silver skid glared back at him, then his stripes tilted. "You heard Shabaz: you're in charge. Take the spotlight, Johnny Drop. It's what you're best at."

Johnny's temperature rose again, but to his surprise Bian tread forward and bumped Albert. "You know, he may not have saved you, Albert, but he saved me. I thought that might count for something. Guess not."

Albert's expression evaporated. "Bian, I . . ."

"Save it," she said, rolling away. Johnny almost felt bad for him.

Almost.

Trying to hide a smirk, he turned to the rest of the room. "All right, guys and girls, listen up. I don't know where we are—or much else for that matter—but we're alive."

"Barely," Brolin, a brown-black Seven grinned.

"Better than vaped," Johnny grinned back. "Now if we're going to survive we're going to have to work together. I know we don't really do that well." He caught some knowing smiles and added ruefully, "And I know that some of us get along better than others, but Bian's right: we have to try. So no more running off solo and maybe we'll get home."

"Where are we?" Brolin asked.

"We'll try to work on that next."

"How?"

"Stop asking good questions." That got a smile from most. "We'll figure it out, skids."

"And what if those black things come back?" Brolin said, not smiling this time.

"We'll figure something out," Johnny murmured. His trail-eye was drooping again. He concentrated and brought it back into focus. *Wouldn't mind figuring out what that is either.*

He turned to the Level Two, who was cream with a dark green stripe. "You're still alive," he said matter-of-factly.

"Yeah," she said, trying not to stare. "Thanks to you and Albert. He got me moving back there."

"Right. Did you follow our path? Inside the storm?"

The Two winced. "I didn't know I was supposed to."

"It's all right," Johnny said. She looked like she was going to faint. "You weren't. So you plowed through the rain."

Her eyes widened a bit at the memory. "Yeah."

"But you didn't get vaped."

"I thought I was for sure," she said, wincing again. "But I just . . . held it together. It hurt—snakes, did it hurt—but I tried to think of you and what happened up in . . . up in whatever that was on the Pipe. What was that?"

"I don't know. But what you did out there," he tapped an eye towards the door, "that was real good. I don't think you're a Two anymore."

"Really?" If her eyes went any wider they were going to explode.

"You get vaped?"

"No."

"Not a Two then. Which means you need a name."

Apparently, they could still go wider. "Really?" she squeaked, her stripes trembling. "I thought GameCorps gave those out."

"I don't think they're around just now." That got him a nervous smile. *Crisp Betty, was I like that?* Johnny couldn't ever remember feeling nervous about another skid. Cocky, sure. Dumb as grease? Yep. But he'd never been awed by anyone. Even Betty Crisp had been a target. "Looks like we're going to have to come up with a name on our own. If you could do one thing, what would it be?"

The green stripes flushed a bit. "I'd like to tread on a podium one day."

A podium. Singular. Yep, this one had a lot more humble than he did. But she'd survived the rain, so there was metal in there somewhere. "All right," he said, smiling, "we'll call you Aaliyah. I think it means 'Exalted One.'"

"Really? That's pretty. I don't know how exalted I am, though."

Johnny nudged forward. "Tell you what, I won't tell anyone if you don't." *Besides, a little cocky might be good for you.*

"Okay," she said, nervous but pleased. "Aaliyah. My name is Aaliyah."

Torg rolled up. "Johnny . . ."

"Torg, nice. Be the first to say hello to Aaliyah."

"Right on. Great name, Aaliyah. Exalted One, right?"

Johnny stifled a laugh as he saw the newly minted Aaliyah blanch, although the joy of hearing her own name followed the shame.

"Johnny, we have a problem."

"You mean other than the ones I already know about?"

"All right, we have a new problem."

"Fantastic," Johnny said, shaking his stripes. "I sure hope it's something that's going to kill us." He saw the look on Torg's face. "Oh, crap."

"Yeah," Torg said soberly.

They rolled back to where the group huddled around a yellow-blue skid. "Daytona got tagged by one of those black things," Torg said. "Not full on, but hard enough. He's a Five."

The skid looked awful. Like the others, he'd been stripped of his skins and glam, and now his colours had paled to the point where it was hard to see where his stripes began. Two of his eyes drooped to the floor, one showing only white. His treads sagged.

All over his body, blooms of black spores.

"Oh, Crisp Betty," Johnny whispered.

"I got tagged, too," Brolin said softly. One of the most laidback skids in the sphere, Brolin was staring at Daytona like he was going to puke. "Not bad . . . but there's something wrong with my Hasty-Arms."

Tagged? I ate one of those things.

Daytona's healthy eye drifted up and focused on Johnny. "I'm . . . I'm only three. . . ." The eye dropped.

"Three?" Johnny said, looking at Torg. "I thought you said he was a Five?"

"He doesn't mean levels," Albert said from the back of the group, his voice rough, staring at Daytona. "He means years. He's three years old. He should have two more."

"We have to do something," Bian insisted. Despite the spores fluttering across Daytona's skin, she'd nudged up to him and was gently running a hand across his body.

Johnny looked around, lost. His gaze, as it always seemed to do, settled on Albert.

The silver-white skid looked back, his damaged eye squinting, until his stripes pulsed once. As if it cost him, he swallowed and said: "Whatever happened after the Pipe, you saved more than me. If anyone's going to try something, it should be you."

And just what the hole was he supposed to try? Daytona's skin was getting worse. Half the skid was black, the darkness rolling around the body, spiky at the edges—blooms branching out from blooms, like the spores that had caused this to happen.

"Okay," Johnny breathed. "I'll try . . . something."

Popping both Hasty-Arms, he reached forward and placed his hands on the wounded Five. "Daytona? *Daytona?*" Nothing. Beneath his hands, the skid's body heaved with irregular gasps, as the blooms continued to spread.

Hold on skid. He took a deep breath. "Daytona, if you can hear me, concentrate on my hands. Try to hold them in your head." Shifting a hand to the left, Johnny tried to place it on one of the black spots, but the bloom rolled away. *Vape it,* he thought, *stay there.*

To his surprise, the bloom froze. *All right,* he thought, trying to remain calm as he slid his hand to centre on the bloom. *Here goes nothing.* He closed his eyes and concentrated on the black beneath his left hand and the healthy skin beneath his right.

Immediately, he could feel the difference. The healthy skin felt warm in comparison, while the hand on the bloom felt like it was being stabbed with a million tiny pinpricks.

Daytona shifted and groaned.

"Stay with me," Johnny murmured, keeping his eyes shut.

In the darkness following the Pipe, he'd done everything by instinct. He had no idea what he'd done, nor how long he'd taken to save each skid. Still, he remembered sending the idea of colour, the idea of a name, urging each skid to hold on. Now, he did the same, quietly repeating Daytona's name like a mantra while trying to transfer the sensation of the healthy skin beneath his right hand to the void beneath his left.

Hold on. . . .

"Betty Crisp," someone whispered, "it's spreading."

Not helping, Johnny thought, trying to shut out the voices. He reached into the black, attempting to pull the healthy skid with him, to reconnect molecule to molecule, to saturate the black with the thought of yellow, the thought of Daytona . . .

The body shifted again.

Hold on . . .

For a second, he had it. For a heartbeat, Johnny reached out and felt Daytona—or the thought of Daytona—somewhere beside him and pulled the areas of healthy skid together, closing the void . . . almost closing . . . *almost . . .*

Then the void bloomed beneath his right hand, right in the centre of the healthy skin. Someone cried out . . .

Vape it, Daytona, hold on!

The yellow in Johnny's mind began to blacken . . .

. . . hold . . .

The skin beneath his hands began to dissolve . . .

. . . on.

Johnny opened his eyes in time to see Daytona evaporate into nothing.

"Snakes," he swore softly, too exhausted to feel any rage. "Snakes, snakes, snakes."

Bian let the hand that had been comforting Daytona drop. She nudged Johnny. "It's all right," she whispered. "At least you tried."

"*It's not all right!*" Johnny yelled, angry at himself, angry at her, angry at himself for being angry at her. It was as if a great big hole was opening up inside his heart and trying to pull everything he cared for down into the dark.

Looking around, he saw fear on every skid's face. Brolin looked like he was going to scream.

"It's not all right," he said again, calmer. "Daytona

died and he was three years old. That is *not* all right. And it's got to stop." His gaze swept the group. "I don't know how, but I swear to you we're going to get out of this. We are not going to die here." He rolled up to Brolin. "I don't know what happened to him or you, but I got tagged, too."

"Tagged?" Torg scoffed. "You swallowed one."

"And my eye's been going spare since." Johnny kept his gaze on Brolin. "We are not going to die here." He held the look until some of the terror faded from the Seven's face. Surveying the room again, he added, "I know that sounds like empty words, but starting now we're going to start figuring stuff out. No one else dies." He glanced at the purple-orange One. "And I don't care what level you are, you need a name, panzer."

"She's got a name," Albert said brusquely.

That stopped Johnny. "You gave her a name?"

"She gave herself a name."

"You let a Level One name herself?"

A snort escaped Albert. "You really think levels matter out here? Why shouldn't she name herself? Or does everything have to get the Johnny Drop approval?"

"All right, fine, I get it," Johnny muttered. "Is this going to be a thing every time? I'm just checking."

The One looked back and forth between them. "Wow, you guys really don't like each other."

Johnny could have said something; instead, he laughed. "Well, that's true. All right, panzer, what's your name?"

"Torres. And I'm not a panzer anymore."

"You're a panzer until Torg says otherwise. Right, Torg?"

"Damn straight, squid."

"See? After nearly four years I've moved up to squid."

He eyed the purple-orange skid. "Torres, huh? Pretty flashy, don't you think, Torg?"

"Doesn't remind me of anyone at all."

Snorting, Johnny said, "All right, *Torres*, you got a name. But whether levels matter out here or not,"—and under no circumstances was he going to let Albert know that he agreed with him—"we still have to keep you alive. Which means you need to learn not to vape yourself."

"Not a problem."

"Not a problem?" Johnny said skeptically.

"Albert taught me a few things," Torres said.

Crisp, this kid's cocky. Aloud, he said, "Albert taught you a few things, did he?" One of his eyes twitched in Albert's direction.

Torres zipped forward and bumped Johnny. "Why? You think you're the only one who can teach me anything?"

Did that panzer just bump me? Fighting the urge to pop her through the wall, Johnny said, "All right, that's enough. Seriously. Not everything I say is an attack on Albert, all right?"

"Can't be more than ninety percent, tops," Torg said.

"Shut up, Torg."

"Sure thing, boss."

Betty Crisp. "Torres," Johnny said firmly, trying to decide whether to laugh or scream, "if Albert taught you anything to keep you alive, that's great." He took a deep breath, flicked an eye at Albert, and said, "Really. It's great."

He was pretty sure they both thought, *Vape me*, at the same time.

"Oh, he taught me plenty. See?" Before they could react, Torres zipped out the door into the same frozen rain that had already killed a Level One today.

"Torres!" Albert and Johnny yelled, even as they heard a roar of pain.

Before they could get halfway across the room, the purple skid came screeching back through the door, roaring at the top of her lungs. With a tremendous crash that flattened her whole body out of round, Torres popped off the wall and swerved to a halt in front of the stunned crowd.

"I did it!" she screamed in a triumphant voice that made it blatantly clear she hadn't been sure she *could* do it. All three of her eyes were wild with glee and terror. "Ow, ow, ow, ow, ow," she half-growled, half-roared, spitting out each 'ow' like a curse. "Ow. Crisp Betty that hurt." She froze, eyes centred on a single thought, then she bounced off the walls again, hard, and popped both Hasty-Arms. "I did it!" she yelled again.

"Wow," Johnny said, stunned. "That was stupid."

Some—but not all—of the glee fell from Torres's face and she rolled right up to Johnny. "I'm alive, ain't I?" she protested. "Now we know."

"And you didn't before?" At least she hadn't bumped him this time. "You could've got yourself killed."

Stabbing a Hasty-Arm towards Albert, Torres spoke— fiercely, like she was declaring war. "He saved me. He told me what to do to save myself. I trust *him*."

Tension rose, but this time it wasn't Torg or Bian who relieved it. It wasn't Johnny.

"Okay, Torres," Albert said, rolling forward. He looked shaken, his damaged eye blinking repeatedly. "That's enough. Thank you, but . . . it's enough." He glanced at Bian, as if offering peace. "Bian's right. We all need each other. Everyone."

Torres glared at Johnny, then the glee won over once more. "Did you see that, Albert?"

"Yes," Albert said, taking a long shaky breath. "It was very impressive."

"For a squid," Torg drawled.

"Hey," Torres said, swinging towards Torg, instantly hurt, "I'm not . . . oh." With a look of innocence that Johnny knew very well, Torg gazed back at her.

"Oh," the purple skid said again. "Okay, I get it. Thanks." A shy but wicked grin crossed her face. "Panzer."

"Old Panzer," Torg corrected her. "Come here, we'll work on the lingo."

As Torg and Torres rolled away, Johnny said to Albert, "You know she was going to do that?"

"No." Staring out the open door, the silver skid looked like he half-expected Torres to jump back out into the frozen rain.

"Right, uh . . . nice work then." Johnny hesitated, then added, "What did you tell her?"

"Same thing we all learn. Start with colour. Feel it, don't think. Hold on. Pull it together. She's smart, she'd have figured it out on her own. But we don't have time."

"Huh," Johnny said. "Well . . . it worked."

"Yeah," Albert said. He exhaled violently. "Stupid squid."

For a moment—just a moment—they made eye contact, each with a faint knowing grin. Then, realizing it at the same time . . . the grins faded and they looked away.

Torres was taking congratulations from the rest of the room. She exchanged names with Aaliyah, each skid grinning like they'd just won the Slope. Bian was talking to Brolin, saying something low and soothing. Johnny caught her looking his way before she quickly averted her gaze. Something was going on there, but damned if Johnny knew what it was.

Torg rolled up. "Interesting skid," he said, an eye on Torres.

"Yeah," Johnny agreed. "She's a lippy one."

Torg barked a laugh. "I could see how that could get annoying."

"Shut up, Torg."

"Sure thing, boss."

Johnny sighed. "You gonna keep calling me that?"

"I'm giving it some serious consideration."

Johnny chuckled; he never could get mad at Torg. Sometimes he wished he had the old panzer's equilibrium.

"Nice to have a positive," Torg murmured, tapping an eye towards Torres.

"Yeah," Johnny said. It was pretty amazing the effect it had on everyone. For the first time since they'd fallen into the darkness, every skid in the room seemed to relax. Johnny began to believe that maybe they'd find a way out after all.

That's when the storm kicked back in.

"Snakes, that's loud," Johnny swore as the wind instantly geared up to a roar.

"Uh, guys?" Shabaz said, perched near the window. "I think there's something out there."

CHAPTER TEN

"White or black?" Johnny said, zipping over to the window.

"I'm not sure," Shabaz said nervously. "Down the street. Whatever it is, it's moving slow."

Outside, the storm thundered at full force. High winds slapped the roof like giant hands, driving the rain, so thick it was hard to see the next house.

"I don't—oh wait, got it," Johnny said, scoping until he found a spectrum that cut through the flood. Opposite from where the knife had disappeared, a single white shape was gliding down the street.

"Doesn't look like the other things," Torg murmured.

"No . . ." Johnny said, not quite so sure.

It resembled the white knives in size and shape, although it was a little larger and much thicker at the core. Like the knives, this new shape floated a metre above the ground; however, it floated flat instead of edge down. And it was more triangular, the thick body flaring out like wings.

And unlike the perfect knives . . . this thing wasn't perfect.

The knives had moved with flawless precision—slow and steady like sharks. This thing had a hitch: every metre or so its glide checked to the left or the right. One side drooped slightly. Whatever it was, it had taken damage: scars and scuff marks stained the white surface.

Johnny frowned. "Either of you get the feeling this thing's . . . different?"

"It's not threatening," Torg agreed.

"It's not?" Shabaz said.

"Don't look with your fear," Torg said gently. "Johnny's right, there's a different intent."

Shabaz stared out the window, her eyes wide. "If you say so." The shape drifted into their block. "Do you think it saw the panzer?"

"Maybe," Johnny said.

"Think it's tied to the storm?" Torg said, peering through the rain.

"Huh," Johnny grunted. "There's an interesting idea." Turning to the room, he said quietly, "Okay skids, I don't think this thing's dangerous but get ready to move, just in case."

"Where?" Brolin asked. "There's no back door."

"Really?" Johnny said, turning back to the window. "Well . . . that sucks."

In front of the house, the white shape stopped, wobbling a bit in the pounding rain.

"Looks like it's been in a fight," Johnny said.

"Looks like it's been in a few," Torg added.

Shabaz started to ask: "With those other—*oh, oh wow.*"

Before their eyes, the shape on the street unfolded. Its front tip swung up, as treads like a skid's emerged from its bottom. Settling onto the treads, four Hasty-Arms popped from its sides. The top twisted and fell back, revealing a head with a mouth and five eyes that resembled holla lenses: two in front, one to each side and the back. A shutter like a thinlid covered the upper edge of each eye, shifting and blinking as it rotated its head towards the house.

"Okay," Torg whispered, "that was pretty sweet."

In this configuration, the damage was more apparent. The upper arm on its left and the lower arm on the right hung awkwardly at its side. The eye on the left face was cracked, the lens-shutter stuck halfway down. A piece above its right-side tread seemed to be missing and there were cracks in some of the treads themselves.

It sat there, facing the house; one damaged arm twitching as the lens-lids vibrated in the rain.

"Now what?" Johnny said.

"We don't have to go out there, do we?" Shabaz breathed.

To everyone's surprise, she got an answer.

"I-We will enter shortly." The creature's mouth moved, although the voice cutting through the storm seemed to come from some deep resonant space. "Fear not. Even the trees have spikes, but I-We am friend. Wish to dispel anticipation of danger. Wobble."

"Good luck with that," Shabaz muttered.

Johnny chuckled. He actually thought the creature was succeeding, but he empathized with the Six.

"Query," said the creature. "May We-I enter? Holes in the system. Answers-answers are incomplete but with merit."

"What the hole does that mean?" Shabaz protested. "We're not going to let that thing in here."

Johnny twisted a bemused eye at her. "And what

makes you think we could stop it?"

"At least it has manners," Torg said. When Shabaz gaped at him, he added: "It did ask."

"Debate is understood but time-time is essence. Ticks in the tocks. Query: May We-I enter? Wobble."

"Everything but please," Johnny said. His stripes tilted. "What the hole, live fast . . ." Raising his voice, he said, "Come in out of the rain."

"Kindness. Warm and fuzzy. Sometimes there are Teddy Bears. We-I will now come-come inside. Fear not. I-We have no harm intention." It spread its working arms as if to show a lack of threat. Slowly, with the same hitch in its treads as when it floated, the creature approached the house.

"Let's meet the neighbours," Torg said.

The creature had to spread its treads and crouch to get under the doorframe, before straightening out with a mechanical whir. Water dripped from its frame as it stopped just inside the room.

A long silence, as the creature and eight stunned skids stared at each other.

It occurred to Johnny that, in the last week, he'd done the most famous Drop in skid history, been given a second name, heard whispers that sounded a hole of a lot like his dead girlfriend and come awfully close to giving Albert a compliment.

Despite all that, Johnny was pretty sure that this was the weirdest moment of his life.

Gears whirred and the creature said, "Business cards and claw-clacking. I-We am Wobble. Wobble."

Johnny couldn't wipe the grin from his face. Wobble? No matter how battered it looked, the thing felt like it had power to burn the world. And it was called Wobble?

"That, my friend, is an awesome name. Uh, claw-clack

back at you." He swept an arm across the room. "We're the skids. I'm Johnny Drop." He heard Albert make a derisive sound. *Vape you too, gearbox.*

Mirroring Johnny, Wobble swept an undamaged arm across the skids. "Lights appearing in winter. Your world is going to die."

Johnny stopped grinning. "What did you say?"

Gears whirred and the lids over Wobble's lenses snapped open and shut. "Inappropriate," the machine protested, but it seemed to berate itself. "Too soon, no port-of-call. There are-are no smoking pipes." It paused. "Please accept apologies. There are loops in time. This conversation has happened-happened but not yet. You need not fear I-Me. We are the good guys. I am Wobble."

"You're insane," Shabaz whispered under her breath.

Johnny thought she had a point. *Though it did say please.* Aloud, he said, "What do you mean: 'Our world is going to die?'"

"Spoken too soon. She got scared and never-never called again." Somehow, the machine managed to look dejected. "There are scars-scars. Breaks in the system. Virus runs-runs-runs everywhere. You have seen them. Black scars. The system is breaking." Without warning, Wobble focused its lenses on Johnny and moved forward a tread. "Not without hope. Clutch the flotsam. She yet lives."

Johnny's heart dropped. *Peg?*

Wobble's head swiveled. Backing up, it said, "Anti are coming. We must leave. Wobble."

"Woah," Johnny said, "wait a minute. Who lives? Who is '*she?*'"

Wobble's head continued to rotate as if he were searching. "We-You must leave. Anti are coming."

"Tell me who you meant by—"

"Hold on, Johnny," Torg said, sliding forward. "Wobble, who are the Anti? Those black shapes?"

"Not virus-virus. Anti-virus. White. Clean. Perfect. Except for the damage." Wobble's head froze. "They are not Teddy Bears."

"Stop talking about Teddy Bears," Johnny snapped. "Tell me who *she* is."

"Answers have been answered soon. Leave—"

"No, answers will be answered now."

"Johnny," Torg said in that calm, firm voice that could stop a bar-fight in the pits after a game. "If those white things are coming back, then Wobble's right. We need to get some place safer. Answers can wait."

Johnny glared at Torg, but his trail eye saw a room of frightened skids. Bian, striving to sooth the wounded Brolin; Shabaz, by the window, trying to fake cocky and looking like a panzer on her first Slope instead; Aaliyah, not far from Shabaz and even more scared; Albert and Torres, the only ones who didn't reek of fear. *Squid might live up to her name after all,* Johnny thought, lingering on Torres for a heartbeat before his gaze came back to Bian.

She gazed back, glanced at Torg, then bobbed an eye.

"Fine," Johnny growled, "let's go. But we're not done with this conversation, Wobble."

"Stored and filed," the machine said. "Conference in the corner, hands on chin. Now we leave." He began to roll, one tread creaking with the sound of metal on metal.

"There's no back door," Bian called. "I checked."

"Always back doors. Side doors too. Sometimes ceiling will open." Wobble's head spun and its face twisted into a metallic smile. "I write the wardrobe. Wobble."

Bian blinked as he rolled into the back room. Abruptly, she laughed. "I think I like him. He's not going to find a door," she added to Johnny, "but he's cute."

"If he keeps us alive I'll take him into the woods," Shabaz muttered.

The back room had almost no furnishings at all, just a sliver of a cupboard and some kind of metallic device that Johnny suspected was visible through the drapes in the front room.

Facing a blank wall, Wobble went still. "See?" Bian said, "No . . ." Her eyes widened. "Crisp Betty."

You can say that again.

One second, a blank wall; the next, a door. Wobble's head spun, still grinning. "See? Pulling sand from the black-black hole. Thunderous applause. Spin the conductor."

"Where's it go?" Johnny demanded, grimacing. He was starting to sound like Shabaz.

"Safety? No." The self-berating tone came back. "Nowhere is safe." Wobble's lenses focused on Johnny and the shutters tilted to one side. "Sometimes it hurts. Hurts." The damaged left arm jerked once. The machine suddenly looked so full of sorrow that Johnny wanted to comfort it.

Instead, it was Bian who spoke. "Wobble, if it's not safe through that door, is it *safer*? For now?"

Instantly, the smile whirred back into place. "Context! One clock runs faster if we stand on the train." The lenses zoomed in on Bian. "*Safer.* You have given I-We context. Warm and fuzzy."

"Glad I could help," Bian murmured, looking pleased.

Wobble's lenses adjusted to take in all the skids. "I-We go first. Trust the light. All is warm-warm and fuzzy. Wobble." He opened the door.

Behind it, a black void.

"Oh, vape me," Brolin groaned.

Johnny was about to agree . . . when he saw that the darkness was different from the one on the Pipe. In that darkness, there'd been broken strings of light, parallel threads twisted and abruptly shorn, sparking like uncapped electrical wires. Inside Wobble's door, the lines weren't cut. And there were more lines. A lot more. As Johnny's eyes adjusted, the dark seemed alive with bands of warm golden light, each perfectly straight, cornering at precisely ninety or forty-five degrees.

"It's beautiful," Bian whispered.

"Some parts hold," Wobble agreed. "Clutching the flotsam." The grin was back. "Drop the fuel cells and set-set them on fire. I-We-We-We're going for a ride." Then he rolled through the doorway and vanished into a flicker of golden light.

Johnny glanced at Torg. "Take the rear. I'll go next."

"If you see any flotsam you might want to grab it," the Nine drawled.

"Right."

Johnny rolled forward. For some reason, right before he crossed the threshold, he glanced at Bian, only to find her looking back. Then he crossed a line and the world streaked into darkness and light.

CHAPTER ELEVEN

Okay, that sucked less.

The trip through the door was near instantaneous. One second, Johnny rolled across the threshold; his vision filling with light and a slight plucking at his skin, as if his front was being pulled forward faster than his back. Then his back caught up—*like rebounding off something in reverse*—and his treads found solid ground.

The strange storm-battered town was gone. In its place, something like the Skidsphere, except saturated in black and gold. In front of them, a black building rose into a black-gold sky. A narrow corridor stretched out in the distance—building after building, each outlined with the same threads that filled the doorway, some thick enough to wash the world with a golden glow.

"Ain't that something to see?" Torg said, rolling up.

Johnny frowned. "I thought you were bringing up the rear."

"Albert told me to go ahead."

Johnny decided to let it slide. "Wonder where we are?"

"Question of the day. Although when everything was white we were getting our gears kicked. So maybe this will work out."

"It was pretty black after the Pipe," Johnny pointed out.

Torg rolled his eyes. "That's what I like about you, Johnny. You help."

Torres came through the door like she was waiting for it to fight back, followed by Albert. "That's everyone," he said, treading over to Bian. She sniffed and rolled away.

Johnny stifled a grin as Shabaz rolled up, her aquamarine stripes appearing brighter than normal. "Now what?" she demanded. "Are we safe now?"

Wobble's gears whirred, the machine's white surface shining dimly beneath his scars. They all glowed a little, Johnny realized. Not just from the golden lines: every skid's stripes glowed like the light that diffused the air. Torg was right: it was something to see.

"Safer," Wobble said to Shabaz. "Nowhere is safe. Now You-We go find answers-answers. Follow."

"Hold on, Wobble," Johnny said. "We get it, we're still in danger. If we know something about the danger, maybe we can help. We're treading blind here."

"Logic," Wobble said. "Answer questions as we go. We are taking the long way home. Wobble."

"All right, but first tell us about the white and black things. You made it sound like they're not the same."

"Black holes and toasters," Wobble agreed. "Black are Vies. White are Anti. Hunters. Good guys wear white."

"What's a vie?" Johnny asked.

"Vie. Virus. Don't touch the monkey."

"Virus?" Shabaz said. "What's sick?"

The shutters on all four of Wobble's working eyes swung wide. "Everything," he whirred, his head spinning.

"Entropy calls. No one is watching." His lenses focused on Albert, then Johnny. "It hurts," Wobble whirred softly, his shutters twisting. "Can you-you make it stop? She said you could make it stop. Wobble."

"There!" Johnny said, shifting forward a tread. "You keep saying: *she*. Who is she?" His heart was pounding.

Wobble's head spun three hundred and sixty degrees. "Answer in the future. She said not to tell." Then the machine actually winked at him.

"Look—"

"Johnny," Torg said, "eyes on the line. Solve the threat first." To Wobble, he added, "Albert said the whites—the Antis—hunt the Vies first, that they prioritize. Is that right?"

"Affirmative."

Johnny very deliberately did not look around to see the smug expression on Albert's face.

"But we were getting attacked by the Vies," Torg continued. "So why did the Antis hunt us? That doesn't make any sense."

"We are all Vies."

Torg frowned. "We're all viruses? Is that what you mean?"

"Systems fail. All are Vies. The cops are corrupt-corrupt. Nowhere is safe." Wobble's head spun and then rotated like a gyroscope. *That's new*, Johnny thought as Wobble continued: "They appear anywhere. The Crocs dropped from the Fourth Wave." The machine rolled down the street. "We-You travel now. Answer questions as we roll. Wobble."

"Just a sec." Johnny said. To the group, he announced, "It looks like we can trust Wobble. But if we get attacked again, stay tight. No solo heroes. Let's go." He saw Albert drop to the back. Good. Johnny didn't want to deal with him, but the silver skid could probably keep everyone together.

The buildings all had long windows, glowing faintly from within. Inside, Johnny could make out vague outlines and shapes. They looked familiar.

"What do you think those are?" Johnny asked Torg.

"Music," Wobble chirped. "Listen-listen to Marley wail. The Dregs sold out. Wobble."

"What?"

"I think he's right," Torg murmured. "That one we just passed. Pretty sure I saw a drum set. They're bands."

"But they're not moving."

"Neither was that storm we hit. If you think about it, it was kind of like a holla on pause."

"Huh." Peering through the windows, he had to agree with Torg. They did look like bands. He glanced at Wobble. "Think we could get him to explain what they're doing here? In a way we understand?"

Torg laughed. "I think we find out where we're going, then try again."

"Right," Johnny grunted, as Bian rolled up. "How's Brolin?"

"I think he's stable. Terrified, but stable. If he's getting worse, it's a lot slower than what hit Daytona." She studied him. "What about you? Shabaz said you ate one of those . . . Vies. Is that what happened to your eye?"

"I'm fine," Johnny said, although he noticed his focus had slipped again. Trying to ignore the nervous flutter in his guts, he fixed the eye. "Thanks for asking."

Her stripes flushed a little. "Speaking of Brolin, we might have something else to worry about. Are you getting hungry?"

"Uhh . . . not really?"

"You?" she asked Torg.

Torg's stripes tilted. "I could eat. Why?"

"Because I'm starting to feel it. Most of the others are feeling the same. It's more pronounced in the Sixes and under."

"Okay . . ." Johnny said slowly, not understanding.

"Oh, snakes," Torg said. "No sugar."

"That's right." Running a hand along the building beside her, Bian tapped a glowing gold line. "I don't know where we are, but it isn't the Skidsphere. Which means we're nowhere near a sugarbar."

Johnny frowned. "So we all get a little hungry. So what?"

"Johnny, we've been out here for what, half a day? What if we don't get back home for a week? Or longer? Everybody here ran the equivalent of a Rainbow Road getting away from those black things. Plus half a Pipe before that. And that's not counting the emotional strain. We're not used to this. Everyone's burning energy."

"That fast?"

Bian glanced skeptically at Torg, who smirked. "How would he know? He's Johnny Drop, remember? Squid's practically a superhero."

"Hey!" Johnny protested, halfway between offended and pleased. "What the hole does that mean?"

"It means no skid here works as efficiently as you," Torg explained. "The higher the level, the more efficient a skid gets, right? So you and I might run faster, longer, and harder than a Six, but we'll burn far longer too. Don't you remember how hungry you'd get after a game when you were a Three or Four? Crisp, I used to sprint for the swizz."

Johnny frowned. "Yeah, I guess I used to suck a lot of sugar. But I don't remember starving."

"There're other factors. Johnny, you're different—we

all know it. Hole, GameCorps knew it. You probably ran cleaner than I do now by the time you were a Six." He hesitated, then swung an eye towards the back of the group. "Come to think of it, you're not the only one. I wonder if Albert's feeling anything."

"Why don't you go ask your boyfriend if he's feeling empty?" Johnny said.

Bian's eyes narrowed. "He's not my boyfriend."

Johnny and Torg stared at her.

Her stripes flushed, then she clamped it down. "Anyway, I just wanted you guys to know what's going on. I don't know how Brolin might be affected, but we're going to need sugar sometime soon, especially if we keep having to push it. See you, Torg. Johnny."

They watched her drop into the pack. "She dumped Albert?" Johnny chuckled. "When the hole did that happen?"

"I'm not sure she's told him yet," Torg murmured, looking towards the back.

"Really? Do you think I can tell him?"

"You're a jackhole," Torg laughed. He looked from Bian . . . to Johnny . . . and back to Bian. "Huh."

"What?"

"Nothing," Torg sighed. "And I thought getting killed was going to be our biggest problem. Hey, look at that."

Halfway up a building, one of the profile lines ended abruptly, glowing like a sparkler against the black surface.

"Uh-oh," Johnny said as Wobble slowed enough for them to catch up.

"Yellow alert-alert," Wobble whirred, his head spinning. "Prime the tubes. Rough sector of town."

"Then why'd we come this way?" Shabaz asked nervously.

"Safest route. In through the outdoor. No Antis. Too few-few Vies. They thought this worm was dead."

"How few-few Vies?" Torg said, spreading his eyes and scanning the street.

"Intention of query: not few enough." Suddenly, Wobble grinned. "Except We-You have We-Me. Wobble."

Johnny considered the hitch in the machine's tread and the arms dangling at its side. "Right," he said. Glancing at Torg, he added, "Let's hope it's fewer than a lot." He clicked his com. "Bian, get them a little tighter. Albert, you see anything back there?"

"I'd probably let you know," replied a dry voice.

"Crisp Betty, you're a panzer," Johnny muttered. "No wonder Bian dumped you."

"You turn off your com before you said that last bit?" Torg asked.

Johnny returned the grin. "I don't remem—"

"Incoming!" Albert barked. "Ten-Eighty-Three!"

In the next few seconds, several things happened at once. Snapping two eyes up and to his left, Johnny scanned the sky. He saw two black shadows peeling out from a building with severed profile lines. "Time—" he started to say, as a third black shape emerged from the broken building.

It was as far as he got. He'd been going to say: *Time to move.*

Wobble beat him to it.

The machine might have been moving before Albert finished his warning. Johnny actually missed the moment when Wobble left the ground, his treads folding seamlessly into his body. What he did see was the end of Wobble's transformation, as his entire body twisted and whirred without a single hitch until it returned to the shape they'd first seen—like a turbo-charged Anti—pointing straight up.

. . . *Sweet*—

Flat and lean except for a central bulge of power, Wobble exploded into the sky.

—*Betty*—

Two projectiles like circular saws on fire dropped from Wobble's underside and screamed through the first two Vies. Wobble tore directly through the third.

—*Crisp.*

Almost as an after-thought, Wobble dropped back to earth, twisting and whirring as he went. He landed on his treads like a dancer.

"Wow," Torg said.

"Affirmative," Wobble whirred, grinning his metal grin. "Screw the cloak, I-We bring the end. Wobble."

Johnny couldn't help but laugh as the machine's broken arm jerked at his side.

So much for damaged goods.

CHAPTER TWELVE

For the next few minutes, all the skids could talk about was Wobble.

"Did you see that?" Shabaz cried, her eyes waving like they were in a parade.

"And you didn't want to let the dude through the door," Brolin laughed, listing a little as he rolled down the street, Bian hanging by his side.

"Hey, I'm just cautious."

Ahead of them, Torg and Johnny tread behind the hero of the hour, holding a similar conversation.

"I'd say we're certainly safer," Johnny mused. He couldn't get over how *fast* Wobble had moved.

"Sure," Torg agreed. "But that was only three of them. Out in that white space we got hit by a few hundred. Those Antis are what saved us. And who knows how he'd match up against them."

"Do you think he could be one?" Johnny frowned under the golden light of the buildings they passed. "They kinda look the same."

"A little. Wobble's thicker in the middle. More power. And none of the Antis did his transforming trick." Torg grinned. "Plus, none of them seemed like they were of the mind to chat."

"Huh," Johnny grunted. "Hey, was it just me or did his wobble disappear there for a moment?"

"Noticed that too, did you? Yeah. *That* reminded me of the Antis."

Up ahead, Wobble hitched to the left. Johnny watched him correct his gait, then murmured, "Good thing he's on our side, I guess."

They came to a new section. The buildings now contained row-upon-row, column-upon-column of hollas, stretching up into the gold-black sky. And now that the buildings were lit, it was obvious they did more than stretch up.

They also stretched down.

"Look at that," someone whispered.

Beneath their treads, they rolled across a semi-transparent floor, like heavily-tinted glass. Through that layer, the columns of hollas sank so far down Johnny couldn't see where they ended. There were millions of them. Looking up, he wondered if the sky was actually just another tinted street. There could be layers upon layers . . .

"Betty Crisp, this place is big," he heard Shabaz breathe.

"These look like highlights," Torg said, running his gaze up and down, his body awash with their flickering light. He tapped an eye towards one. "That looks like some kind of race."

The hollas showed hundreds of different types of creatures. Many were upright like Wobble—like Wobble they had four Hasty-Arms, although they seemed to tread on two of them.

Some of the displays were definitely competitions. In some, creatures fought. In some, creatures looked out, as if they were trying to speak directly to Johnny. In some, there were no creatures, just images.

"They're not all highlights," he murmured.

"Look at that one," Aaliyah whispered. "It's just like the Slope."

"No, it's not," Shabaz said, although her voice was also hushed. "It's too flat."

Johnny found the one they were talking about. Shabaz was right—the environment was flat and empty. Plus, the dust didn't cover the whole area.

In one, a creature stood and pointed at another holla within the holla. In another, some kind of construction. In another, two creatures seemed to fight in close quarters, although both appeared to be enjoying it at times.

"Well, at least some of them are," Torg said.

"What?"

"Highlights."

"Why?" Johnny said, tearing an eye away from a holla where two creatures appeared to be making out. Why would you show highlights of that?

Torg pointed. "From me: eleven up, six left."

Johnny found the image. He'd seen it before: The Rainbow Road.

"I don't think it's current," Torg said. "Don't recognize anyone."

"Think it's a 'Best Of?'"

"Maybe."

A queasy feeling began to churn in Johnny's gut. With an eye in each direction and one fixed on the Rainbow

Road, he looked up and down the street.

Highlight shows weren't made for skids. Oh sure, they showed them in the sugarbars and skids got a snort out of seeing themselves play. But even the most vain skid knew that the 'lights weren't for them. The highlights were made for . . .

"Torg," Johnny said slowly. "You don't think this could be the Out There, do you?"

"I was wondering when you were going to mention that." Torg followed his gaze. "Not a lot of company, is there?"

If anything, the flickering from the hollas made the streets feel even more forlorn. With the exception of the Vies, they hadn't seen another living thing since the house in the storm.

Where they also hadn't seen another living thing.

The sick feeling rose as Johnny peered down the street. Millions of hollas and no one watching them run. A cold shiver shot through his stripes. *No one is watching.* Wobble had said that. Somewhere in the twisted mess of his speech, Wobble had whispered: *No one is watching.* He'd been speaking nonsense; the words had slipped by without Johnny really thinking about them. Now . . .

What if Wobble was right? What if GameCorps didn't exist? What if no one was in the Out There?

What if no one was watching?

Because if that was true, then just what the hole had Johnny been striving for all these years?

"This can't be the Out There," he muttered. "It can't be," he insisted again as he caught Torg staring at him. "Somebody gave me a second name. I didn't do that." He ran his eyes over the hollas. Someone had to be watching all this somewhere. They had to be . . .

He stopped, staring at a wall.

"What are you doing?" Torg said. "What do you—oh. Well . . . damn."

On the opposite side of the street, dozens of hollas up, another highlight from the Skidsphere. This time of the Skates, a game that was closer to the artistic qualities of the Pipe than the raw-power of the Slope or Tilt. Although it wasn't without violence.

For all intents and purposes, skids skated a routine meant to display strength and beauty and grace. It would have been purely artistic except for one thing: each skid skated their routine along with fifty other skids. Who, in addition to doing their own routine, were trying to pummel you off yours.

Dozens of skids streamed around a massive ice-surface like a parade of kaleidoscopes. Some completed their intricate series of flips, loops, and spins. Some were knocked off trick. Some were plowed into the boards, where moves were awarded extra points due to the risk of collision. If you popped someone hard enough into the boards you could vape them. It wasn't common, but it happened often enough and was highly rewarded.

The highlight took turns centring on different competitors. But it kept returning to one skid in particular: a bright pink skid with cherry red stripes.

"Peg," Johnny whispered, a space in his heart seeming to empty and fill all at once.

Johnny had never been particularly good at the Skates. Grace wasn't really his thing: he was all about power. That was true for most skids; the ratio of games that rewarded power over grace was significant. Johnny almost never thought of his kind as graceful.

Except when he'd watched Peg.

"This looks like the one—" Torg started to say.

"I know which one it is."

With all three of his eyes, he watched her launch spinning into the air. Watched two skids zero in on her in mid-flight—*Was that Boti? Crisp Betty, I forgot about that old panzer.* Watched as Peg spun, almost as if she'd created a hole within herself, out from in-between the attack—the two skids colliding almost comically in the space she'd vacated—to continue her pattern as if the attack had been part of the pattern all along.

He heard Bian roll up. "Why did we . . . oh. Oh, snakes."

"What did we stop for?" Shabaz said. "What are we—?"

"Shabaz," Albert said. "Shut up."

Far above them, Peg floated across the ice for a few more seconds, then the holla cut away. Johnny watched for a moment more, praying it would cut back. But it didn't.

"Crisp Betty," he whispered.

Skids didn't hold on to other skids. They went through relationships like they went through life: brief, hard, and fast. Johnny remembered thinking it made good drama for the Out There.

But Johnny had held onto Peg.

Turning his eyes away from the holla, his trail-eye fell on Albert, who was watching him. An old rage flared in his gut.

He might have done something then, for his hatred of Albert was one of the core parts of his life. And Peg was at the core of that hate. But as one eye fell on Albert, the other two found Wobble looking at him, the machine's face twisted.

"All-all is not lost. She is waiting. Wobble."

Hope flared inside Johnny's skin. Dead was dead, that had to be true. But days after Peg had disappeared, a stone had appeared with a name etched in its surface.

And six months later, a group of skids had fallen into a black darkness, eviscerating everything it touched, and yet eight of them were still here.

Albert had always claimed that Peg had fallen through a crack that had just opened up . . .

Glancing a final time at the holla, Johnny looked at Wobble. He took a long, shaky breath. "Fine," he said. "Let's not make her wait any longer."

That's when the ground collapsed beneath their feet.

CHAPTER THIRTEEN

The entire world bucked to the left—*hard*—and then to the right. *Corpsquake*, Johnny had time to think before the street beneath them cracked like a sheet of ice.

"Negatory, Negatory," Wobble cried, his body already twisting and transforming. "Betelgeuse is stable, sir. She won't nova-nova for a million years."

Well, she's going nova now, Johnny thought as the ice shattered and skids began to fall. "Go thin, people," he yelled. "Control it as much as you can."

"Crisp, I'm tired of falling," Torg sighed, spreading thin.

Remarkably, Johnny remained calm, even as hollas above and below exploded out from buildings in fireworks of incandescent light. Whatever this was, he was pretty sure it wasn't an attack, which made it more like a game.

Except that some skids were better at the games than others.

"Aaliyah!" Bian cried.

"Help!" the cream-green skid screamed, plunging into the abyss below.

Snakes, Johnny thought, eyes scoping. Of course Aaliyah couldn't go flat yet, most skids didn't think in any shape other than round until Five or higher. Nearby, Albert clutched onto Torres with a Hasty-Arm, giving her instructions.

That's what I should have done. Hole, that's what we all should be doing.

"Everybody grab somebody!" he yelled, well aware it was a little late. Angling his body, he dived after Aaliyah. Instinctively, he popped off a chunk of falling street, stealing its energy. Gaining speed, he popped back and forth, accelerating faster than Aaliyah could fall.

Drop Johnny Drop, he grinned. "Hold on, sugar, I'm coming!" Of course, once he caught her, how were they going to get back up to the others?

Fortunately, Wobble solved that problem. "Salutations," the machine said as it tore past Johnny at twice his speed, his body narrowed down to a spike, his arms stretched forward. He caught Aaliyah and turned. "Stay here," he said as they passed Johnny on the way up. "We-I will return."

"Sure thing," Johnny laughed as he flattened out to slow his fall. "Glad I could help."

He watched Wobble fly back to the pack of falling skids—*wow, we dropped a long way fast.* The machine handed Aaliyah off to Bian then returned to Johnny.

"Of all the gin joints," Wobble said as he grabbed Johnny's Hasty-Arm. "Very brave. Useless but brave."

"I'll make that my slogan," Johnny laughed. "Hey, if we all grab hold of each other, can you carry us?"

"Affirmative," Wobble said. "Must find solid ground. Flee. This should not transpire." The hitch had disappeared from his speech.

Wobble levelled out with the other skids and Johnny grabbed onto Torg. "Has everybody got hold of everybody else? Support the low-level skids. Torg . . ." He calced the weight and swallowed his pride. "Albert?"

Albert passed Torres off to Brolin. Together with Torg, he and Johnny each grabbed onto Wobble with one hand and the pile with the other, distributing the weight as much as they could.

"All good, Wobble, hit it!" Johnny cried, and the machine soared up, cutting through the wreckage. Somehow, Johnny found himself pressed up against Albert. Staring into the Eight's damaged eye, he fought the urge to ask how things were going between him and Bian.

Wobble cleared the falling debris and sailed back over a solid street, flying another hundred metres before touching down. The hollas around them were lit but flickering, strobing the street like a dance pit. It seemed as if every third line of golden light had splintered.

"We must move quickly. Nothing stable remains." The ground bucked even as Wobble spoke. "Must find exit. This should not transpire."

"Gear up, squids," Torg barked. They increased their speed.

"Can't you just grab us if we fall again?" Bian asked.

"Falling not danger. Region unstable. Systems fail. Where the stars fall, there be dragons."

"What kind of . . ." Johnny started to say. The flickering hollas made it difficult to focus. "Oh . . . great."

Behind them, Vies peeled out from the broken street. Without a word, Wobble twisted and released three of his fiery sawblades. They tore through the Vies, but not before more emerged even closer to the pack.

There were far more than three.

"Negatory-negatory! Red Alert." Wobble yelled, beginning to spin so fast it was hard to follow.

"You seem to have it under control," Torg murmured. It wasn't too often you saw awe on the Nine's face.

"Too many Vies. Anti alert. They come for the Vies, then We-Us."

He wasn't kidding. Johnny blinked and suddenly there were white shapes falling from the sky, hollas mirrored on each surface as they streaked towards the Vies.

"Street's end," Wobble announced. A laser shot from his body, cutting a path down the vibrating corridor. "There will be a door. Safety." The Antis fell on the Vies, slicing through them like the knives they resembled. "We-I will hold them off. Screw the Spartans, they'll remember the Gor-Vien. Run-run-run, little games."

"You heard him," Johnny said, bumping Aaliyah to give her some more speed. "Gun it, skids. Bump your neighbour, boost it up!" Skids began popping off walls, accelerating beyond their normal speed. *We should have done this the first time the Vies attacked.*

Behind them, carnage. The Antis ripped through the Vies, but occasionally a dozen Vies converged on a single Anti, soaking into it until the knife went dark and died. Still, the Antis were clearly stronger.

And Wobble was something else entirely. The machine annihilated the Vies and did almost as much damage to the Antis. A giant pinwheel of destruction, projectiles shot out of his body in every direction.

But even he couldn't get everything.

"Heads up," Torg yelled.

A black shape fell from above. The Vie landed in the middle of the pack, clipping Shabaz, who screamed before darting ahead. Before Johnny could act, a white

Anti appeared from nowhere and sliced into the Vie. The black spore turned pale white, then evaporated.

The Anti rotated, the tip of its point pointed at Bian.

"No!" Albert and Johnny both yelled, accelerating towards the Anti. Albert hit it first, near the back. The Anti spun and surged forward. Johnny caught it and sent it into another spin, but not before it clipped Albert.

Johnny had never heard Albert scream before.

A cold bolt of terror sped through his stripes as the Anti turned his way. "That's right," Johnny snarled with a bravado he no longer felt. "Come get me." He waited a heartbeat to make sure the Anti was focused on him . . . then he fled.

"Get to that door," he yelled into the com. "I'll be along in a minute."

"Where the hole do you think you're going?" Torg snapped back.

Johnny sliced around the first corner he found, the Anti right behind. *Crisp Betty, these things are fast.* "I've got a plan. Get through the door, Torg!"

He banged off a wall, gaining speed. He was already topping out and the vaping thing was still *faster.* "You think you can catch me, you grease-sucking spare!" he cackled, banging around another corner. His treads were burning. "I'm Johnny Drop, jackhole!"

The Anti didn't seem impressed. It clipped him going around the fourth corner, barely cutting his skin. Johnny thought he was being vaped. His whole body felt like it was being sliced apart by a scalpel.

"Vape you!" Johnny screamed, holding it together and gaining more speed. The ground beneath him bucked, hurling him into the air. Johnny used the force to bang around another corner. "Is that all you got?! You got nothing, squid! Nothing!"

"Johnny, we can see the end of the street," Bian said over the com. "Get back here, you idiot!"

"Working on it." His skin where the Anti clipped him felt like it was on fire—Albert had taken a direct hit. *How the hole did he hold it together?* "Where's Wobble?" he demanded.

"He's coming now."

"Any Vies or Antis?"

"No, I think he took care of them."

"Right. Uh . . . hold on." Screaming into an intersection, he scanned and turned in the direction of the pack. The tip of the Anti's point feathered his skin. *Crisp, that was close.* "Get through the door. Trust Wobble: I'll be right behind. Can he close the door behind us?"

A heartbeat of silence, then Bian said, "He says he can."

"All right, I've got you guys on scan. Get through the door and tell Wobble to get ready to slam it shut behind me. I'm coming in hot."

The ground bucked him into the air again. Five metres back, the Anti gleamed glossy white in the flickering light of the hollas. "I don't care how pretty you are, you're still a jackhole," Johnny spat, banging around a final corner.

Up ahead, he could see the last of the skids funnel through a doorway framed by solid gold lines. Bian was last, looking back. "Go!" Johnny screamed. "I'm coming." She ducked through the door.

Now only Wobble waited. The machine looked absolutely battered. Johnny wondered why he didn't blast the Anti; maybe he was out of ammunition. Didn't matter. He had half-a-dozen lengths on the Anti. It would be enough.

On that thought, a Vie dropped into his path.

You have got to be kidding.

The Vie began to turn his way. *Vape it,* Johnny thought. *I-We bring the end.*

He plowed into the Vie, agony lancing through his body, this time tearing instead of slicing. *Not a chance,* he thought, burying the pain and holding together. *I did this once, I'll do it a million times if I have to.*

The Anti became a blur in his trail-eye, but he didn't have time to think about it as Wobble went through the door. Johnny followed, his skin on fire as the doorway flared shut behind him.

CHAPTER FOURTEEN

"Are you all right?" Bian said, rolling up as Johnny came through the door.

He popped the Hasty-Arm without thinking, the hand travelling twice as far as he intended. He almost punched her in the face. "Just . . . wait," he hissed. The tone shocked him, so he took a deep breath. "Just wait," he said again, more gently this time.

His body felt like it was filled with hornets. The focus off in at least two of his eyes. There were black sunbursts on his skin—*on his stripes!* He retched but nothing came out. No surprise there. It was, what—hours? days?—since he'd had any sugar. Even though he was at rest, his left tread kept hitching forward.

Just like Wobble. He took a shuddering breath. Then, because it had worked before, he got mad.

Drawing all his attention inward, he hit the tearing sensation with what he could only describe as a mental fist. Ruthlessly, he crushed every ounce of Vie he could feel, then he pulled himself together, cell-by-cell. He focused on his stripes and willed them white.

When he turned his attention back to Bian, this time she was clear.

"Uhh . . . wow," she said.

"Better?" Johnny asked, exhausted.

"Yeah," she breathed. "That was . . . I don't know what that was." Her eyes bobbed and weaved, examining him. They focused on his trail-eye. "This looks almost perfect. If I didn't know you were injured, I wouldn't see anything."

It was true. The eye wasn't completely healed, but it was closer, much closer than when he'd fixed it at the storm-house. "Let's hope it stays that way. How're we doing?"

"Not so good." She swallowed. "Brolin got hit again. So did Shabaz."

Black spores flared all over Brolin's skin. Johnny shuddered. Daytona had looked worse than that, but not a lot worse. Shabaz had a single bloom near her upper eye and looked as if she was going to blow chunks at any moment. Johnny actually felt sorry for the lippy Six.

"And then there's Albert."

They all surrounded the silver-white skid. A long razor-thin scar, perfectly straight, marred the left side of his body. *Betty Crisp*, Johnny thought, staring at the scar.

Albert's whole body vibrated with pain. "Back . . . *up!*" he snapped when Aaliyah got too close.

"I'm just trying to help," she said, her eyes wide.

"Give him some space," Torres demanded, her eyes as wide as Aaliyah's, all three on the skid that had saved her life. "Let him breathe."

"I don't need you to speak for me," Albert snarled, and Torres jumped back like she'd been slapped.

"Sorry, I . . . I . . ."

A sound like a mine collapsing escaped Albert's lips. "No . . ." he gasped. "I'm sorry. Just . . . just give me some space."

Johnny couldn't take his eyes off the scar. It took a lot to permanently mark a skid, he knew that intimately. Albert looked like he'd been cut in half.

He caught Johnny looking. "What are you staring at?" he snarled. "Happy?" An eye swung at Bian. "Got out just in time didn't you, sweetheart?" A violent shudder snapped through his body.

Johnny's stripes twitched. Albert might be a jackhole, but this . . . the skin on Johnny's back still burned where the Anti had nicked him. "All right folks," he murmured, backing up. "Give him all the space he needs."

"Thank you," Albert rasped. His body continued to spasm as they backed away.

"That's not the same as what happened to you," Bian whispered.

"The Antis are different. The Vies feel like they're eating you. It's horrible. But for straight up pain, the Anti was far worse. It's like getting stabbed in the eye with a thousand knives. Getting vaped doesn't hurt that much."

Bian glanced back at Albert and shivered. "It left a scar. How is that even possible?"

Johnny's stripes tilted. "I have no idea."

"And I thought Wobble had it bad."

Wobble was a mess. Scorch marks covered his body. One lens had been knocked out of alignment and both the machine's shoulder flares were bent.

But he was getting better.

Amazed, Johnny watched as the shoulder flares straightened out with the sound of metal-on-metal. "No need to link-link the nurse, old fellow," Wobble grinned. One of his metallic teeth dangled and then reset. "I-We will be-be fully-op soon. Wobble."

"Thank goodness we have him," Bian said. "I have no idea how many Vies and Antis he took down."

"Yeah, he's pretty crazy-impressive."

"Not to mention crazy," Torg said, rolling up. "You guys should see this."

It finally hit Johnny that they weren't in the city of hollas anymore. Instead, they sat inside in a small room, the black walls glowing with a familiar golden light.

Torg took them over to a window. "Looks like we found some company."

The street outside was filled with . . . he wasn't sure what it was filled with. Hundreds of box-shaped creatures, floating like the Vies and Antis, zipped by in every colour of the rainbow, all bathed in gold. Something with eight Hasty-Arms tickered past; another had six. Many resembled the creatures they'd seen in the corridor of hollas: four Hasty-Arms, striding around on two of them, although everything had a box-like quality.

And if the street was busy, the sky . . .

It's like Tag Box, Johnny thought, picturing the Skidsphere's most chaotic game. Layers upon layers of traffic—all boxes, all travelling in perfectly straight lines—starting ten metres above the street and rising into the distance.

"At least we know this world isn't empty," Johnny murmured.

"Nice to see some colours other than black, white, and gold," Torg said. "I wonder if they're friendly."

"Everyone is Teddy Bears," Wobble said from directly behind them, making them jump. *I have to stop looking at things with all three eyes*, Johnny thought as Wobble added, "We-You have arrived. She is waiting-waiting. Come. Time is diamonds."

The door nearby faded out. Johnny glanced at the others. "I guess we're leaving. Albert, are you good to travel?"

"I'm *fine*," came the rasping reply.

"Fair enough." Johnny followed Wobble out the door.

He expected a reaction from the traffic. After all, the eight skids didn't resemble anything else on the streets. But three boxes whizzed by his head without pausing.

"No one seems too worried about Vies or Antis," Torg said, his eyes swinging around cautiously.

"No Vies," Wobble whirred, spinning his head. "No Antis. The parent-parent's never found out. Everyone is Teddy Bears. Wobble."

Something crossed in front of Torg and Johnny that blocked out most of the block. The ground shuddered as they watched the massive box with four arms stomp through traffic. "I sure hope that's a Teddy Bear," Torg murmured.

Johnny glanced at him. "Do you know what a Teddy Bear is?"

"No idea. But I believe they're on our side."

"Who's on our side?" Bian asked, rolling up.

"The Teddy Bears," Johnny grinned.

"I thought we were all Teddy Bears." She swung an eye towards Wobble. "Do you think he's completely sane?"

"I have no idea what he is," Johnny admitted. "But I'm pretty sure that he, at least, is definitely on our side."

"He's certainly taking the punishment," Bian agreed.

"He's not the only one. How's Brolin?"

Bian's stripes paled. "I'm . . . I think he's pretty bad. We need to get him help."

"Yeah. Hopefully we're on our way there now."

Her expression changed. "You know, I haven't thanked you for saving us, for saving me. Again." She smiled.

"Careful, it's getting to be a habit."

Something about the way she looked at him made Johnny's stripes flush. "Yeah, well . . . it was Albert who took the big hit."

She swung an eye in Albert's direction then sniffed. "Good for him. Besides, he seems more interested in the panzer than me."

No matter how much he hated Albert, even Johnny thought that was just a little frosty, given the scar the other skid was sporting. Just a few days ago, Bian had asked him to cut Albert some slack—now she was treating him like tread-grease. What gave?

"I'll go check on Brolin," she said, leaving an eye on Johnny as she rolled away.

Beside him, Torg sighed.

"What?"

Torg blinked emphatically. "Just what we need. More drama."

Wobble came to a halt. "We-You are here. Ticker-tape and everyone dance. Gurg made it through the Antaries in one piece. Wobble." His head whirled in a full three-sixty, obviously pleased. "In we go. She is waiting."

Johnny's heart skipped a beat. *Peg,* he thought to himself like a promise.

They entered a long, narrow room cluttered with debris, workstations and hollas. Lines of muted gold traced the contours and the floor, flickering softly. Opposite the door, resting in a booth just like a sugarbar, surrounded by hollas, was a female skid.

It wasn't Peg.

"Crisp Betty," Johnny swore softly as he took in the flat-black body with the shining pink stripe.

"Well," said the skid, rolling out from behind the booth. "It's nice to be recognized."

CHAPTER FIFTEEN

"Sweet Snakes," someone swore.

"*Vape me,*" said someone else.

"Watch your mouth," Torg said, his voice soft and reverent.

Betty Crisp, the greatest skid who'd ever lived, popped two Hasty-Arms and spread them wide. "Wobble. It's good to see you. You did a wonderful job."

"Claw-clacks and rub-rub-rubbing tens," the dilapidated machine beamed. "Farsi got 'em home, Sarge."

"He certainly did," Betty said. "You can rest now, my friend. Repair what you can, we'll need you soon."

The broken smile dropped from the machine's face. "It hurt-hurts still."

"I know. Rest now. Make it better if you can." As the machine rolled away, hitching to one side as he did, Betty turned her eyes toward Johnny.

"Betty Crisp," he said. It took everything he had to stop his third eye from swinging in her direction. "You're Betty Crisp."

The only Level Ten in skid history laughed with delight. "Didn't you just have this conversation a few days ago, Johnny Drop?"

"What? Oh, the Combine. Right." He grinned sheepishly. "I guess I kind of . . ." He stopped. "Wait, you know about that?"

Betty waved an arm at the sea of hollas surrounding her banquette. "I know about a lot of things." Her eyes narrowed. "Let's start with your wounded."

She rolled over to Shabaz and Brolin, Bian hovering nearby like a protective mother. Shabaz's grey skin looked pallid and dull and the bloom under her upper eye had grown, but she was holding on. The same couldn't be said for Brolin. Two of his eyes hung limp as black spores flared all over his skin.

Betty examined him, her gaze filled with sorrow. "See those cells along that wall?" She pointed to three compartments outlined with thick gold lines. "Put them in there. They should . . . help." Bian bobbed an eye and gently led Brolin away, with Shabaz following behind.

"Help?" Torg said. "How much?"

"Not enough," Betty said grimly. "Not here."

"Then you have a place," Johnny asked. "A place that will . . ." he glanced towards Wobble, repairing himself in a corner, ". . . cure them?"

"Maybe."

"Then let's go there."

"It's not that simple," Betty said, watching as Bian guided Shabaz into the cell beside Brolin. The lines surrounding the cells took on a hint of each skid's hue.

"It is if it saves their lives," Johnny insisted. He'd made a promise to Brolin, he didn't intend to break it.

Betty's gaze came away from the far side of the room. "No, Johnny," she said, "it's not." Seeing his expression, she added more gently, "Those cells will help. If nothing else, they'll kill most of the pain. Given time, they could heal Brolin and Shabaz completely." Glancing at the hollas surrounding her booth, she sighed. "Unfortunately, time is not something we have in abundance."

She swung an eye. "I'd offer you the third cell, Albert, but I'm afraid they can't ease your pain." She examined his scar, a strange expression on her face. "I wish they could."

"That's all right," Albert rasped, his voice tight. "I'm sorry to be a nuisance."

"You're not a nuisance, Albert. I'm very glad you're here."

The injured Eight winced, then bobbed an eye. "Thanks." Behind him, Torres stared at Betty with very un-Torres-like awe.

"Speaking of here," Torg drawled, "where exactly would that be?"

"You're in a lost node," Betty said, rolling back towards her hollas.

"Ahh," Torg said. "Well . . . that explains that."

Betty stopped, her second eye swinging around. Torg gazed back at her innocently. A single bright pink stripe cocked to one side. "You're Torg, right?"

"Most of the time, yes, ma'am."

Betty held the gaze for a minute, then the corner of her lips twitched. "Kinks, I've missed talking to skids. Okay, Torg, wrap your eye-stalks around this: you're in a place called the Thread, which is made up of information. A node is a place through which a great deal of information tends to pass, in one way or another. But here's the catch: the Thread is broken. So a lost node is a node that, to the system, no longer exists. Better?" Now she was the one wearing the innocent look.

Torg blinked. "I think I just sprained something." And grinned when Betty laughed with delight.

The laughter died as Bian rolled up. "How are they?" Betty asked.

"They said they feel better," Bian sighed. "But Brolin still looks terrible. They need . . ." Her eyes flinched. "I don't know what they need." She took a deep breath. Exhaled loudly. "So . . . where are we?"

"We're in a lost node," Torg drawled.

Bian considered this, then her stripes tilted. "Could be worse."

"Really?"

"Sure," Bian sniffed. "Lost is better than dead." When they stared at her, she added, "What? Am I the only one who thought that we might be dead and all this was just the Hole?"

"You're not dead," Betty said, studying Bian with a contemplative look. "Though the Skidsphere thinks otherwise." The hollas around her booth spun and a single image jumped out to hover just above Betty's head. It was a replay of the Pipe: a black void swallowing the white surface as the words, "JOHNNY DROP, THOUSANDS OF SKIDS MISSING!" scrolled across the image.

"Nice to be missed," Albert spat, staring at the holla. "Thousands of skids," he added, his voice dripping contempt.

"Don't be snide, Albert," Betty laughed. "Johnny didn't write the tag. Besides, they mentioned you and Torg in the broadcast."

"Really?" Torg said.

"Really," Betty said, winking at the Nine.

"I don't get it," Johnny said.

"What do you mean?" Torg grinned. "I'm very marketable."

"Not you, gearbox. This." He looked at Betty. "You said this place was called the Thread? So is this like another version of the Skidsphere?"

"No, Johnny," Betty said. "The Skidsphere is part of the Thread. A small part."

He stared at her. *The Skidsphere is small?* The Rainbow Road alone was five hundred kilometers long. Then he remembered columns-upon-columns of hollas, buildings stretching up and down . . .

"Can I ask a question?" Torres asked.

"Certainly, Torres," Betty said.

The orange stripe glowed with pride. "She knows my name," she whispered to Albert.

"I'll bet she knows a lot of things," Albert said, wincing. His colour was coming back, but the scar still marred his body.

Torres looked at Betty Crisp, blinked once, and said, "Why aren't you dead?"

The sound of Torg choking on his tongue. All three of Johnny's eyes went wide as Bian murmured, "Torres . . ."

"What?" Torres protested. "She's like . . . ancient! She *is*," she added, when Aaliyah nudged her treads. "I mean, if you're alive then you're . . . you're . . ."

"I'm fifty-five years old, relative to the Skidsphere," the ancient skid said, amused.

"See!" Torres nudged Aaliyah back, staring at Betty. "What level are you now?"

"I'm afraid levels don't really exist out here. Not in the way you think."

"Oh," Torres said, disappointed. "Still, if they did . . . you'd be higher than Level Ten, right?"

Betty smiled. "A little higher than Ten, yes. I suppose I would be."

"Cool . . . can I call you Betty?"

"I'd like that very much, Torres."

Torres looked at Albert and beamed. "She'd like that very much."

"Torres?"

"What?"

"She didn't answer your question yet." As the purple-orange skid worked that out, Albert said to Betty, "It's a good one. How are you still alive? And how did you get here? Did you fall through the black like we did?"

Betty took a long, shaky breath. "Those are good questions, Albert." A beat, then she added, "Would it be all right if I didn't tell you at this exact moment? I will, but . . ." her smile came back, "it's not really a first date story."

Albert held her gaze, then winced and bobbed an eye.

"Can you at least tell us what happened to the Skidsphere?" Bian asked. "Thousands missing? That's horrible." She bit her lip. "Did . . . did anyone else . . . survive like we did?" Unconsciously, her trail-eye scanned the entire room.

"No," Betty said softly. "The only skids that came through what hit the Pipe are the ones Johnny and Albert brought with them. The rest, unless they somehow fell right off my grid . . ." she tapped an eye at the bank of hollas, ". . . the rest are dead."

"Crisp Betty," Torg whispered, then cast a guilty glance at Betty.

"It's all right, Torg. I've had fifty years to get used to it." Betty took a deep breath, her gaze still on Bian. "Thank goodness the break finally stopped. Although not before it took out ninety percent of the Pipe and a chunk of the Rainbow Road."

"The Road as well?" Johnny said, stunned.

"Yes," replied the skid who had once performed the Leap, her face grim. "They won't be running either of those for some time."

Johnny frowned. "Why not? I mean, Bian's right, that many skids vaped is . . . is insane . . . but GameCorps can repair the structural stuff within a few hours." He didn't like the response he got at all. "Can't they?"

Betty held his gaze. "They should. But this might be a little bigger than GameCorps."

An ugly feeling was starting to build in Johnny's gut, one that had nothing to do with any residual effects of getting tagged by the Vies and Antis. "Betty . . ." he said slowly. "One of the first things Wobble said to us was: 'Your world is going to die.' Is that . . . is that what's happening?"

"Yes, Johnny," Betty said. "That could be happening."

"Snakes . . ." Aaliyah whispered, her eyes wide with terror. "We aren't going to be safe even if we go home?"

Betty gazed at her with a strange look for a skid, something very much like affection. "Well, Aaliyah, I have good news and bad news. The bad news is that no . . . you can't go home. The good news is that the Skidsphere won't be dying anytime soon."

"Why not?" Bian said suspiciously. "What's to stop another one of those black things from hitting the Slope? Or a packed sugarbar?"

Betty looked back at her. "Me."

Bian blinked. "I'm sorry?"

"Me," Betty said. "I stopped it. I stopped the Skidsphere."

A deep silence. "Uh . . ." Torg said. "You want to clarify that a bit?"

Betty pointed at the bank of hollas. "Six hours after the break on the Pipe ground to a halt, there was a corpsquake. A big one. Unfortunately, corpsquakes are poorly named: they have nothing to do with GameCorps. They're a symptom of a sick and broken system, breaking more. Things were happening too fast. I couldn't take any chances."

She rose on her treads and her whole body seemed to swell until it filled the room. "Five minutes after the quake, I did something I never, ever wanted to do. I placed the entire sphere into stasis. If everything is shut down then, in theory, nothing else should break." The single pink stripe radiated like a star as her eyes swept the group.

"My world is not going to die," Betty Crisp declared. "Not on my watch."

CHAPTER SIXTEEN

"You . . ." Johnny started to say. Stopped. He couldn't wrap his mind around what he was trying to ask. He tried again. "You stopped . . . *the Skidsphere?*"

"Think of it as a holla on pause," Betty said helpfully.

I can't, his mind protested. A flutter of panic surged through his stripes as he glanced at Wobble, quietly humming to himself as he healed in the corner. *Sweet snakes, what if they're both insane?*

"How?" Torg said, bringing Johnny back. His magenta skin had paled.

"How did I do it?" Betty asked. "Or: how could I do such a horrible thing?"

"Start with the first one," Torg said levelly.

Betty swung an arm. "Look around. Everything you see is information. Those boxes whizzing by outside? Information. This booth?" She rapped a finger loudly off the booth's surface. "Information. That storm you hid in, every line of golden light, the Vies, the Antis: everything's a metaphor for some specific collection of data. Including the Skidsphere. Including the skids."

"What am I a metaphor for?" Aaliyah whispered.

Instantly, Betty's expression softened. "For a skid," she said, smiling. "A good one." She reached out and placed her hand on Aaliyah's stripes, held it there, then looked back at Torg.

"If you know where to look and how to do it, you can manipulate the data. Theoretically, with the entire Thread. I've spent the last twenty years focusing on anything related to the Skidsphere. So I can protect it." She glanced at Johnny, hesitated, then said: "Six months ago, something happened that scared the sugar out of me. So I came up with a last-chance scenario: if I thought the sphere was going critical, I'd put it in stasis to try and save it. After the Pipe and the quake that followed . . . I did it."

No one had to ask what happened six months ago. Sitting at the back of the group, his scar bright against his silver skin, Albert steadfastly refused to look Johnny's way.

"That's horrible," Bian protested, staring at Betty. "All those skids. It's like they're dead."

"It is horrible, Bian," Betty agreed. "And the worst part is: it might not work. The entire Thread is slowly breaking down. Putting the sphere into stasis should protect it from Vies, but if things keep breaking around it . . ." She took a deep breath. "Still, it should buy us some time to do what we have to do."

"And what is that?" Johnny said, his stripes still spinning.

Betty grinned. "Save the Skidsphere. And not by keeping it in stasis. By repairing the damage that's been done. Getting rid of any virus that crept in with the break. By making it whole and as healthy as anything inside the Thread can be."

"And just how are you going to do that?"

"Actually, I was hoping you could help me."

From the back, Albert groaned. "Great, you're going to make him a vaping hero."

"Actually, Albert, I was hoping to use you both." Betty's grin widened. "I'm afraid I need you boys to kiss and make up."

Torg barked a laugh. "Yeah, good luck with that."

"What about the rest of us?" Bian said, scowling.

"You'll stay here. You should be safe. For what I have planned, I only need Johnny and Albert."

Ouch, Johnny thought, watching Bian's stripes darken. "We can help too," she said, her voice cold, two eyes squarely on Betty. "We're not invalids." Then, realizing what she'd said, she sent a guilty glance towards the cells holding Brolin and Shabaz.

"I didn't think you were." Betty sighed. "I'm sorry, that was . . . I haven't had a lot of experience recently talking with people. Except Wobble, of course." From the corner, the machine looked up and waved a damaged arm. "You *can* help. Someone needs to watch over Brolin and Shabaz. Someone needs to care for the younger skids."

"Hey," Torres protested, bumping forward. "Whatever's going on, I'm in!"

"Not this time, Torres," Betty said gently.

Bian continued to glare. "And just how long are we supposed to sit here while the three of you go save the world?"

"Actually, it's four. We'll be taking Wobble."

"Fine, whatever. How long?"

"I don't know."

"You don't know?" Bian said, her voice rising. "So we're just supposed to—"

"*Stop it!*" Johnny barked. Popping a Hasty-Arm, he held

up a hand. "Everybody just . . . slow down for a minute. This is . . . this is . . ." He took a deep breath. "Look," he said to Betty, "thanks for the vote of confidence. I don't know what you think I . . . Albert and I . . . can do but, hey, great to think we can do it. But why do we need to? Why the hole do we have to fix the problem? That's *insane*. Where's GameCorps? It's their job."

"GameCorps only takes care of the Skidsphere, Johnny. The problem is bigger than that; what's attacking the sphere comes from *outside* of the sphere. GameCorps can't fix the Thread."

"*Then who takes care of the Thread?*" Johnny cried, furious at not being able to understand a single vaping thing.

Betty had gone stock-still. "That," she said softly, "is a very good question."

"Where's the Out There in all this?" Johnny demanded. "They exist, right?" His heart was pounding.

"Yes, Johnny, there is something beyond the Thread. Out there. And whatever they are, we're pretty sure the Thread is their creation."

Thank Crisp, Johnny thought, too emotionally charged to catch the irony. "So . . ." he said, drawing out the word, trying to calm down. "You said everything is information, we're all information, fine. I don't understand that at all, but I don't need to. GameCorps takes care of the Skidsphere. The Skidsphere is part of the Thread. The Thread is broken, sick, whatever. If the Out There created the Thread, why aren't they fixing it?"

Betty held his gaze for a long moment. They might have been alone in the room.

"I've spent most of the last twenty-five years trying to answer that question, Johnny. It's the most important one you could ask. The Thread is huge—I can't begin to explain how vast it is, how complex. Something, somewhere, invested a lot of effort in creating it. Whoever they were, they were obviously intelligent. Why would they let it break down? What possible reason could they have for letting it decay?"

A knot of ice began to settle inside Johnny's stripes.

"There's a few possibilities, but in the end . . . there's only one that makes sense."

"Vape me," Torg whispered.

"Not possible," Johnny spat. "It's not possible."

"I'm afraid it is," Betty said. "The only reason something gets left to rot is because something left it to rot." She waved a hand at her booth. "I'm sorry, Johnny. The hollas run, but no one is watching."

"Not possible." It came out as a snarl now. "You said it yourself—the highlights are still running!"

"Because GameCorps is still running."

"GameCorps doesn't watch the highlights!"

"No," Betty sighed. "But they do run them."

"But . . . but . . ." He was reaching, desperate. There'd been that nervous, empty feeling in the city of hollas, but this . . . "They gave me a name."

"Did they?" Betty asked. "Johnny Drop. Was the announcement on the 'lights really the first time you heard that name?"

"Uh . . ." Johnny flinched with the memory: lying half-vaped on a ledge, his eye flapping in the wind, grinning as he thought about what he wanted to be named.

"You gave yourself your name," Betty said.

"How? I never said it out loud." When the others swung a stunned eye his way, he explained, "I thought it, though. After the race, I thought the name Johnny Drop."

"And GameCorps read his mind?" Torres whispered. "Sweet."

"It's all just information," Betty said. "I was called Betty Crisp because I used to say it all the time. It was my favourite expression: if something was right, it was *crisp*. I dreamed of having that name." Her gaze swept the group. "We are our own program."

"Nice," Torres said. "I'm giving myself a second name."

"Why don't you get comfortable with the first, squid?" Torg drawled.

"All right, fine," Johnny said, taking a long, ragged breath. "We name ourselves. That still doesn't mean no one Out There is watching. I mean, why would the games continue if . . . ?" He threw his hands up, his stripes twisting with a dozen emotions at once.

The only emotion Betty showed was sympathy. "Because the Skidsphere is practically autonomous. It might be a small part of the Thread, but it's a sophisticated one. It's a self-sustaining, self-enclosed entertainment mem. The only one of its kind I've found. From what I gather, there was a time when it was incredibly popular."

"But not now," Bian said, glancing at Johnny. They all knew how much this mattered to him.

"Probably not. You need to understand, most of the Thread's inactive, like that weather-mem you drove into. Other parts are stuck in a permanent loop, some decades long. That block of hollas you passed through? Most of those images happened years ago. In many cases, centuries. Maybe longer."

"Vape me," Torg whispered.

There was a long silence as they tried to absorb what they were being told. Betty gave it to them. Johnny found himself staring at one of the hollas hovering over Betty's booth.

He had absolutely no idea what he was staring at.

"All right," Bian said finally. "I don't understand half of this but I guess we have to trust you. Not much choice. So, fine, we stay here. Polish our treads. Whatever. But before you go, there's some things we need to take care of. You mentioned sugar. Do you have any, some of us are starving."

"There's no sugar here," Betty said. "I used to synthesize it at my other safehouse, but I don't have the equipment here."

"Then how did you survive?"

"I don't need it. None of us do."

Bian stared at her. "Uh, I'm pretty sure I do."

"No, you don't," Betty insisted. "Haven't you been listening? Bian, what happens when a skid doesn't get sugar? How would you even know—GameCorps keeps everyone stripes-up in sweet. You think they die? Who cares: *You've been dying your whole life.* You've all died dozens of times and survived. Once you hit Level Three, there's only one hard death."

"Five years," Torg said quietly.

"Five vaping years," Betty said, her voice dripping contempt. "It's all programming. You've got control of every molecule in your body. You don't . . . need . . . sugar." Her eyes swung to each of them, then dipped. "But you don't believe that . . . so of course you do."

A beat of silence, then Aaliyah whispered: "I haven't died a dozen times."

"I haven't even died once," Torres added.

"Trust me, it's overrated," Torg said.

Bian and Betty continued to stare at each other. "Maybe it's all programming," Bian said flatly, "but we need sugar."

"Well, you're going to have to hold on without," Betty sighed.

Bian glared at her for a moment more. "I'm going to check on Brolin and Shabaz." Betty watched her cross the room, her expression somewhere between annoyed and amused.

Funny, but for the first time something Betty had said made sense to Johnny. He knew Bian was feeling it, obviously others were too, but Johnny hadn't had a single hunger pang. Of course, that didn't mean he was feeling good.

He turned to Torg. "Are you understanding any of this?"

The magenta-gold skid pursed his lips. "There's a thread . . ." he said slowly.

Johnny laughed. Trust Torg to make him feel better. "All right," he said, looking at Betty. "I guess I'll figure all this out later. The Skidsphere comes first. You said you had a plan." He grimaced and added, "Involving me and Albert?" He could have sworn he heard Albert snort.

A quirk played across Betty's lips. "Well . . ."

Behind her, every holla went red. In the corner, Wobble's head came up, his lenses spinning.

"Oh, kinks," Betty groaned. "Oh no." She zipped over to the booth, hollas flashing past her eyes.

"What . . ." Johnny started to say.

"Red Alert!" Wobble screamed. "Burgs in the tockhouse! The Ventari slipped the block!" Dozens of probes sprang from his body, spinning and whirring.

"*Bian!*" Betty yelled. "Get Brolin and Shabaz, we're leaving. Torg?"

"On it," the Nine said, moving to help Bian.

"Vies or Antis?" Albert said, staring at Betty's hollas as

if he could read their secrets. Unconsciously, he reached towards Torres.

"Antis."

"I thought this place was safe from Antis," Johnny said. "It's a lost node, right?"

"It was," Betty said grimly. "However, about an hour ago there was some fairly specific traffic."

"Oh, crap," Johnny said, his heart falling. "Us. We led them here."

"Don't," Betty said, swiping a hand across the booth. Every holla shrunk and then dove into her stripe. "Don't beat yourself up. You needed to get here, I needed you here. I was hoping you might arrive unnoticed, but hey, we got unlucky. No one said SecCore was completely stupid."

"What's SecCore?"

The voice seemed to come from everywhere. "DID YOU THINK YOU COULD ESCAPE ME FOREVER, BETTY CRISP?"

"That guy," Betty muttered, pulling out from behind the booth.

Bian rolled up with Brolin. He looked better, but several spores still ebbed and flowed across his skin. *Crisp Betty*, Johnny thought.

"WE ARE COMING FOR YOU, LITTLE SKID."

"Figured that out, jackhole," Betty spat. Her pink stripe blazed. "Wobble, get ready."

"Who's the loud-mouth?" Torg asked casually, holding onto Shabaz.

"SecCore." She popped a holla and examined it. "It runs the Antis."

"But not the Vies?"

"Not the Vies." Betty shuddered. "Nothing controls the Vies." She swept the holla away and looked around.

"Everyone stay tight. Move fast. Do everything I say." She winked at Wobble. "You want to go shut that son-of-a-snake up?"

The machine winked back. "Pop the top, let's show them the circus. The clackers should have stayed in the Hoag. Wobble." His body rose off the ground and began to transform. Betty pointed at the ceiling. As she did, the surface flared bright gold then vanished.

Dropping from the sky above: Antis. Lots of them. *We're screwed*, Johnny thought, as Wobble roared into the sky.

"Let's move," Betty said, leading them outside. Above their heads, Wobble began to single-handedly attack dozens of Antis, with dozens more falling in the distance. "Wobble," Betty said calmly, "you have to draw and hold them here. I need time and they can't see what we're doing."

"Affirmative," came a voice over the com, as the sky filled with wheels-of-fire. "I-We bring the end."

"I know you do," Betty said softly, a quiet pride gracing her face. She looked at Johnny. "I never thought we'd leave here under fire. We were going to take a Thread Line, but we need to get someplace they won't see us do it or there's no point. Stay tight—"

An Anti dropped from the sky, right between Johnny and Torg.

Ah snakes, Johnny thought, moving even as he saw Torg do the same. He didn't have time to warn Torg to stay clear. As it was, it didn't matter.

He and Torg were too slow.

Quicker than Johnny could believe—quicker than he had *ever* moved—Betty surged forward, popping a Hasty-Arm as she did. In it, she held a long straight blade that glowed with golden light. "Rrraaggh!" she snarled, slashing into the Anti. The white knife peeled in two and vanished.

"Kinks," she sniffed violently. "I hate doing that." The Hasty-Arm popped back into her body, taking the golden beam with it.

"Vape me," Torg said, staring at her. "You killed it."

"Don't be amazed and maybe you'll figure out how to do it too."

"What was that . . . that light thing?" Johnny breathed. He'd never seen a skid with a weapon before.

"Type of sword. I've learned a few tricks." Betty grinned. "Stole a few, too."

"Can I get one?" Torg asked.

Betty winked at him. "We'll see."

The battle above their heads continued to mount. Johnny had no idea how Wobble survived. The sky looked like a snow-globe.

To his amazement, the streets weren't alive with creatures fleeing, trying to escape the carnage above. Instead, the traffic continued exactly as it had before. The zippy little boxes continued to zip from place to place, the lumbering hulks continued to lumber. Even more stunning, the flying traffic carried on, even where its path crossed the battle. Johnny watched, stunned, as a glowing yellow box disintegrated as it ran straight through one of Wobble's fire-disks.

"What the hole's wrong with these panzers?" he breathed, as they rushed through a crowded intersection.

"They're automatic," Betty said. "Every aspect of the Thread sees it differently. Those Antis probably don't see Wobble the same way we do. And most of this clutter doesn't see that battle at all." Her trail-eye grew angry. "That's one of the reasons the Thread gets broken. That transport won't get where it was supposed to go and the system fails a little more."

"THE TRAITOR IS FAILING, LITTLE SKID."

"You're a terrible liar," Betty muttered. "Besides, the traitor only needs to hold on for a few more minutes."

"Traitor?" Johnny said, glancing at Torg.

"Beats me." The magenta skid's stripes tilted. "Wobble?"

Why would Wobble be a traitor? Johnny thought as they darted into an alley. Betty stopped at a round door in the surface of the street. Dozens of glowing circlets, connected by lines of light, pulsed on the door's surface.

"All right," Betty said. "We're going to change locations several times, very quickly in succession." She looked apologetically at Brolin, hanging on Bian. "This probably won't feel good for you."

The wounded skid tried a game smile. "What does?"

"Good man," Betty said. "There should be a number of these doors in succession. After the second or third transition, it'll start grinding hard, but we've got to do at least half a dozen before I can look for a smoother run. Everyone stay together." She glanced at the sky. "Wobble, we're leaving. Drop in twenty."

"Affirmative. Tell Ripley to blow the doors."

"Stay together," Betty said, letting an eye run over everyone. "Bian, take Brolin and Shabaz through first, it'll give them a few seconds to rest between transits. Albert, will you follow, please? Johnny, you cover the rear with me." Reaching down, she touched one of the circlets. It pulsed once. The door dissolved. "In you go," she said to Bian.

The red-yellow skid did not look happy, but she took Brolin and Shabaz by the arm. The doorway flared gold when they jumped in.

"I SEE YOU RUN, LITTLE SKID. YOU WILL NOT ESCAPE."

"You'd be surprised what might happen," Betty snarled softly. The doorway flashed as skid after skid jumped through. To Johnny, she added, "One day, I'm going to pop that jackhole."

Wobble came screeching down from the sky, folding back into his smallest form. "Jammed corsets and ground tremors," he whirred. "The whole Uug-xhal fleet is right behind." Half his body was smoking.

"That's all right, Wobble," Betty said. "You did great." She patted his head as he dropped through the door. "You're the baddest knife there is."

"WE WILL FIND YOU, BETTY CRISP."

The oldest skid in the universe flicked a contemptuous eye towards the heavens. "You do that," she said. Then she gave Johnny a nudge and took them through the door.

CHAPTER SEVENTEEN

They went through one transit after another, each time emerging into a small hallway with doors everywhere: on the ceiling, the walls, the floor. All covered with glowing circlets, connected by lines of gold. After each transit, Betty would land, turn, and send them through the next door.

"The first three were completely random," Betty said after the fifth. "We needed a new start point as best we could."

Every hallway had gaps where there'd been doors in the other hallways. *Breaks in the system?* Johnny wondered, staring at an empty space on the floor.

After the sixth transition, Bian reached out and grabbed Betty. "How many more?" she said. "We're killing Brolin."

"I'm fine," the Seven hissed, but his skin blossomed with spores.

Betty looked down at the hand clasped on her arm and then up at Bian. She held the gaze until Bian let go. "I didn't choose the number of transits on a whim.

And you're not the only one who cares about Brolin and Shabaz."

"You've got a hole of a way of showing it," Bian muttered, rolling away.

Betty watched her tread over to Shabaz, then sighed and rolled her eyes. "I'm going to need a minute," she said. Her hollas popped up, seemingly from nowhere.

"Where do those come from?" Johnny said.

"I carry them with me," Betty said, as image after image cycled by. "Like I said, it's all data. We are the program."

"Nice," Torg said.

"Isn't it?" she grinned at him. "Technically, I could run these internally. You wouldn't see a thing."

"Oh? And why wouldn't you do that?"

"Two reasons. One: this looks sweeter. Two: it gives me a massive headache." She winced. "Never been able to shake it." The hollas stopped on what looked like a map. "Finish line," Betty said as the hollas snapped away. She rolled over to a door in the ceiling, tapped a pattern in the circlets, then double-tapped the centre. The circlets flashed and rotated.

Turning to the group, she said, "This transit will take a little longer. You might have the weird feeling you're being stretched." She looked at Bian. "But it should be easier on the wounded."

"Whatever you say," Bian sniffed. Holding Brolin's arm, she reached up and was pulled into the door.

Johnny leaned into Torg. "Notice Bian seems a little sketch?"

"Who isn't?" Torg said. "It's like we're trying to play ten games at once and no one gave us the rules. Our nerves are shot. Now, Bian's got a huge heart and stepped up to take care of Shabaz and Brolin . . . but she's also a Look-At-Me-Girl." He grinned. "Not going to happen with Betty Crisp around."

"She's jealous? But she's always hanging around the higher Levels."

"Not the girls."

Johnny stared at him and then chuckled. Who the hole was going to match up with Betty Crisp, anyway? Shaking his stripes, he reached up for the door.

It was different this time: as if each side of his body was gently being pulled. Then, for the first time since the weather-mem, they popped into a world dominated by more than black and gold.

They emerged from a door built into a crumbling building. Rectangular with rounded edges, the door looked solid even though it's half-ceramic, half-metal surface was red with rust stains. Peering closely, Johnny could still see gold lines, but they were faint. Dirt and detritus piled up against the building.

"Betty Crisp," Torres whispered, looking up.

They were in a vast complex. Far, far above their heads: a ceiling perforated with massive holes. Entire parts of it appeared to be missing. Through the gaps, a hazy white sky cast the roof into a skeletal silhouette. Around them, huge frameworks of machinery stretched up towards the ceiling.

"Where are we?" Bian breathed.

"That's a little tough to explain," Betty said. Her hollas were up, though they flickered in and out of focus.

Bian glared at Betty. "I'm not stupid."

"I didn't say you were stupid, Bian." Betty glanced away from the hollas. "Are we going to keep doing this? I'm just checking." She waited a beat then added, "I didn't say it was tough to explain because I thought you were stupid. I said it's tough to explain because it's tough to explain and we need to move. If you'd like, I'll try to put it into words as we go. All right?"

This time, Bian at least had the grace to look embarrassed as she bobbed her eyes.

They rolled down a wide artery that centred the superstructure. Hazy white light streamed in through holes in the roof, the walls; at times, even the floor. The far end of the highway—hazy in the distance—seemed partially open. The wash of light bathed humongous machines, hundreds of metres high. Unlike the roof or the crumbling building, most of the machinery seemed intact, if unused.

"We call them ghostyards," Betty said as they tread past an unmoving conveyor belt. "I don't know what they're supposed to be called because we're not sure they really exist."

"Looks like it exists," Torg said, grinning as his eyes swung in every direction. "Imagine the game we could play in here."

"Yeah," Johnny murmured, staring at a bin bigger than the Skates rink. "Some kind of hide and seek. Like the Tag Box."

"Why don't you think it exists?" Bian asked Betty.

"Whatever was built here, it was physical."

"Maybe they built the Skidsphere."

Betty nodded. "We thought about that. It's certainly possible. Except remember, the Skidsphere isn't really physical. It's data."

"Yeah, but we don't see it that way," Bian insisted. "You said that, right? Skids see things different than other parts of the Thread. So maybe this is how we see our own factory."

Admiration lit Betty's face. "Now that's a hole of a thought. Really. And we're not counting anything out, so you could be right. We're gearing toward the ghostyards being symbolic. A metaphor within the metaphors."

"I don't get it."

"We've never found one that's in operation. While a lot of the Thread is inactive, even the small part that remains is massive. If the ghostyards were a real part of the Thread, at least one of the hundreds we've found should have been working."

"You keep saying *we*. Who's we?" Torg said.

Betty's stripe flushed. "Me and Wobble. I always think of him as part of the team."

"We're better than Cuddle and Squeak." Wobble's head whizzed around and a grin split his face. "Wobble."

"I try to think in the plural as often as I can. It's better than spending ten lifetimes alone," Betty said, looking at Torg. "Can you understand that?"

"Yeah," Torg said sombrely. "I can understand that."

A beat of silence passed as Bian watched them with a perplexed expression, then Betty continued. "Anyway, we're pretty sure this is a representation of factories that exist in the Out There. Which is another reason why we think no one is watching."

"So what does it do?" Torg said, confused. "I mean here, in the Thread?"

"That's the point. It doesn't do anything. It's not even here. In many ways, the ghostyards don't even scan as part of the Thread. They're . . . quirky."

"Quirky?"

"Quirky," Betty said. "In the past, I've used them as hideouts because the Antis avoid them, but it was hard getting any work done. Nothing works the way it should. That's why my hollas are acting spare." She glanced peevishly at the flickering displays, then sighed and swept them away. "Plus it gets depressing pretty fast."

"I could see that," Torg agreed, as they rolled under a pipe large enough to fit a dozen skids side-by-side. "So where are we going now?"

"We've got to try my original safehouse. I can't think of any other way to keep Brolin and Shabaz alive. There's only one problem: SecCore. Ten years ago, he found the safehouse."

"The cops-cops are corrupt," Wobble said from the front of the pack.

"That they are, Wobble," Betty agreed.

"So you're saying we could be rolling into a trap," Bian said.

"Possibly. Or SecCore could be long gone. I didn't leave a lot of data behind; he may not realize how important that particular safehouse was. I've had many since." Betty sighed. "But most likely it's a trap."

Bringing up the rear, Johnny stayed out of the conversation. He even dropped back a few metres. He knew he should pay more attention, but if Betty was right, then they weren't in danger here and they'd probably have a better picture once they neared her safehouse.

The gap between him and the group was a small but important distance. It was all a lot to absorb and, right now, Johnny needed space.

Nearby, Albert rolled alongside Torres, the younger skid pointing at something new every few seconds. Albert remained largely silent, although that wasn't surprising: Albert saved most of his talk for inside the games; outside he tended to roll quiet. Johnny had always been the loud one.

Surreptitiously, he glanced at the scar running the length of Albert's body, splitting his stripes. Half his thoughts followed a familiar path: *Serves you right, gearbox.* The other half . . . he grimaced.

He hated feeling sorry for Albert.

Johnny knew he wasn't completely rational about his feelings for the silver skid. But way too many skids seemed to forget that Albert was the one who'd attacked Johnny first, not the other way around. Had anyone else made the nine-nine comment, Johnny probably would've laughed, popped whoever it was in the next game, and then forgotten about it. Coming from Albert, though . . .

"Betty's right," he sighed, looking around. "This place is depressing."

They rolled past a derelict mechanical arm. The arm was big enough to pick up an entire Mart, but it hung at an awkward angle. He wondered how long it had hung that way and why. *Because no one's coming to fix it,* he thought, two eyes trailing as they left the arm behind. The Out There was gone. In a place like this, it was hard to deny.

He put a little more distance between himself and the group, trying to sort out the thought. On many levels, he couldn't accept it. No one was watching? The whole reason skids played the games was to be watched. Sure they enjoyed the competition—they lived for it—but the first thing every skid did after a race was check the boards. Look for yourself on the hollas. You didn't need to *see* the Out There to know that it was . . . out there. Watching. Otherwise, what was the point?

And if every skid had hoped for the Out There's recognition, then Johnny . . .

He couldn't remember a time when he hadn't dreamed of a second name. But he could remember being less than a month old and popping a Five—and month-olds never tried popping any skid on the Slope, let alone a

Five—then rushing to check the hollas, screaming when they'd shown the play. If the other skids wanted the Out There's approval, then Johnny had bled for it from all three eyes.

So if there was no Out There out there . . . then who the hole was Johnny Drop?

Johnny . . .

Instantly, all of his eyes came up. In time to see a pink-red flash disappear behind a stack of crates.

"Oh, snakes . . ." he whispered, looking around. No one else reacted. Up front, Betty was still talking with Bian and Torg. Wobble was rolling up to random pieces of machinery, examining them as if they were long lost relatives. A dozen metres away, Torres continued to pester Albert.

"You're imagining things, squid," Johnny muttered, even as he dropped back. "This place has got you—"

Johnny . . .

Down a corridor between the crates, a flash of pink . . .

"I'm going crazy," Johnny sighed, sprinting down the corridor. He followed the flash of colour around a corner, only to discover it had gained on him, fleeing behind a crane. "*Peg!*" he hissed, gunning it. Again, the flash of pink and red had increased the distance, darting behind a bin.

"Peg!" he cried, louder now. *Last one*, Johnny thought grimly. *I am not going to be* . . .

Not far from the bin, resting under a conveyor belt, a skid sat with her back to Johnny. Six cherry-red stripes pulsed against bright pink skin.

Johnny . . .

"Peg," he said, reaching out as he rolled forward.

The skid vanished.

"No!" Johnny barked, reaching . . .

"Johnny?"

Johnny swung his trail-eye back where it belonged, too keyed up to care that he'd had all three looking forward.

Torg sat by the bin, stripes cocked. "You all right, squid?"

Keeping his trail-eye on Torg, Johnny swept the area under the conveyor belt with the other two. Nowhere to hide . . .

"Johnny?"

"Yeah, just a minute." Nothing. No pink, no cherry-red . . . "You see anything? Other than me?"

"I'm seeing a lot of things, Johnny," Torg drawled, swinging an arm to encompass the ghostyard. "Did you mean something more specific? You took off pretty quick back there, sport."

"No, I . . ." Johnny bit his lip, then swung an eye and turned. "Never mind. It's nothing."

"All right," Torg said, eyeing his friend. "Just be careful taking off. Everyone's scans are going spare. Easy to get lost."

"Yeah," Johnny said, his trail-eye now on the conveyor belt, bathed in hazy white light. "I guess it is."

"You sure you're all right?" Torg said, as they started to tread back to the group.

"Yeah, I'm just . . . it's a lot to absorb. I mean . . . Betty Crisp."

Torg chuckled. "I hear that. Put all the weird stuff together—all the Everything's-Just-Data-Wobble-Talk—and the freakiest thing is that five minutes ago I was talking to the chick who did the vaping Leap."

"Yeah," Johnny agreed. "Hey, you notice she's only got one stripe?"

"I did. Maybe after Ten you go back to being a panzer."

Johnny thought about Betty popping her arm, her hand filled with light as it sliced into an Anti . . .

"I don't think that's what happens," he said dryly. "I mean, she's supposed to have been dead for fifty years. Hole, if she's still alive, maybe . . ." He gazed up through the holes in the distant ceiling. The Thread was so large it contained hundreds of ghostyards. So huge, the Skidsphere was considered small. Surely, it was possible that somewhere in it . . .

Torg had stopped. "You still on that, Johnny?" he said softly.

Johnny's gaze came down from the sky. They were in an intersection between crates, not far from the centre causeway.

"Let it go, brother," Torg said, his voice somehow both gentle and firm. "She's dead."

"We don't know that." The words came automatically.

"Yeah, we do."

"If Betty Crisp—"

"Betty Crisp was a Level Ten," Torg said. "Maybe higher. No one knows what a Ten can do, Johnny. Even you don't know that yet. Peg was a Six when she died. A *Six*. And . . ." He hesitated. "And she wasn't you."

"What the hole is that supposed to mean?" Johnny said, his stripes flaring.

"It means that even if she was the most beautiful skid on the Skates I ever saw, she wasn't as strong as you. Or Albert."

"Torg—"

"No, listen. I'm not vaping her memory for Crisp's sake. The truth is none of us are as strong as you or Albert. You were better than me when I was an Eight and you were a Five." Torg took a deep breath. "Johnny, without you there, I don't make it through the black. And I'm a Nine. Peg was a Six. She's dead, brother. Let it go."

Looking away from Torg, Johnny studied the ground. "Maybe she didn't fall into the black."

"You serious?" Both eyes facing Johnny rolled and the third twitched. For the first time, the older skid looked angry. "Are you talking about Albert? Are you still on that? After all we've seen, everything we now know, are you seriously going to stay on his skin about Peg?"

"We don't know . . ." Johnny began, but his voice trailed off. Deep down, in a place he didn't want to admit existed, he knew he was just repeating the same arguments he'd been making for the past six months, arguments that no longer made any sense at all.

Torg stared at him, his eyes set. "You know, squid, I'm going to say something I'm pretty sure skids don't say to each other too often—you're my friend. I mean that. Whatever plays out here, whatever we have to do to get out of this alive and save the sphere, I'll stick with you all the way to the sea." He paused. "But sometimes you're a jackhole."

Watching Torg roll away, Johnny found it hard to argue with him.

CHAPTER EIGHTEEN

Johnny came back to the main artery about twenty metres behind the pack. Torg had gone to the front. Wobble tread along not far from Johnny, emitting a low keening noise, followed by barely spoken words, rapid and sparse.

Wobble was talking to himself.

"Wobble?" Johnny said, pulling up. "You all right, buddy?"

Gears whirred and Wobble's head spun. The lens-shutters twisted. "It breaks slow-slow-slowly," the machine said softly, his voice a high, tight whine. "A thousand-thousand years before the shelf fell into the sea. Valporin still looks like a moon." His fractured arms twitched. "It hurts."

"What hurts?" Johnny asked. Whatever he was suffering through, it was a lot more than a damaged limb. "What's breaking, Wobble? The Thread?" *Can he feel the Thread breaking?*

A chill went through Johnny's entire body. He

thought of the black void attacking the Pipe. Whatever had hit the city of hollas, wiping out millions of mems. The yellow data-box, plowing into one of Wobble's own fire-wheels.

Daytona.

He tried to calc how many Vies they'd seen since landing in the white. Failed miserably. Had Wobble felt all of that? Johnny gazed down the ghostyard, stretching out for kilometers. They seemed no closer to one end than when they started. Already, they'd seen so much, but that was a fraction of the Thread's true breadth. And if the damage matched proportionally . . .

What if Wobble felt it every time something, somewhere broke?

As if reading his thoughts, Wobble's lenses suddenly focused on Johnny. "Can you make-make it stop?"

Johnny stared back, his heart full. "I'm sorry, Wobble. I don't think I can."

Wobble's lenses retracted and his head turned away. "Somebody should," he said, in a voice that didn't waver at all.

Johnny watched him tread away as Betty dropped back from the group. "It's all right," she said, keeping an eye on Wobble. "There's nothing you can do for him right now. He'll . . ." She took a deep breath. "Well, he's tougher than he looks."

"I heard that," Johnny said. "I've known him a day and he's already saved my skin . . ." He tried to math it. "Three times? Four?" He shook his stripes. "Where'd you find him, anyway?"

"Actually, I prefer to think we found each other— saved each other, really. I honestly don't know what I would've done for fifty years without him. I'd have gone crazy. Probably would have ended up talking to the boxes."

Johnny glanced at Wobble, his stripes tilting.

"He doesn't count," she said, following his gaze and rolling her eyes. "Lesson for Johnny: it's all right if a lady calls herself crazy—it's less wise for the man to point it out."

Johnny grinned. "If you say so."

Betty's laugh was sharp and echoed off the ghostyard. "Kinks, you're like I was. Cocky little spare."

She was still smiling so he took it as a compliment. He grinned back . . . and that's when it hit him. *I'm flirting with Betty Crisp. You dumb squid.*

"Stop that," she snapped.

Johnny blinked. "Stop what?"

"Hero worship. You look like that Two when she saw you at the Combine."

"Oh. Sorry."

"You don't have to apologize, I get it, just . . . try not to make it a habit. We don't have time for it, and, yeah—I am *Betty Crisp*—and given that I'm fifty years past my due date I guess that makes me special . . . but I'm not that special." She chuckled. "In a weird way, Bian's attitude is kind of refreshing."

Rolling his eyes, Johnny said, "That's one way of putting it."

"No really," Betty said. "I get it: at her level, I would've acted the same if I met someone like me." Her stripe tilted. "We're designed for jealousy, we skids—girls, boys, doesn't matter. Made for good watching."

"When somebody was." Johnny's gaze wandered up to the holes of light, silhouetting the ceiling.

"Yep." Betty studied him for a moment. "You going to be okay with that?"

His gaze wandered down the underside of the roof

until it disappeared into the haze. The place was so huge. So empty.

"I don't know," he said softly.

Betty bobbed an eye. "That's fair. By the time I had to deal with it, I'd already moved a little past the glory-seeking stage. But when it's been a part of your entire life . . ." Now her gaze wandered. "For the first five years of my life I was so desperate to do something . . . different. By the time I hit Eight, I wasn't competing with the skids around me, I was aiming somewhere else. I'd started to move past that by the time I left the Skidsphere, but it still hit me hard. Took me years before it didn't bother me." She paused. "The personal aspect of it. The rest still vapes my gears."

They rolled in silence for a bit. Ahead, Albert had taken the lead with Torres and Aaliyah in tow. Bian remained near Shabaz and Brolin. Torg rolled near the back, leaving Betty and Johnny their space.

"How'd you do it?" Johnny said suddenly. "Leave the Skidsphere?"

Betty pursed her lips. Looked ahead to the group. Then her stripe tilted and she sighed. "I have a feeling you already know. I've seen you contemplate it a few times in the last few months."

Yeah, he knew exactly where she was talking about. "The woods?"

"The woods," Betty agreed. She hesitated, then said, "It was about three weeks shy of my birthday. You know which one. Five years. Game over." Her pink stripe darkened until it was almost as black as her skin. "Most skids think the Rainbow Road happened and I died right away, but I actually had two months left. Got my second name that night. You'd think it would've made me happy.

Not so much." She looked at Johnny. "Sound familiar?"

"Yeah," Johnny said. He remembered watching hollas in the pit, then screaming at Albert like he wanted to kill him.

"Don't know why," Betty continued, "but it just pissed me off. Almost immediately I thought: is that it? That's when I started going out to the Spike every day."

Above them, vast machines hung, bathed in a ghost-white haze.

"I'd been having odd thoughts for a skid for some time. You're not the first Nine to stop by the Combine, although I never went so far as to actually help another skid." She frowned. "Why'd you do it?"

"I don't know." He caught her look. "I really don't."

"But it felt good, didn't it? Helping?"

"Yeah," Johnny said, thinking about that moment and how it had surprised him. "It did. Weird."

"It is weird. We're not supposed to do that: care. Certainly not for panzers and squids. Friendly rivals, sure—bump-and-gos with the other sex every few months, hey, that's great watching. But *caring* . . . that's a whole deeper level of relationship."

Johnny's stripes twitched. He hadn't thought about it that clearly before, but it echoed some of what he'd been feeling lately.

"It's like death. We're not happy about it but we never really think about it. Sevens spend most of their energy trying to get to Eight before they die; Eights worry about making Nine. Only the Nines who get there early think about dying, because they know they're not going to make Ten. No sane skid really thinks they're going to make Ten." She smirked as she said this, deliberately not looking his way.

"Hey . . ." he protested.

"It's all right, Johnny, I was the same. Still, like I said, most Nines given the time stop thinking about advancing. They think about how they're *not* going to advance. Here, I'll show you. You got a count?"

"Sorry?"

"A count. How many days until you die?"

Johnny blinked. "Uh, more than a year?"

"Right. Watch this." Betty's eyes swung towards the pack. "Torg, do you have a count?"

"Of what?" When Betty remained silent, his eye-stalks dipped. "Oh, right. Huh." His stripes tilted slightly. "Four months, sixteen days."

Johnny's eyes widened as Betty said, "They go fast, don't they, Torg?"

The gold stripes dimmed a little. "Yeah. They come quick. Least recently they do."

Johnny stared at Torg, a sudden wave of sorrow washing over him. He'd never thought about death seriously. It was like Betty said: there were races to run. Live fast, die fast: it was their motto for a reason. Even after Peg died, he'd never considered his own death. He'd only thought about Peg.

Torg's stripes remained dim for a moment, then a smirk split his face. "You boys and girls are having a conversation just filled with sugar."

"Come join us," Betty smiled back. "Johnny asked me how I got out of the Skidsphere and we got a little off topic."

"Just a little," Johnny grinned, as Torg dropped back.

"Not as far as you might think," Betty said. "My point is that I was thinking differently than most skids think—than most skids get a *chance* to think. And most of it was death." She took a deep breath. "For more than a month after the Rainbow Road, I would go out to the

Spike, any time I could. And every time, I got angrier and angrier. I'd accomplished everything that a skid could ever possibly hope for in my lifetime, but I was pissed off I was going to die. Despite everything I'd done, I didn't feel done. So . . . I went for a roll."

"Into the woods," Johnny said. He could see it. He might never have consciously considered it, but the thought had been there, at the back of his mind. He could see it.

"Into the woods," Betty agreed. "I'm sure thousands of skids have wondered how far back they go. I'm sure I'm not the first skid to have tried it. But I doubt if any skid ever wandered more than a few hours." She paused, her stripe darkening once more. "I rolled for a little longer than that."

"How long . . . ?" Johnny started to say. "Wait a minute, when did you say you did this—three weeks from your birthday?" He stared at her.

"It didn't take three." Betty smiled grimly. "It took one. I rolled for a week solid, never stopping, never resting. Without any sugar. That's when I knew: sugar was a lie. And if sugar was a lie, then it probably wasn't the only one."

Her eyes swung forward. "Every single metre I tread, I got angrier. And angrier. And when my clock hit a week, I remember thinking: *Go ahead*. Put another tree in front of me. I don't care: I'm not going to stop. I'm going to keep going until you kill me. I'm going to make you create another fourteen days' worth of trees, you grease-sucking spares. So why don't you stop wasting everybody's time and kill me now, because I'm not going to break. And I didn't." She took a deep breath. "But the woods did."

"The woods . . . broke?" Torg said.

"The woods broke. There was a sound like thunder, then the ground shook and a tree split open right in front of me. Inside that space—a darkness like night, but instead of stars . . ."

She let it hang and Johnny completed the thought. "Lines of gold?"

"I didn't even think twice. You'd think I would've at least paused, but nope. Barely broke rhythm. I thought: *Vape it,* and plunged right in."

"Wow," Torg said.

"This wasn't like what you went through. The edges of the break were clean, the golden lights inside the black were unbroken. There was a flash of pain and a feeling that something was *wrong,* but nothing like what you all went through. Just a few seconds, then I landed . . . well, it doesn't matter where I landed, just that it sure the hole wasn't the Skidsphere." Her eyes swept over the ghostyard and she shivered.

"Still," Torg said, amazed, "you got out. And you survived."

"And in the process . . . I broke my home."

"What?"

Betty's eyes swung. "That feeling of wrong. I can't be certain, but I'm pretty sure when I broke out . . . I broke a lot more than that. Before me, there were no corpsquakes. None. There wasn't any black moss." She hesitated, then glanced at Johnny and added, "There weren't any disappearances."

Johnny's stripes flinched. "Peg?"

"She wasn't the only one," Betty said grimly. "I know you thought she was unique—sorry, she *was* unique, that was cruel. But she wasn't the only skid to disappear. Sixteen have vanished like Peg since I left."

"*Sixteen?*" Johnny and Torg said together, stunned.

"Sixteen. Nine disappeared in one day alone during Tilt, about twelve years back. That's when I first started thinking about putting the sphere in stasis."

"Impossible," Johnny said. "We'd know about that."

"Would you?" Betty said, her voice getting hard again. "How much do you know about the past, Johnny? How many skids could you name from before you were born?"

"Uhhh," he said, stalling as tried to remember all the records he knew. "Twenty? Thirty?"

"Exactly," Betty said, her voice filled with bitterness. "We remember the ones on the records until they wipe the records clean and that's it. Thousands of skids, millions maybe if you count the squids and panzers, since I died and we remember a couple dozen."

"And only one we could cite from memory," Torg added.

"Right," Betty said. "Peg wasn't the only one to fall into the black. And I'm pretty sure I caused the black to happen to the sphere." She waited for Johnny's reaction.

He should have felt furious. Instead, he just felt empty. An eye twitched in Albert's direction, but Johnny roughly pulled it back. He didn't care to think about Albert right now and he sure the hole wasn't about to give him an apology.

"Do you think . . ." he said. His eyes swung around the ghostyard, staring through the holes in the ceiling. "We made it through. I keep . . . I keep seeing . . ."

"Johnny . . ."

And now he got mad. Because in addition to guilt, Betty's tone contained a resignation that sounded way too much like Torg. "Don't want to hear it," he said, popping an arm.

"Johnny—"

"Hey! I said no." He gunned his gears, grinding them.

"Forget I asked. Tell me about Wobble. How did you save him?" Vape it, that's where the conversation had started. The focus was out in his eye again. He corrected it so hard he felt a brief stab of pain as he did.

Betty watched him for a moment, then her stripe tilted. "I didn't do much," she said. "Not nearly what he's done for me. I found him about fifteen years after I entered the Thread. He'd been left for dead. I managed to drag him to a safehouse and get his self-repair systems online. He did the rest."

Nearby, Wobble's head spun. "Magnum came back, sir. Teddy Bears and lights in the distance. Wobble."

"Who tried to kill him?" Johnny asked.

"SecCore. Wobble's an Anti."

"He doesn't look like them."

"He does sometimes," Torg said.

"He does," Betty agreed. "Somewhere along the line, when the Thread hit a critical point, SecCore started developing different types of Antis to deal with different things. It was a brilliant move and may have actually saved the Thread. Wobble's type was the most sophisticated."

"Okay," Johnny said. "So why'd he try to kill him?"

"Not him. Them." Betty's stripe darkened almost down to red. "There were thousands of Wobbles. Maybe more. But they got *too* sophisticated. When they became sentient, some disagreed with a few of SecCore's methods. So SecCore had them destroyed. All of them."

"I'm beginning to develop a serious dislike for this guy," Torg murmured. In the distance, a long, glowing light appeared in the haze, cutting across the thoroughfare.

"You and me both," Betty said grimly. "Had that kind of development continued, maybe they would've eventually evolved into something that did more than just kill Vies. They might have fixed the Thread. Apparently, that was the direction Wobble and his kind wanted to go. But SecCore was in charge. His ideas. No one else."

Wobble had paused at a mechanical arm like his, but thirty times his size. The former Anti was trying to line up his arm with the mechanical one. He appeared to be humming.

"I've never found another Wobble," Betty said, watching her friend. "Not in thirty-five years. I don't know what they did to him, but I know it hurts, and it hurts me that I can't stop it. As I said, without Wobble, I might not have stayed sane. I wasn't in much better shape when I found him."

Satisfied that he'd matched the arm-angles just right, Wobble hooted, spun his head, then beamed a broken grin as he sped to the front of the pack. "Pings from the probe. I-We are here. Wobble."

The far end of the ghostyard appeared no closer than when they'd started. Nonetheless, cutting across the causeway was a translucent tube, ten metres tall, pulsing softly with golden light. It looked completely out of place with the rest of the ghostyard. Without pausing, Wobble tread right though the walls of the tube and stopped inside.

"What's he doing?" Bian said, eyeing the tube skeptically.

"Calling a pulse," Betty said.

"What's a—?"

The whole ghostyard boomed and washed gold with light. When the glare cleared, Wobble stood inside a ball of luminescence that pulsed in time with the tube.

"That's a pulse," Betty said, grinning as Wobble waved. "It's the fastest way around the Thread. As far as

I can tell, in real time it's near instantaneous, although time is slower inside the pulse. We'll have about fifteen minutes to get ready before we arrive."

"Arrive where?" Bian said. Beside her, Brolin lay on his treads breathing heavily, black spores blooming and fading on his skin. "We can't keep bouncing around like this."

"Brolin and Shabaz made it this far. This is the last trip; my safehouse is near where we'll arrive." She held Bian's gaze. "This is the fastest way there, Bian. And we need that time to scan ahead and see what we're getting into."

"And if there are Antis there?" Shabaz asked nervously. She looked better than Brolin, but she didn't look great.

"That may not be likely. I left very little to indicate that this safehouse was more important than my others. I haven't been back in ten years. There's really no reason for SecCore to be there."

"Unless he planted Antis at all your safehouses," Albert said.

"I got your back," Brolin rasped, lifting one of his eyes.

"That's my brave boy," Betty said, placing a hand on Brolin's skin. "Even if there are Antis, Wobble and I can handle anything short of an army. Once we're inside, SecCore will find it difficult to breach the house. You'll be safe, at least in the short term, and Brolin and Shabaz can get some care. When the boys and I leave, we shouldn't be gone for long."

"What if the Antis do get in?" Aaliyah said quietly. "How are we supposed to fight them?" She glanced at Albert's scar.

"I left a few hidden goodies behind." Betty grinned. "Hole, there might even be some sugar."

Bian rolled her eyes. "Do we at least get to find out

what you're going to do?"

"We'll have time inside the pulse. My hollas should work again; I'll show you everything. It won't take long." She smiled, as if at a private joke.

Torg glanced at Johnny, his stripes tilted. "Ride the lightning?"

"Live fast," Johnny murmured, looking down the tube. He followed Torg through the translucent walls. The seemingly large pulse was cramped once nine skids and a turbo-charged Anti fit inside.

"All right," Betty said, bringing her hollas up, "Wobble, let's go."

"Fire in the hole-hole." Wobble grinned and, instantly, the ghostyard stretched out in a stream of golden light, like a picture pulled apart from the sides.

The world outside went black.

Immediately, Wobble screeched: *"ALARM! ALARM! They bombed the bridge, this worm is dead!"*

All three of Betty's eyes opened to the max and spread like she was trying to read every holla at once. "Oh no. Oh no."

"What's going on?" Bian said.

"The pulse is a dead end." The hollas flew around Betty's head like a storm. "We're running through the black."

"Then why did we take this thing?" Bian demanded, her voice rising with fear.

"Because it was fine last time. Wobble, we need an exit. Now."

"That might not be a problem," Torg murmured, staring at the walls. Blooming along the pulse like spores, black fissures met and formed.

The walls were being eaten.

"Everyone hold hands!" Betty bellowed, grabbing

Brolin and Torg. "Focus on that contact and think of your colours. Wobble, find us a path and clear."

As Johnny took Bian in one hand and Aaliyah in the other, Wobble rose into the centre of the sphere and spun. His body flared out and took on his sleek knife-like form. Spinning like a gyroscope, his nose stopped abruptly, pointing down at an angle.

"Hold on," Betty whispered. "Colour."

As the pulse in front of Wobble's nose evaporated, the machine lit up like a flare and plunged into the darkness. Thinking of colour, Johnny and the others plunged after him as the last fragments of the pulse fizzled into the black.

CHAPTER NINETEEN

It wasn't as bad as when they'd fallen from the Pipe.

For one thing, this time they had Wobble. Johnny wasn't sure what the machine did but there was a white light ahead—a beacon in the black—burning a space for them to follow. And this time he knew what was coming. Hole, he even had a little warning. Not much, but enough to focus: on his colours and the colours of those around him. Plus, he wasn't alone. Through the line, he could feel Betty anchoring them like a stone. Albert too: struggling along with Johnny to help as many as he could. So, no, it wasn't as bad.

But that didn't mean it was good.

The pulse died and instantly Johnny felt the empty darkness of the broken Thread tearing at him from the sides. A heartbeat, maybe two, and spores began to flurry across the light ahead—black on white—like a snow-storm in negative.

Hold on, Johnny sent along the line, as the sides of his skin began to fail. It was inside him, he could feel it—

burrowing inside, eating away at his colour, at his name. Aaliyah's hand started to slip; it felt like it was growing thinner . . .

Hold on, he thought, clapping down, sending her name—so new, so newly named—time and time and time again.

The black snowstorm began to blot out the light.

Hold . . .

They broke through, hitting the ground hard. The air was crushed from Johnny's lungs and he had a visceral memory of the end of the Slope. Sucking in air, he smelled burnt metal. His cells were on fire, parts of him felt hollow; he was going to throw up—nearby, someone was retching air. None of his eyes were clear.

I'm getting sick of doing this, he thought bitterly, attacking the hollow sensation inside, pulling his eyes into focus, one-by-one. His third fought him, staring up at a blurry darkness until his anger surged and his vision snapped into clear. *Then again,* he thought, looking up, *maybe it was in focus.*

Off to his left, he heard Bian call, "Everyone here?" her voice ragged and raw. In his left hand, Aaliyah's twitched; he hoped that was a good sign. Above them, black on black.

And some of the black . . . moved.

"*ALERT!*" Wobble cried. "Incoming!" Every part of his surface had been scored with acid and smoke; despite this, a dozen fire-wheels spun into the dark. From his sides, two gun emplacements of four barrels each appeared, rotated upwards with a high-pitched whine, and began to fire. The sound of pounding artillery filled the air.

"Vies," Betty said grimly. "They follow the breaks." Her upper eye stared into the falling sky, filled with rage. "Get everyone together; wounded and kids in the middle. You'll need to take out anything that gets past Wobble and me."

"What are you going to do?" Torg breathed, an awe-filled eye on Wobble.

"The two of us?" A black splotch on her stripe evaporated. Her left Hasty-Arm disappeared, replaced with a gun that made Wobble's look like a toy. "We're going to bring the grease-sucking end."

Her treads transformed into cylinders, ignited, and she roared into the sky like a rocket. Wobble's guns folded back into his body and he followed, his white surface beginning to glow like a star.

"A little higher than Ten," Torg murmured, watching Betty as her gun shattered the air.

"Maybe we should . . ." Johnny started to say.

"*Johnny!*" Bian screamed. "Albert, somebody get over here!"

They all were in bad shape. Torres had spots appearing and disappearing across her stripe like some horrific version of a pond splattered by rain. A hitch had developed in Torg's treads like Wobble's; his magenta skin was washed pale. One of Bian's arms drooped. Albert's scar looked like it might crack open.

But Brolin and Shabaz . . .

Spores criss-crossed Shabaz's body and the two eyes that still worked were tearing up with fear and pain. And Brolin . . . Brolin resembled a deflating balloon, his brown skin almost completely black.

Johnny couldn't see his stripes.

"They're dying," Bian cried, tears streaming down her face. "Help them."

But Johnny had already tried to save a dying skid. And failed. He couldn't . . .

He couldn't do it alone.

The thought struck like a tuning fork through every cell in his body. He couldn't do it alone.

But that didn't mean it couldn't be done.

Swallowing his pride, Johnny kept one eye on Brolin and turned the other two on Albert. "You got skids through the dark. You took out Vies and took a hit from an Anti. I need . . ." He took a deep breath. "I need your help. I can't do this on my own."

Albert didn't even smirk. "Now or never," he said, placing a hand on Brolin. The skid seemed to be shrinking before their eyes.

"We can help too," Bian said, rolling up with Torg.

"No," Johnny said. "You both need to get your own systems clear." When she started to protest, he barked: "I can't have you dying too. Besides, someone needs to help Aaliyah and Torres." Although, remarkably, Aaliyah looked clear of spores. Summoning a cockiness that he didn't really feel, he winked at the cream-green skid. "Get fixed, get focused. Try to help Torres do the same. Then protect Shabaz and watch our backs."

"Johnny, I think we need to do this," Albert said quietly.

Torg bobbed an eye, but Johnny was already turning back to Brolin.

He put both hands on the dying skid; Albert did the same. "Brolin," Johnny said, "hold on, sport." He tried to coat his thoughts in the colour of Brolin at his best: light, sandy brown, like the dust they scattered across the Slope to make it look good. He thought the Seven's name, sending it through his hands.

Then he closed his eyes and drove his thoughts into the black. He heard Albert whisper, "Stay together, Brolin, stay strong." Then the silver skid followed him in.

With Daytona, Johnny had tried to connect the healthy with the unhealthy, grafting the one over the other. But he'd concentrated too much on Daytona's skin—too much on the surface. If he just went after the virus . . .

Diving into the black, hard and deep, Johnny attacked it with the colour of sand and that single, all important word: *Brolin*. From somewhere outside his body, he thought he heard someone shout in fear. *Focus on the race you're running,* he thought grimly.

Unbelievably, Brolin was worse than Daytona. A million pinpricks of pain surrounded Johnny; instinctively, he lashed out at each one. That seemed to work, he felt the virus retreat, there was still so much— *where the hole was Albert?*

A wave of sandy brown that didn't come from him. *About time.* He sent the name Brolin out and felt Albert there. And then . . . and then . . . from somewhere even deeper, he had a fleeting image: a dusty brown core with black stripes—*healthy* black stripes—circling the core.

Johnny and Albert dove for the core like they were repeating the Drop, each screaming: *Brolin!* There wasn't much left, but the core surged as Johnny and Albert arrived; washing it with waves and waves of sandy brown. They attacked the black—it was amazing how clearly the difference between the virus and the healthy black stripes stood out. Johnny could feel Brolin trying to fight too, weakly at first, then stronger. This was going to work . . .

A spore bloomed on the core and Albert and Johnny both fell on it instantly. But instead of supporting each other, it was as if they'd crashed together on the Skates, both of them careening away. *You're getting in my way,* Johnny thought. And it was true—suddenly, they were stumbling, tripping over each other. They each shouted Brolin's name so often and out of sync that they cancelled the other out.

From outside, someone screamed: *"No!"* More blooms appeared on the core. One of the black stripes unravelled. *Vape it, Brolin, hold on!* But he wasn't holding on. Johnny and Albert stumbled again—this time it felt like they drove through each other—and another stripe unravelled, then another, then another . . .

Someone said, "No," again; this time like a dying prayer.

The remaining stripes broke apart as the core turned black and imploded. A spike of pain tore through Johnny and he drove his concentration away from Brolin so hard that his body flew back. He opened his eyes just in time to see Brolin shrivel away into nothing.

"Ah, snakes," he whispered. Closing his eyes, a wave of drained sorrow washed over him.

"Ohnoohnononononononono," Shabaz wailed, her voice keening with fear as she backed away from the spot where Brolin had been. Her battleship skin was the colour of ash, her stripes so tight they looked like one.

Johnny heard a deflated sound and swung an eye. Bian was weeping. Torg stared at an empty space, his face filled with despair. At least they looked healthier. And Torres seemed . . .

"Wait," Johnny breathed, surging up on his treads. "Where's Aaliyah?"

Bian made a guttural noise like a wounded animal. Her whole body shook.

"Where's Aaliyah?" Johnny said again, his voice rising.

"She took on a Vie," Torg said, stunned and raw. "By herself. One dropped from the sky—Bian and I attacked that together—but another dropped just as we finished, right by Torres. Aaliyah attacked it, wiped it out completely. Saved Torres. But she . . . she was just a squid . . ." Torg's voice broke and his gaze ripped away.

The battle above their head continued. Torres sat huddled nearby, her face a mask of guilt and sorrow. Shabaz continued to keen.

Something began to burn deep inside Johnny. "No one else," he spat softly. She'd been right . . . *here*. He'd winked at her . . .

"No one else," he said again, his eyes coming up. "*Shabaz!*" he snapped, rolling over to the Six who was collapsing more and more with every second, blooms bursting all over her body. "Shabaz, hold on," he said in a voice that was calm and certain and true. "You're going to make it."

"No, no, no," the terrified skid wailed. "You couldn't save Brolin, there were two of you and you couldn't—"

"Shabaz," Johnny said, amazed at how calm he felt, although there was something burning . . . "No one else dies today."

"Johnny," Torg said, "you can't, you and Albert look like you've been hit with—"

Three eyes swung. "No . . . One . . . *Else*." He held Torg's gaze for a heartbeat, then said, "You and Bian keep Torres alive."

His eyes swung again, settling on Albert. "We got in each other's way. That can't happen. One of us needs to lead and one needs to follow and support, make sure nothing gets in behind. Couldn't care less who does what. Pick. Now."

Albert stared at him for a second. Then . . . "Go."

Johnny didn't even acknowledge it. He put his hands on Shabaz and drove his will into the black, his mind burning with rage. Without hesitating, he dove straight for her core. He found it immediately: a tiny sphere of battleship grey, six aquamarine stripes whipping around its surface. Surrounded by black.

Shabaz! Johnny thought, screaming the name. *Your name is Shabaz!* He felt her respond, fighting for her life.

Then he held himself as close to the core as he could, turned out . . . and pushed. He was tired of trying to fix things, he just wanted to get the virus out. Gathering the rage burning inside, he attacked the black in all directions, forcing it back. He felt Albert slipping in behind him, supporting the core, washing it with waves of battleship grey. Shabaz was fighting . . .

It wasn't enough. The searing black retreated, then surged inwards once more, a million pinpricks . . .

Whatever had been building inside Johnny went off like a bomb. From his very centre he screamed: *Get out of my friend!* and like a star gone nova, a shockwave radiated out, plowing through the black. Some parts of the virus leaked through but Albert was there, catching each one. Shabaz was screeching her name. Johnny rode behind the shockwave, burning, burning, burn—

Three skids screamed as one.

Johnny's consciousness ripped out from Shabaz like a tsunami. Again, he was thrown back from a skid he'd tried to save, but this time when he opened his eyes, he saw Shabaz whole and complete, grey and aqua and not a single shadow of black.

"I . . . I'm alive," Shabaz said, popping an arm and examining it in amazement. "I'm alive!" All three of her eyes went wide and stared at Johnny. "You saved me."

"You did it!" Bian cried, and suddenly her arms were around Johnny and she was laying a huge kiss on his stripes—kiss after kiss, crying in-between each one: "You did it, you did it, you did it!"

"He wasn't the only one," someone said softly.

Albert sat on his treads nearby, eyeing her and Johnny. A black spore ran along his scar and then disappeared.

Bian's expression flattened as she unwrapped her arms from Johnny. "I'm sorry. Not getting to your parade fast enough for you, Albert? I thought the important thing was that Shabaz got healthy."

Woah, Johnny thought.

Albert's gaze remained steady. "Of course it is. You know that's not . . ." Two of his eyes swung away and then swung back. "What did I do, Bian? What did I do to deserve this?"

"Oh, for Crisp's sake, why don't you wear your wounds a little louder?" Bian snapped. "Fine. You helped Johnny—"

"Hey," Johnny started to protest.

"—save Shabaz," Bian continued, relentless. "Congratulations. You're a hero, Albert. Happy?" She started to turn away, then looked back. "And heal that vaping scar already—it makes you look ugly."

Johnny watched her roll away, stunned. He couldn't believe it: he actually felt sorry for Albert. They'd both saved Shabaz. If anything, Albert had swallowed his pride and allowed Johnny to lead—Johnny couldn't imagine how much he must have hated doing that. Albert had done it without thinking. If he was honest, Johnny wasn't sure he could've done the reverse. Eyeing the silver skid, he said, "Listen . . ."

"It's never enough with you, is it?" Albert whispered.

Johnny blinked. "I'm sorry?"

"You just take and take and take. You can't let anyone else have anything." He made a twisted sound: half-laugh, half-snarl. "And she said I'm the one looking for a parade."

"Look, Albert . . ."

"Save it." He rose on his treads. "I couldn't care less."

He rolled past Shabaz—poor Shabaz, who'd been stuck there, her now healthy eyes filled with guilt and pain. "Hey, Albert . . . I didn't mean . . ."

"It's all right, Shabaz. Like Bian said: what matters is you're healthy again. And I'm glad. Really. We're good." A wry smile. "Honestly, Shabaz, we're good." He rolled away.

Shabaz turned to Johnny, looking miserable. "I don't . . ."

"Don't worry about it," Johnny murmured, one eye watching Albert stop opposite from where Bian rested. He sighed. "I don't know what's going on and I'm in the middle of it." When that didn't seem to make the Six feel any better, Johnny added, "They both said it: you're healthy, that's what matters."

"I heard that," Torg said, rolling over. "You look good, panzer."

Pleasure rushed across Shabaz's face. "I feel like one." Her stripes were glowing. "Seriously, Johnny, you and Albert—I owe you guys."

"We get home, you can buy the sugar," Johnny grinned. "Panzer."

A high pitched whine split the air. Betty and Wobble descended from the darkness above—a darkness no longer swirling with Vies. Every centimetre of Wobble's body was battered and scarred, although he sported a huge, mangled grin. One of Betty's Hasty-Arms was twisted at an awkward angle, but her grin matched Wobble's. The massive gun she held in the other hand trailed tendrils of smoke.

"Where the hole did you get that bad boy?" Torg said, eyeing the gun.

"We aren't the only entertainment sim out there," Betty said, tucking the weapon—twice her size—inside her body. "Some are a little more . . . nasty than the Skidsphere. I borrowed their BFG."

Johnny frowned. "What's the 'F' stand for?"

Betty's stripes tilted. "Vape if I know." Two eyes swept the sky as her third swept the group. "Wobble and I took out every Vie in the area. We've sealed off the space as best we could, so we should have a little time . . ." Her voice trailed off and one of the upward eyes came down to join the third. "Where's Brolin and Aaliyah?" she said in a soft voice that already knew the answer.

"Brolin . . . Brolin couldn't hold on," Johnny said. "And Aaliyah . . . she saved Torres when Albert and I were working on Brolin."

"Are you all right, Torres?" Betty asked. Suddenly, she looked tired.

The cocky skid was sitting near Albert, unsure what to do, where to look. "Yeah," she said in a little voice. "Aaliyah . . . she was amazing . . ."

"Well, I'm glad you're all right. I'm sure you'd have done the same for her."

"Johnny and Albert got Shabaz clean too," Torg added.

"Together," Johnny said quickly, glancing at Albert, who sat with his back to the group.

"You healed her completely?" Betty said, brightening once more. "Shabaz, come here." The grey skid rolled over. Examining the Six's entire surface, a wide smile split Betty's face. "This is wonderful. There isn't a cell of Vie left."

"Yeah, I feel good," Shabaz said, embarrassed.

"This is truly wonderful," Betty said to Johnny. "Both of you have done something . . ." Her voice trailed off as she finally registered Albert's posture. A calculating look fell across her face as she took in the group: Albert, ten metres away, his back turned, his scar stark against his skin; Bian, ten metres in the other direction, her back turned as well. Torres, huddled near Albert, uncertainly glaring at Bian; Shabaz, unsure whether to feel joy or shame.

Betty glanced at Torg. "Do I need to ask?" she sighed.

"Probably not," Torg drawled.

CHAPTER TWENTY

Betty studied Bian. She studied Albert. She looked like she might say something to either one or both, but then she laughed. "You know," she said to Johnny and Torg, "I never thought fighting the Vies was going to be the easy part."

Torg chuckled as Betty popped her hollas and worked on where they were. Johnny excused himself and rolled over to Bian. He wasn't sure if this was a good idea; in fact, he was pretty sure it was a bad one. Albert sat on the other side of the group, staring out, but that wouldn't last. Johnny was surprised by how much he wanted to avoid antagonizing the silver skid.

"Hey," Johnny said softly. "You all right?"

When Bian turned, her eyes were red. "No. No, I'm not all right," she said, her voice scraping the back of her throat. "I'm tired of being so vaping useless."

"You're not useless," Johnny protested. "You kept the group together when we first got here. You took care of Brolin and Shabaz . . ."

"I said a bunch of meaningless words that didn't change anything," she said, her voice a snarl of self-loathing. "And Brolin died anyway."

"Shabaz didn't."

"Because of you."

And Albert, Johnny thought, but this probably wasn't the time to make that particular point again.

"You told me to keep Torres and Aaliyah safe and I couldn't even do that. At least Aaliyah saved Torres. And as for her . . ." Her gaze flickered towards where Betty sat with hollas of data swirling around her like a halo.

Johnny laughed. "Bian, I don't think any of us can really compare to Betty."

"It's different for you. It's . . ." She sniffed. "Snakes, I'm such a bitch." She cast a guilty glance at Albert, then her stripes twitched violently. "Never mind. It's not important." She sniffed again and looked around. "Any idea where we are?"

"Betty's working on it."

"Right," Bian said. "And then you and Albert and her get to save the world while the rest of us . . . hide."

"Bian," Johnny said firmly. "Bian. You haven't been useless thus far and you won't be useless in the future. Let's just all get home, okay?"

Her gaze changed, settling on his. "You've really been amazing though all this, you know." She tread a little closer.

"Uhhh . . . listen . . ." Johnny said, treading back. "I came over to check on you 'cause I was worried. You've been acting a little . . . strange lately."

"Am I acting strange now?" she said, her stripes tilting to one side as she tread closer still.

"Bian." He said it firmly enough that she stopped. "Look, I don't know exactly what's going on with . . . with you and Albert. If you broke up . . . if he did something to piss you off . . . well, all right. But I'm not really comfortable with you using me to hurt him." He found that a remarkable thing to say. He was pretty sure a week ago he wouldn't have given a spot of grease about being used to hurt Albert.

If anything, her stripes tilted even more. The corner of her lips twitched with amusement. "Is that all you think I'm doing? Really?"

"Uhh . . . yeah." Or at least, he hoped that was it.

The twitch curled into a smirk. She rolled close, paused . . . then kissed him lightly on the corner of his mouth. "Thanks for the pep-talk, Johnny. Let's see if the queen knows where we are."

I'm pretty sure I used to understand girls, Johnny thought as he followed her.

"Well?" Bian said, rolling up to Betty with a hint of a challenge. "Bad news or good news?"

An eye flickered in her direction as Betty filed through her hollas. "We're not going to get attacked for a while, so that counts as good news." She smiled a wry smile. "That might be it for the good column."

"Where are we?" Torg asked.

"I'm not sure yet. When you shunt through a break, any data gets messed up. You can come out anywhere. There are landmarks throughout the Thread, but I can't find any. Which can only mean . . ." A hand reached out and swiped at the hollas. Several flew by, then she reached out again and flicked one back.

"Yep," she said shortly, staring at the holla. "We're in a bad place."

"How bad?" Johnny asked.

"Nowhere near where we were going bad. We're not lost, but we may as well be." That struck them into silence, save the odd creak or crackle as Wobble slowly built himself back into shape.

"Wait a minute," Bian said suddenly. "We can still get there, right? Your safehouse?"

"I can find a route," Betty sighed, "but it's going to take too long."

"Too long for what?" Bian said. "We're not in the same situation anymore. Brolin . . . Brolin is dead. And Shabaz . . . you said you were feeling better."

"I feel great," Shabaz said, then her face flushed with guilt. "I mean, you know . . ."

"It's okay, Shabaz, you don't need to feel bad for surviving," Betty said slowly, one eye on the grey skid and another on Bian. "And Bian's right. The clock has changed. As long as . . ." Almost absent-mindedly, the hollas swung once more. Then one settled in front of Betty and all the colour drained from her stripe. "Oh kinks," she swore softly. "That gearbox."

"What?" Johnny said.

The most powerful skid in the universe stared at her hollas as if she could will them to change. "He turned off the stasis," Betty said, stunned. "SecCore. He took the Skidsphere out of stasis."

"What?" Johnny lurched forward, staring at the hollas.

"Why would it do that?" Torg said. "Why would it try to destroy the Skidsphere?"

"It wouldn't. Not directly," Betty murmured. "But I'm sure it wouldn't be disappointed if the Skidsphere vanished. SecCore's scared of any part of the Thread that can function independently. It hates me. Same with Wobble."

"I-We be terrifying," Wobble said, grinning. One of his teeth flapped with a tiny *creak, creak, creak*.

"So why doesn't SecCore just wipe it out?" Torg asked. "We wouldn't stand a chance against an army of Antis."

"You never know," Betty said. "Or, more importantly, SecCore can't. One skid and a beat-up Anti caused it plenty of headaches. Plus . . . attacking the sphere outright counters its programming. SecCore is supposed to protect all of the Thread. It might be corrupt, but that core program holds."

"So why turn the stasis off?" Bian asked. "Can't you turn it back on?"

"There's no point, he'd just turn it off again." Betty's stripes tilted. "It can probably justify this as returning the sphere to its normal state. And if the sphere gets destroyed because SecCore was focusing its energy somewhere else . . ."

"You know," Johnny said, "seems to me the Thread needs a new caretaker."

"You bet your gears," Betty agreed, her voice hard with hate. "But that . . . that's a battle for another day. For now, we need to take care of home. Which means . . ." She sighed. "I think we need to change the plan."

"Shouldn't be hard," Bian said. "We didn't know it in the first place."

"Fair enough," Betty said. One of her eyes kept staring at the hollas as if she hoped something would change. Apparently, nothing did. "Okay . . . the safehouse wasn't going to keep you permanently safe anyway. But you probably could have held it long enough for the rest of us to do what we have to do."

"Which is?" Johnny said dryly.

"We're going to go into the Skidsphere's programming, wipe out any sign of Vies, and then rebuild what's broken."

Johnny laughed. "You make it sound easy. And just

how are we going to do it?"

"For the first part, we're going to fight our way in with Wobble. For the second part, we fight anything we find inside. As for the third part . . . I haven't nailed that down yet."

They stared at her. "Uh . . ." Shabaz said. "Isn't fixing the broken stuff kind of important?"

"Yes, Shabaz. Still, I have a few theories which are starting to look more promising. Because of you."

"Me?"

"You're healthy. You look as good as new. Feeling hungry?"

Shabaz blinked. "Hey, not really."

"Exactly." Betty looked at Albert and Johnny. "The two of you not only wiped out the virus inside Shabaz, you restored her to complete health. I don't know how you did it—do you?"

"Not really." Johnny glanced at Albert. "You?"

"Me?" Albert said bitterly. "I was just along for the ride."

Johnny rolled his eyes. "Are we really going to go back to this?"

"Stop it," Betty snapped. "Both of you. Whatever issues you had just lost their grace period. The clock's running and I need you both. And as for the rest of you . . . well, I guess you're coming with us now."

Bian scoffed. "I thought—"

"We don't have time to get you to the safehouse; the sphere could fail at any moment. We need to get to the Core as quickly as we can. We can't leave you here. So you all come with us as far as you can. That way, if we have to leave you, it's for the shortest possible time."

"Can I ask a question?" Torres said hesitantly.

"Sure you can, Torres."

"You said there was going to be fighting. You can do that, you got that crazy gun. Wobble can do that. Albert and Johnny . . ." She blinked several times. "What am I supposed to do?"

Betty grinned at her. "Well . . . I guess we better find you a crazy gun."

CHAPTER
TWENTY-ONE

Betty led them a few hundred metres until the ground folded up into a long corridor lit by familiar golden lines. Johnny stared at the spot where the corridor ended and the break began: the solid lines of light abruptly torn, sparks flying from each mangled stump.

"That . . . is just not right," Torg said, following Johnny's gaze.

"No," Johnny murmured, eyeing the stumps for a moment longer before catching up with the group.

They rolled in silence, five metres behind the pack. Bian and Shabaz huddled together; nearby, Betty spoke softly with Torres. Wobble came next, humming to himself. Albert rolled out in front, alone.

After a few minutes, Torg said, "Do you want to talk about it?"

"Hmm," Johnny said absently, two of his eyes following a thick line that ran midway up the wall. "Sorry, talk about what?"

Torg chuckled. "Take your pick. Weight of the world, Albert, the Out There, Bian . . . Albert . . ."

"Oh," Johnny said. "Actually, I wasn't thinking about any of that. I was thinking about what happens if we win."

"Positive thinking, well done. That's the Johnny I know."

A smirk crawled across Johnny's face. "I'm not sure if positive's the right word. I was wondering if it mattered."

"I'm sorry?" Torg blinked. "We are talking about saving the Skidsphere, right?"

"And then what? I mean yeah, obviously, saving the sphere matters. But what happens after that?" Beneath their treads, line after golden line went by, all the same. "Go back to running down the Slope? Banging off things in Tilt until what . . . we die?"

"Wow. The nobody's Out There really messed with your treads."

"Maybe," Johnny said. "I mean sure . . . that sucks large. But even if Betty's wrong, even if someone *is* still watching . . ." His stripes tilted. "So what?"

Torg's second eye swung. "What have you done with my friend Johnny Drop? Who cares? Even if someone is watching? Are you serious?"

"I know it's . . . okay, I don't know what it is. But I know I was feeling weird even before we got here. You saw me the night I tied Betty—I was off my tread. Why was I so angry? I mean sure, it was Albert, but I think I was just . . . mad."

"No argument here," Torg murmured.

"Yeah," Johnny said. "You ever feel this way? Just kind of: what are we doing?"

Torg's eyes reflected the walls, lines of light against the black. "Ever since I made Nine."

"Yeah?"

"Yeah. I was happy for about a week. Topped out. Made Nine. Maybe one in a hundred do it. For a relatively normal skid who isn't pursuing ghosts—"

"Hey!"

"Squid, you pursued two of them. You aren't normal. For most of us, Nine's the summit." Torg took a deep breath. "Like I said, for a week it felt good. Then I thought . . . what now? I made Nine pretty early. I was like: okay, I got ten months 'til I die, what do I aim for now?" His face seemed to tighten. "Then I started thinking about dying. A lot. Five years seems like a long time when you're running the race. Hasn't seemed that long lately."

"No," Johnny said. "I guess not." *Then again, it's more than some get.* His gaze wandered over the group—six skids left from the dozens that had fallen from the Pipe. "Hey," he said. "How'd you get Torres so clear? She looks great."

Torg's stripes tilted. "Mostly it was Albert, he's been talking her up pretty much the entire time here. She's seen both you and Albert do it several times. Plus, Torres might be a panzer, but she's a tough one. You can see it already. I liked Brolin as much as the next skid, but he was going to die an Eight at best." He tapped an eye towards the group. "But this lot? We might not be you or Al, but you're still looking at the best the sphere has to offer. Amazing really. Even Shabaz."

"Yeah," Johnny said, eyeing the grey-aqua Six. "How about that?"

"Skids surprise you sometimes." Torg pursed his lips. "That's what I realized when I was trying to figure things out: I like skids. Not the games . . . skids. We ain't perfect: we're shallow and self-absorbed and cocky and . . . we're great. Maybe if we had more than five years we'd be even better. Maybe if we helped each other . . . so that's what I decided to do. I decided to help someone."

"Really?" Johnny said. "You went to the Combine too?"

"No."

"Then who'd you help?"

Torg held the look, blinking in that innocent way he had.

Johnny stared. "You did not."

"It's not like I ran interference for you on the Slope. But everyone for the last six months has been talking about Betty's record. I didn't know how much pressure you were under, but I knew it wasn't the only thing you were dealing with. So I decided to just . . . be there. If you needed me." He grinned. "I'm surprised you haven't noticed. Sure, we partied a few times before, but recently . . ."

"You've been there," Johnny said, bemused. "Huh. So you were like, what, my own guardian angel?"

"Something like that. Tried to do it with Albert, too. To a certain extent I did, but . . . he's a little more self-contained than you."

"He's a little something," Johnny said ruefully.

"Now that sounds like the Johnny I know." Torg glanced at Albert, then over to Bian and Shabaz. "Can I ask you something? Is there anything going on between you and Bian?"

"Vape me—you too?" Johnny snapped. "Look, I don't know what's going on in her mind and, yeah, it seems like she's playing me off Albert, but me . . ." He waved an arm as if it could encompass the entire Thread. "I gotta few other things to worry about than bumping Albert's ride."

Torg was grinning. "All right, squid. Had to ask—ain't

that long ago that you'd have done anything to twist his gears."

"I would not . . ." Johnny started to protest. Torg simply gazed back, the corner of his mouth twitching.

There had been two times when Johnny had hated Albert the most. Right after Peg disappeared—all right, he wouldn't have been with another skid then, under any circumstances. But a few months before, just after Albert dropped the first Nine-Point-Nine?

Yeah, he thought, *I'd have jumped on that.* He sighed. *You're all class, Johnny.* Aloud, he said: "Fine. Maybe I would. But now . . . I'm not interested. Besides, Betty says we need Albert, so we need him. At his best." He shook his stripes. "I can't believe I'm saying that."

"Gotta run the race you're in," Torg drawled, as up ahead Betty gave Torres a pat on her stripe and dropped back. "Wouldn't worry about it too much. Al's tough. He'll get over it."

"Maybe not," Betty said. "Bian?"

"It's not nice to eavesdrop, young lady," Torg grinned.

"Kind of hard not to," Betty said, winking at him. "I spent the last five decades trying to pick up everything. Not used to tuning stuff out."

"What do you mean, maybe not?" Johnny said.

"Torg was right: you and Albert are different. There have been other Level Tens in the past—"

"What? Really?"

"From what I can tell, there's one every fifty to seventy years." Betty's stripe flared down toward red. "Then they flush the records. Every fifty to seventy years."

"*They what?*"

"Yeah," Betty sniffed. "We're not even allowed to learn our own history." She stared forward, her stripe dark against her skin. "Anyway, once I was outside the sphere, I learned to access a lot of stuff, a long way back. Not all the way, but . . . long enough. There have been Tens before: dozens if not hundreds. But I've never seen any record of two Ten potentials born in the same generation. You and Albert are unique."

"Huh," Johnny said, looking towards the front, where Torres had rejoined Albert. Bian and Shabaz were still locked in conversation.

"And because of that," Betty continued, "well, you both act a little different. Like Torg said, most skids that make Nine get a little reflective before they die." Her stripe darkened even more, almost invisible against her skin. "Makes you wonder what they might be like if they got a few more years than five."

"Yeah," Johnny murmured, glancing at Torg. He'd just said almost the very same thing.

"Granted," Betty said, "most skids don't run that deep. But you and Albert, you started another level of thinking by the time you hit your third birthday. Both of you have shown an interest in helping other skids. And both of you hold on." Her third eye swung. "Don't you?"

"Uhh . . ." Johnny flushed. Torg took that moment to let his eyes wander.

"Peg," Betty said. "It's been six months since she died. Most skids wouldn't have mourned for six days. We're not designed to."

Popping an arm, Johnny ran his fingers along a line of gold. "And if she's not dead?"

"Let me guess: you keep hearing her voice? Maybe even seen her a few times?"

Johnny looked up, his heart pounding. "Yeah."

Betty's gaze saddened. "Talk to her yet?"

He swallowed. "No."

"No," Betty said gently. "And I'm afraid you're not

going to. That wasn't Peg. It was you."

"Sorry?"

Betty took a deep breath. Exhaled roughly. "A couple of years after I landed in the Thread, I started seeing skids. Everywhere. It was ridiculous: I'd see them disappearing around every corner; I heard conversations coming from buildings I passed by. It took me years to realize I wasn't seeing or hearing other skids. I was creating them."

"Creating them?" Torg said. "Nice."

"No," Betty said sadly. "Just one lonely skid. Remember, we are the program: we have the potential to create what we need. Or what we think we need." She looked at Johnny. "I call them ghosts. Because they're like the ghostyards: they're not real, they're just a memory of something that isn't there anymore. You're not seeing Peg, Johnny; you're creating her from memory. Because you're holding on." She swung an eye. "What's the longest relationship you ever had, Torg?"

"Couple months." He grinned and winked at Betty. "I'm sure if I tried I could do better."

"I'm sure you could," she said, looking pleased. "Johnny, you haven't even had a fling since Peg died. And as for Albert . . . looks like he felt pretty close to that with Bian. Only one problem."

"Ain't her code," Torg said.

"Ain't her code. Nothing wrong with that; first four years of my life, I was the same, bumping from one guy to the next. But I don't think Albert's going to let go so easy."

"So what do you want me to do about it?" Johnny said. "It's not like I'm encouraging her."

"I know," Betty said. "Just keep trying to be sensitive. It's tough on her, too. Right now, she and Shabaz are talking about how each of them feels useless."

"That's ridiculous," Johnny protested. "I told her that."

"Doesn't matter. Brolin and Aaliyah—especially Aaliyah—they're both claiming part of that guilt. And skids do guilt about as well as we do team. So just try to keep a delicate touch. While I see if I can't find something to make them both feel more proactive. Speaking of which, we're here."

As Betty tread towards a glowing door, Johnny looked at Torg. His stripes twitched.

"Delicate touch. Yeah . . . 'cause that's my strong suit."

CHAPTER TWENTY-TWO

"Okay," Betty said. "This place is a little intense."

They faced a door with broad, thick outlines. Slashed into the centre of the door: a golden 'A,' throbbing in and out, softly thrumming at its brightest point.

"It's an entertainment sim. Like the Skidsphere, but . . . well, you'll see. The key is quiet—we move *real* quiet. If something happens, Wobble or I will handle it. We've been here before and we're good at stealth. From the looks of things," her hollas zipped around her head, "it's a good time. Not a lot of action. Albert, you still all right bringing up the rear?"

"Where else would I be?"

"Good," Betty grinned. "Wobble will ride with you."

"Shabaz and I will just hang out in the middle and swap stories, then?" Bian said wryly.

"Not for long," Betty assured her, ignoring the sarcasm. "In a few minutes, you can ride where you like." She swept her gaze over the group, held it, then bobbed her eyes. "All right, let's go."

They emerged from a sterile two-tone hallway into a world that hit them in all five senses. Trees and plants surrounded them, obscuring the door. Huge, thick, ridiculously green trees and plants. The heat was oppressive; Johnny had never felt anything that hot. And the humid air reeked of . . .

"Sweet snakes," Torg breathed. "You can taste it."

"Sure can," Johnny murmured. Sunshine pierced the green canopy with spears of light.

"It's like the woods by the Spike," Bian said, her eyes trying to cover all points on the compass at once. "But . . . more."

"This is the jungle," Betty said. "And there are things in here that want to kill us. Unless we get hit with the heavy stuff, they probably can't do it, but even the little things hurt like a jacked gear. And some of them can hit you from kilometers away."

"Really?" Torres said, staring at the plant life pressing in. "How would they see us?"

"You'd be surprised," Betty said. "Stay close. Wobble and I can jam a lot of signals and take care of just about anything that can track us. Trust me, they're expecting us a lot less then we're expecting them. Turn on your coms, I'll explain as we go. Keep your voices low—if you speak at all—and we should be fine."

"How're they going to hear us?" Torres said. The jungle was a symphony of hoots and trills and creaks.

"Everything has ears," Wobble said. Floating a few centimetres off the ground, his skin bristled with probes. "Takers got scan-scans like nobody's seen. Wobble."

"Our target is about half a kilometer this way," Betty said. "This is a combat sim. Imagine a game where everyone gets vaped. Unlike the sphere, I'm pretty sure the Out There participated in this. Some player-mems are independent but some the Out There could slip into. We won't run into any of those."

"But if the Out There isn't there anymore, why is the sim still running?" Johnny said.

"Why's the Skidsphere still up?" Betty's stripe tilted. "Because the program kept running. Now the mems just vape each other."

"Then how come everybody ain't dead?" Torg asked, ducking under a broad green leaf dripping with moisture.

"The sim resets once everyone dies. Then they do it all over again. Some things move around, the terrain changes, but basically the same sim runs every time." She shuddered. "Imagine doing the same Slope, with the same skids, over and over, forgetting after each race is run."

"Betty Crisp . . ." Johnny whispered.

"Yeah," Betty said. "Me." Her stripe twitched. "Anyway, the sim usually takes a week or so to run. We're here towards the end of a cycle, after most of the big action. Some mems left, but there shouldn't be any packs. Plus, the warehouse might be unguarded."

"What ware—"

The jungle went silent.

That can't be a good thing, Johnny thought, as Betty held a finger to her lips. Rising off the jungle floor, Wobble tilted on his axis, absorbed his probes, then disappeared into the green.

All in dead silence.

Albert immediately took off after the machine, pushing past Johnny. "Albert!" Betty hissed, then rolled her eyes and moved to follow. The others fell in behind, trying to stay silent.

Somewhere off to their left, there was a low wet thud.

Johnny broke through the dense undergrowth behind Betty and Albert.

Wobble hovered over a body lying face-down in the mud. As the machine rotated back into his upright shape, his motors quietly whirred. "All dead-dead now. At least until next time. Wobble."

The body looked nothing like a skid—in fact, it more resembled Wobble in his neutral position. Four Hasty-Arms: one on each side and two extending from the trunk. A mottled glam patterned like the jungle covered its entire body, including the top of the tiny head. A black rifle lay by one of the arms.

"You know," Torg drawled, "I don't know who the Out There were . . . but they had themselves some messed up fantasies."

"Not as messed up as you think," Betty said softly, examining the body. "Or at least, not in the way you're thinking. What you're looking at isn't some stretch of the imagination. Most likely, it's them. The Out There. That's probably what they looked like."

"You're kidding," Johnny breathed. He wondered what the face looked like.

"That city of hollas you came through. How many times you see a skid?"

"A few times."

"Right. And only on Skidsphere highlights. We're the fantasy. But that, right there,"—she stabbed a finger at the body—"shows up everywhere. One head, long body, legs instead of treads. In just about every type of mem, that body structure appears. Sometimes the details change: the shade of the skin, the shape of the ears or eyes—but in the end, this guy is what you see."

"Weird," Torres said, trying to peer closer.

Betty's stripe tilted. "Who knows what weird is? I'm a

fifty-five year old skid. You're a panzer who's been vaped at least once and is still here." Torres beamed. "We know the Out There had more than one type of creature, but we're pretty sure this one played a major role—if not *the* major role. More sure of that than understanding why they did what they did."

"Let me get this straight," Albert said, staring at the body. There was a strange, flat quality to his gaze. "Everything in here vapes pretty much everything else, forgets about it, gets brought back to life, and then it happens all over again?" He looked at Betty. "That about right?"

"That's about right," Betty said, watching him.

Albert's flat expression didn't change. His stripes twitched. "Fine," he said softly. He turned and rolled away. Betty and the others followed, leaving the dead mem behind.

Johnny could understand Albert's disgust. The whole idea revolted him. Sure, skids vaped each other every day, but something about this . . . maybe it was the way everything seemed brighter, smelled stronger . . . somehow Johnny doubted there was anything clean about getting vaped in this place.

"Ah," Betty whispered, as the foliage began to thin.

They peered through the growth into a small, sunken clearing. In the centre, a long, rectangular building made from the same ceramic-metal that they'd seen in the ghostyard. Like the ghostyard, the building was weathered, although the wear and tear seemed deliberate—it fit the surrounding jungle.

This whole place is designed. Johnny stared at the light angling down from the sky, flashing off the rusted roof. *Amazing.* The Skidsphere was beautiful, but the details here . . .

Another four-limbed mem stood by the door, facing the jungle on the far side. It had a glam like shaded thinlids over its eyes and another of those long, black rifles cradled in one arm. In the opposite hand, a drift of smoke rose from a small device. The creature lifted the device, inhaled—causing the device to flare—and blew smoke from its mouth.

Crazy.

It just looked so weird. Nothing at all like a skid. "It makes no sense," Johnny murmured.

"What doesn't?" Betty asked.

"Skids." When Betty's stripe tilted, Johnny pointed at the guard. "If that was the standard, then why skids? I mean, we're popular—were popular—right? The Out There created GameCorps, the Skidsphere, this whole complicated system: one of the most sophisticated in the entire Thread, you said. Then they ran three or four games a day, all day, every day, for . . . centuries. Maybe more. And we were popular." He heard Albert snort and he snarled, "Stow it, Albert. I'm not stroking my ego, I'm trying to understand something."

Betty had a peculiar look on her face. "Yes, Johnny. We were popular."

"Why?"

"Because they liked watching things die," Albert said softly.

Johnny's eyes swung. "Uhh . . . that's a bit harsh."

"Is it? What's the main thing about the games, Johnny? It ain't you, jackhole. It's the squids. And the panzers. And the dying. How many Ones and Twos die every game? Seventy or eighty in games like the Road or the Slope. More in Tilt or Tag Box, less in the Skates or on the Pipe. Seventy or eighty, three or four times a day. All day. *Every day.* That's what, sixty or seventy thousand a year. More? Seventy thousand panzers and squids that never see Three." Albert's eyes were stark white against his silver skin. "How many Level Three-to-Nines at any given time? Four hundred? Maybe five? That's less than one percent. The lucky freaks who get to live represent less than one percent of the skids that play the game every year."

"And we die at five," Torg whispered.

"And we die at five," Albert finished, his voice like judgement. "That's why we look so different from them. So they can watch us die and not feel bad about it."

Johnny stared at the silver skid. That was the longest speech he'd heard from Albert in years. Maybe ever. "Then why not make all the sim-mems different?" he said, trying to make sense of a universe that seemed to get deeper and uglier with every second. Betty was watching them like she knew every word Albert was going to say. "This place is about death, even more than our world. But here they look like them."

Albert's stripes rocked like he couldn't care less. "Here, they used to play too. With us, they just watched. Maybe just watching their own kill each other made them uncomfortable."

"But none of this is real!" Bian protested. She stabbed a finger at Betty. "You said that. It's all just information."

"Not real?" Albert hissed. "That how you feel about Brolin? Aaliyah?" His eyes narrowed with rage as he jabbed a finger of his own at Johnny. "That how you'd feel if he died?"

Bian's stripes flinched as she cranked back a tread in the face of Albert's anger. A moment passed where all they could hear was the jungle.

"Uhh . . ." Shabaz said nervously. "I don't want to interrupt anything, but that guard's still there . . . she's got a gun . . . and I don't."

"All right," Betty said calmly. "Shabaz is right: let's get what we came for." She swung an eye towards Albert. "Once we're out of here, if you want to talk about it, we'll talk."

Albert blinked several times, as if suddenly realizing where he was. "Forget it. Doesn't matter."

"Actually it does. But first things first. Wobble, take care of the guard."

"*Wait!*" Albert hissed.

Wobble, who'd begun to transform, stopped. "Inquiry?"

Albert turned on Betty. "He's just going to kill her?"

Johnny had yet to see Betty confused. "Albert," she said, frowning, "that's the nature of this place. Everything in here is going to die. Then it's all going to happen again."

"Yeah, but we don't have to do it. Do we? Wobble, you can take that guard out without vaping her, right?"

Wobble's lenses slowly opened and closed with a single mechanical *clink*. "Affirmative."

"Then why the hole aren't we doing that?" Albert snarled, swinging towards Betty.

"Albert . . ."

"*No.* Nothing else in here dies by our hand. That never should have happened in the first place. They might look like the Out There, but they aren't them. They're us. *They're skids.*" The glare he sent at Betty could have cut her in half. "And you shouldn't have to be told that."

Betty stared back, and then her eyes bobbed in acceptance. "Wobble, put her out until we're gone. She's going to die . . . but we're not going to kill her. Make it enough simtime that we'll be long gone."

"Affirmative," Wobble said, and a thin tube emerged

from under one of his Hasty-Arms. A soft *wuft* of sound and the guard's hand snapped up to her neck. Before it got there, her knees collapsed and she crumpled to the ground.

"Let's go," Betty said.

They paused by the unconscious guard. *Crisp Betty, they look odd*, Johnny thought. A curl of smoke still drifted from the cylinder in the guard's hand.

"For most of the sim, there'd be dozens of guards for a store this size," Betty said. "This late, she was probably just here for effect."

"Effect?" Bian said, looking at the body like it was going to jump up and bite her.

"Like dust on the Slope," Betty said. "Doesn't serve much use, but it looks good. Let's go."

As the others rounded the building, Albert lingered over the body.

"Doesn't look very fast," Johnny said.

"No," Albert said slowly. "Though I bet it goes side-to-side better than us." He continued to stare at the creature, his eyes demanding answers that they were unlikely to get. The light around them softened as the sun descended towards the horizon.

More effect, Johnny thought absently, watching Albert. Then he asked a question that a few days before he wouldn't have asked in a billion years.

"What are you thinking?"

A heartbeat passed, then one of Albert's eyes came up. He started to say something, stopped, smirked a familiar smirk, started to say something else . . . then the smirk dropped away like it was being abandoned. Finally, he said, "Don't worry about it." His last eye came up from the body. "Let's go find out why we're here."

The inside of the warehouse was dappled with light

shining through dirty windows that topped the walls. Stacks and stacks of containers were piled in what had once been long tidy rows. Half the building's stockpiles had already been raided.

Still plenty left for a few skids, though.

Albert and Johnny caught Betty pulling a set of needles out from a locker. "Most of the tracking weapons won't work on the Antis and Vies. But there are a few that seek out anything in the area that isn't to code." She handed out the needles. "Everyone take one of these. Jab it anywhere, with us it won't matter. We'll sync the weapons to the code. That should let you do some real damage."

"What should we take?" Torres whispered, looking at all the crates with a mix of wonder and fear.

"Simple," Betty grinned, ripping open a box of rifles. "More than we think we need."

"How're we going to carry it?" Bian asked, tentatively peeking under a lid.

"A lot easier than the other mems do," Betty laughed. "Wobble?" The machine's gears whirred and a compartment opened along one entire side of his body. "I don't have time to teach you how to carry it yourself, but we could stuff this entire storehouse in Wobble if we wanted. If it fits through that door, we'll take it."

"How does that work?" Torres asked.

"It's all data," Johnny murmured, staring down the long row of stacks.

Betty stopped loading Wobble, a slow smile gracing her face. "Now you're getting it."

"Well, if that's true, then I want one of these babies," Torg said appreciatively, yanking a gun nearly the size of Wobble out from a crate. He hefted it once in his arms, then winked at Betty. "Feels like she's got heart."

Betty laughed and pointed down the row. "Grab some time-proximity rounds and you'll have your own battle-fleet. Last stack of crates on the left."

For the next ten minutes, the skids grabbed every weapon they could. "When the boys and I leave you," Betty explained, "we'll dump everything and try to fortify where you are. Try and find at least one weapon you feel comfortable carrying. No, Torg, not the cannon." She rolled her eyes. "I think you can take care of yourself with something half the size."

"Yes, ma'am," Torg drawled, settling for a piece that still looked like it could take out a sugarbar.

"All right," Betty said finally. "That should do it. I'll show you how each thing works once we're out—"

The voice came from behind them, low and harsh.

Now what the hell are you?

The mem stood in a semi-crouch at the end of the row. Larger than the guard outside—quite a bit larger. The rifle in its hands descended slightly from one of its eyes, though it remained centred on the skids.

Then the mem's gaze settled on Betty and filled with wonder. "Do I . . . do I know you?"

"Well, I'll be," Betty whispered, staring at the mem.

The gun slid back up to the mem's eye: a crisp, clean movement with nothing wasted. "Whatever you are, everyone drop every—"

He got no further. A soft *wuft* of sound from Wobble and the mem collapsed.

"He recognized you," Johnny said, as they tread over to the body. It really was *much* larger than the other two mems they'd seen. A vicious scar ran along its jawline. "I thought you said they had their memory wiped every time the game reset."

"They do," Betty said slowly.

"Then how could he remember you?"

"He shouldn't. Except . . ." Betty's lips pursed as she studied the unconscious body. "He's the main mem in this sim. Even has a name: Kruger. Not many mems have them. And in some ways, he's deeper than a skid. He's got a history seven times longer than a skid's lifetime, despite the fact that he never lives more than a few weeks at a time." She chuckled. "Wrap your eye-stalks around that."

"So he's . . . evolving?" Johnny said. "Like you did?"

"Our last encounter was pretty memorable, for both of us. He nearly vaped me—you saw it, he just snuck up on seven skids and Wobble. And remember: in here, we're Vies. Every time I show up, I break the system a little." One of her eyes swept the stacks. "We're changing things."

"Huh," Johnny grunted, looking at Kruger. "Pity we can't bring him with us."

Betty's eye swung. "Now that is a really interesting idea." She paused, an eye on Kruger, one on Johnny. Then she sighed. "Not now. We don't need to make this more complicated. Keep that one for the future."

"As long as we have one," Torg drawled.

"As long as we have one," Betty agreed. "Okay, let's go."

"Uh . . . where's Albert?" Torres said. Her eyes swept the group.

"Anybody?"

CHAPTER TWENTY-THREE

They all stared at her.

"Seriously," Torres said, her voice starting to rise. "He was right here." She sped down the row, her gaze darting left and right.

"Albert!" Shabaz called, treading onto a crate. "You all right?"

"Think Kruger got him?" Torg said, glancing at the rifle in the mem's hands.

"I thought Albert was behind us," Johnny said. "Like always."

"Albert?" Torres came down another row. "Dude, where are you?"

"He isn't here," Betty said. Her eyes slowly closed then opened once more. "He left."

"*He what?*" Torres screeched.

"He what?" Johnny said, with a little more surprise than panic.

"There's a door in the back of the warehouse. He

probably used that. He isn't inside or in the near vicinity." She sighed. "He's gone into the jungle."

"He's gone . . ." Torres started to say. "You can find him, right?"

"I don't think he wants to be found, Torres," Betty said softly.

"What? Why?"

Betty's stripe tilted. "For the same reason he still wears that scar."

"What does that mean?"

"Bian was right," Betty said. "Albert sports that scar because he wants to. Same reason he sports that damaged eye. He got that in a fight with you, didn't he, Johnny?"

"Yeah," Johnny said. *Nine-Nine*, he thought, and shuddered.

"So . . . how many skids do you know who have a scar?"

"Scar does," Torg said.

Betty's eye swung at Torg and held the look. "I'm pretty sure that was a deliberate choice," she said dryly. Her eye swung back to Johnny. "Even before he got here, Albert had the ability to heal a scar like that. Hole, most Threes could do it. It wasn't caused by a virus, it was caused by an Anti. Clean cut. But Albert didn't heal it." Her stripe tilted again. "Albert wears his wounds because he wants people to think he's wounded."

"What a jackhole," Bian muttered.

"Hey," Johnny snapped, suddenly out of patience. Every time anything remotely got settled, something else went wrong, someone else disappeared or died. It was enough. "How about you ease off a little, all right?" Beside him, Torg's eyes widened in surprise. "Does that sound familiar, Bian? 'Cause I'm pretty sure that's what you begged me to do just a few days ago. Yet ever since we dropped here, you've treated Albert like tread-grease. You're probably the reason he took off."

Silence, as Bian stared at Johnny, her eyes flinching and glassy with tears.

"Maybe you should ease off a little," Shabaz said quietly. As Johnny's eye swung, she added, "Some of us aren't adjusting to this place as well as others."

Johnny stared at her. "Shabaz, none of us are adjusting to this place."

The grey skid held his gaze. "At least you're not baggage."

"Shabaz . . ."

She cut him off. "Don't make the same speech twice." Then her stripes tilted and she hefted the rifle in her hands. "Anyway, at least now we're armed." She hesitated, then added, "I appreciate what you were about to say. Just . . . cut her a little slack. We should all cut each other some slack."

"Well, twist my gears," Torg drawled. "Johnny defends Albert and Shabaz becomes the voice of reason." He glanced at Betty. "Two miracles in twenty seconds."

"Good," Betty said. "Let's go make another. Shabaz, you're right. We're all under enough stress without us taking it out on each other. And as for Albert, he's responsible for his own decisions." She sighed. "He can live with them."

"Wait," Torres protested. "We're going to go find him, right? We can't just leave him in here. What . . . what if it does that reset thing before he leaves?"

"Torres," Betty said gently, "he left for a reason. When he wants to find us, I'm sure he will."

"You're sure?"

"I hope so."

As they retraced their path through the jungle, Betty explained how each weapon worked. The sun disappeared behind the treetops, casting the thick green into shadow. They reached their starting point, but Albert didn't reappear.

"Should we wait?" Bian said hesitantly, glancing at Johnny.

Betty grimaced. "We can't. We have no idea how long the Skidsphere holds out. Every second counts."

"Then maybe we shouldn't have come here," Shabaz said. "This was all just to help a couple of us defend ourselves. I'm not more important than the Skidsphere."

Johnny was amazed. With every second the grey Six seemed to get deeper and deeper.

Apparently, Betty agreed. She smiled with unfeigned warmth. "That is a very noble sentiment, Shabaz." Her stripe tilted. "Anyway, we came here. What's done is done. But no . . . we can't wait for Albert."

"Oh," Bian said softly. "Okay." Her eyes swung and then froze in place. "Wait, where's Torres?"

Even as he scanned the jungle, Johnny realized he wasn't surprised. At least this made sense. "She must have gone to find Albert. Hard to blame her, she's been under his wing since they got here. Don't worry about it, Bian. This isn't on you." He looked at Betty. "That's two. You really want to leave them in here?"

Suddenly, Betty looked all fifty-five of her years. "We're out of time," she said softly.

And the fact you said we needed Albert? But he didn't say the thought out loud. Betty knew her plans better than he did. If Albert was that essential . . . "All right," he said. "Then we go. Can Albert find us once we leave? Could he follow us through the Thread?"

"I think so," Betty said. She didn't look anywhere

close to certain. Behind her, a golden door opened in the jungle. "I guess we'll find out." Without looking back, she rolled through.

She led them down now familiar tunnels, black-lined with gold, then through a series of doors like those they'd taken when they'd fled the lost node.

Johnny rolled behind everyone else, a black mood seeping through his skin. It didn't fail to dawn on him that he was in Albert's usual place, the back of the pack. He wasn't sure if that was ironic, but it sure the hole felt like it.

Some of us aren't adjusting to this place as well as others. Johnny couldn't believe Shabaz had said that; couldn't believe she thought it was possible that any of them would have found adjusting to this place easy.

He could understand it was hard for the others. Shabaz had gone through more suffering than any skid had before without vaping themselves. Torres should have been learning how to grease her treads in the Combine. Bian had tried to take care of other skids and instead had watched them die. Or get saved by someone else. And obviously all the dying—not just the skids— had tweaked something in Albert. That or it was just Bian. Or he was just a jackhole.

Probably the last, Johnny thought with a bleak grin.

Both Bian and Shabaz felt like baggage. That wasn't surprising, given that every time Betty spoke of her plans, it was Johnny and Albert and not much else. He got how that would bother the others—it would've driven him nuts. The only one it didn't seem to faze was Torg, although things didn't tend to bother Torg.

Or maybe he just hides it better.

The funny thing was that only a few weeks ago Johnny would've been cocky as snakes about the whole thing.

Damn right, Johnny Drop was the one to save them: *who else?* He didn't need Albert—hole, he probably didn't need Betty-Vapin'-Crisp. He was Johnny Drop baby, gear it up and bring it on. A few weeks ago, he would have felt just like that. Now . . .

Now he was beginning to realize just how terrified he was.

Skids fought for themselves. Johnny had done that better than any skid alive and maybe—just maybe— better than any skid ever. But now Johnny wouldn't be fighting just for himself: he'd be fighting for other skids. And that scared the crap out of him.

He'd failed Daytona. He'd failed Brolin. Without Albert, he'd have failed Shabaz.

And now he was supposed to save the Skidsphere? He knew one thing: whatever Betty had in mind, she'd better get real specific about his role soon before he lost his mind.

Of course, that feeling wasn't helped by the fact that, for the past several minutes, Peg had been shadowing him out of the corner of his trail-eye.

Finally, he couldn't take it anymore. He stopped. Turned around. He was expecting her to be gone. After all, Betty had said she was a figment of his imagination, created by his inability to let go. Like all the other times, he'd round the corner and she'd disappear.

Except this time she didn't.

She sat in the centre of the corridor, about ten metres away. Golden light glinted off her deep pink skin and her six red stripes. All three of her eyes faced his way, all of them blue like the sky they loved to hang over the Pipe. A small, crooked smile that Johnny had always loved graced her face.

Betty had called her a ghost. She sure the hole didn't look like one.

A long moment where there was nothing but a soft hum from the walls, pulsing gently like a tide.

You're not real. It broke Johnny's heart to think it, but he had to accept it sometime. *You're not real.* Sadly, he opened his mouth to say the words . . .

"I miss you too," she said.

Johnny stared at her, stunned.

Talk to her yet? You're not going to.

Peg sat in the centre of the hall, her lips twitching somewhere between laughter and sorrow. Johnny clicked forward a tread . . .

"Johnny!" Shabaz called. "Johnny, where are you?" She came around a corner. "There you are, what the hole? You sight-seeing?"

One of his eyes swung to Shabaz, but two stayed fixed on Peg. If Shabaz noticed her, she gave no sign. "Let's go. Betty says we're here." She started back up the hallway, pausing at the corner. "Johnny?"

He hesitated, then moved to follow. "Okay," he murmured, two eyes trailing behind. "Okay, I'm coming."

He'd thought that she would disappear when he'd first turned around. Or when Shabaz had appeared, surely then. He was waiting for her to disappear now.

But Peg remained where she was, sitting in the centre of the hallway, bathed in golden light. All three eyes on his until he followed Shabaz around the corner . . . and then it was he who was gone.

CHAPTER TWENTY-FOUR

Johnny was shaking when they caught up to the others. If there was a door anywhere nearby, hole if he saw it.

"Good," Betty said. "You're here. We're on the outskirts of the Core. Now what I'm about to do is going to seem a little—"

"No," Johnny said. "I'm not going anywhere." It seemed as if his whole body was vibrating at the wrong frequency. His eyes felt out of focus and it had nothing to do with a virus.

I miss you too . . .

"Johnny?" Betty said, staring at him with concern.

"You keep talking about the Skidsphere. You keep saying you need me and Albert. Well, Albert's not here. And me . . ." He took a deep breath, his body expanding to nearly twice its size. "I don't know what you want me to do. So I'm not going *any*where until I understand *some*thing."

Betty's gaze on him tightened. "What happened?"

His stripes twitched. "It's not important. If there's a plan, I want to hear it. Now."

"Me too," Bian said. "I'm with Johnny."

"Me too," Shabaz said firmly.

Betty's expression hovered somewhere between amusement and exasperation. "I can explain on the way. We have time." Johnny, Bian, and Shabaz didn't say anything. They might have been carved in stone.

Glancing at Torg, the oldest skid asked, "You want in on this?"

Torg leaned against the wall. "If you need, I'll defend your honour, sugarlips," he drawled. "Otherwise, I think I'll join the mutiny."

"Sugarlips," Betty murmured. "I like that." She studied them for a moment, then her stripe tilted. "All right, you asked for it. The plan, such as it stood, was to get to the Core. Theoretically, you can access the entire Thread from there, including the Skidsphere. Wobble and I would clear a path for you and Albert to follow. If I got killed, then Wobble would get you and Albert to the sphere. Then . . ." An embarrassed grin split Betty's face from arm to arm. "Then you and Albert would fix it."

Johnny stared at her. *Then you and Albert . . .* "Please tell me there's more than that," he breathed.

"It does seem to be lacking in specifics," Torg agreed. "Not to mention, I didn't hear my name once."

"Join the club," Bian muttered.

Johnny didn't have time for self-pity or jokes; he felt like his eyes were going to burst. "Lacking specifics doesn't even begin to cover it. *Albert and I would fix it?*" His hands clenched and unclenched. "Just a little vague, don't you think?"

Betty's grin didn't fade one bit. "Well, that was *your* part of the plan."

I'm going to hit her, Johnny thought. *I'm going to punch Betty Crisp right in the eye.* "And just how long," he said aloud, "has that been part of the plan?"

"Since about the time you hooked up with Wobble."

Johnny took a deep breath. Blinked several times so that his eyes didn't dry into a desert. "Look . . . let's ignore the fact that the plan relies on Albert . . . who isn't here. Let's ignore that apparently Albert and I—who have an absolutely fantastic record of working together—were supposed to figure something out. That's not what's wrong with the plan."

"What's wrong with the plan?" Betty said innocently.

"*It doesn't make any sense!*" Johnny cried. "It's backwards—makes it sound like you're expendable. Which is insane, you're the last one we can lose. You're so many levels beyond any of us, if anyone is going to fix the Skidsphere, it's you. Hole, Albert and I should be clearing a path for you."

"No," Betty said firmly, and her grin finally faded.

"Why not?"

"Because of what you just said. You're right, when it comes to fighting, I'm way beyond your level. I've got lifetimes of experience fighting Antis and Vies, and I've got lifetimes of experience fighting with Wobble. In a fight, all you and Albert do is get in each other's way. No, if we're going to make it to where we need to go, Wobble and I are in the lead."

Johnny started to protest, but she held up a hand to prevent him.

"Because," she continued evenly, "you were wrong about the other thing. I *am* expendable. I'm not the last person we can lose—you are. Albert would be too, if he were here. Because when it comes to saving skids . . . you and Albert are far beyond my level."

"That . . . that doesn't make any sense," Johnny said, though he saw both Shabaz and Bian unconsciously bob an eye.

"Doesn't matter if it makes sense," Betty said. All the flippancy she'd shown a few minutes before was gone. "It's true."

"You saved all of us!" Johnny protested.

"No," Betty said. "I've killed Vies and Antis to cover you. But I never saved anyone but myself. I broke out of the Skidsphere. By myself. I've survived dives through the black. By myself. But you and Albert . . . you brought skids through with you."

"Ahhh," Torg breathed, as if everything in the universe suddenly made sense.

"Before you even met me," Betty continued, "you almost cured Daytona single-handedly. Then, together with Albert, you did cure Shabaz."

Something about the way she said that bothered Johnny, but he couldn't pin it down and he didn't have time. He was trying to listen to everything Betty said because apparently sixty or seventy thousand lives depended on it.

"I have no idea how you cured her," Betty admitted. "None. I wouldn't have known where to start. You and Albert went *inside* her. Exactly the way someone is going to have to go inside the Skidsphere." Her gaze was locked on his own. "Do you see it, Johnny? I don't matter. You and Albert are the only ones who can do what needs to be done. And Albert isn't here. So it's you. Johnny Drop."

There was a moment of silence, then Torg swung an eye towards Shabaz and drawled, "I think we should get him a cape."

"Now then," Betty said, drawing a deep breath, "we can sit here all day and work out our issues . . . or we can go get it done. What's it going to be?"

Johnny didn't feel any less rattled than he had before. But she was right: regardless, they were running out of time. "Okay," he said. "Let's do it. Whatever. Wherever we're going, whatever we're doing, let's go and do it now." He looked around. "Where's the door?"

"There isn't one," Betty said. Stretching out a Hasty-Arm, she plunged it right into the wall. A glowing square appeared, surrounding her arm. "This . . . this is going to be a little mind-blowing." She twisted her arm.

Immediately, every line in the walls pulsed, fractured into a million pieces, then scattered up and out. The walls seemed to expand and fall away at the same time, opening up a world . . .

"Vape me . . ." Johnny breathed.

They were in a vast space. Embedded under the ground beneath their treads, dim but clear squares of light sectioned a perfectly flat plain, no two the same size. Far above them—so far that Johnny's mind did boggle at the sight—an arch of sky domed the expanse, lined and dotted and pulsing with the Thread's golden glow.

"Welcome to the outer core," Betty said.

"Where did the hallway go?" Johnny said. Doors he could understand. But this . . .

"Remember, space is an illusion. There was no hallway; just a hidden and relatively safe path for information to travel. We experience the Thread in a way that means something to us."

"So what the hole does this mean?" Shabaz whispered, staring at the sky like she was afraid it was going to reach down and swallow her whole.

Johnny didn't blame her. There were *billions* of specks of light, shining from distances he couldn't even begin to comprehend. And they were layered: there was a depth that could only be registered by instinct. It was almost as if he were in the sky, looking down on the entire Thread far, far below.

"How did we get here?" he asked, trying to wrap his mind around something he could understand.

Betty's stripe tilted. "Like I said, if you know how, in theory you can appear here from anywhere in the Thread." She grinned. "I haven't gotten quite that far yet, but I'm working on it."

"Not much cover," Torg murmured. Around them, a barren landscape stretched out, the horizon as distant as the lights above.

"But not so easy to find, either," Betty said. "You can disappear in space."

"I'll bet you can," Bian said softly.

"Plus, Wobble and I are jamming any scans. We won't be invisible, but at least until we get close to the Core, someone's going to have to look directly at us to see us."

"Well," Johnny said, taking a deep breath. "We didn't come here to gaze and gawk. Which way's the Core?"

Betty pointed and immediately they all saw it. A glimmering of light rising from the surface, more vivid than those against the horizon behind.

"Guns out," Betty said as they started to roll. "Although if the Antis catch us this far out, we're probably grease. SecCore will have too much time to swing a defence our way. The good news: the megalomaniac has pretty much eradicated any Vies around the plain. So we won't have to worry about them. Probably."

"That doesn't make any sense," Johnny scowled. "We know there are viruses in the Core. I mean, the cops are corrupt, right?"

"Like dandelions," Wobble agreed. His skin bristled

with probes, his head slowly spinning to take in the entire plain. "There are no Teddy-Teddy Bears. The shields are down. Wobble."

"Right," Johnny said. "And everything else is breaking down, so there have to be other parts of the Core that are infected or broken."

"All I said was that SecCore managed to get rid of the Vies on the plain. As for the Core . . ." Betty's eye-stalks swayed as if she were remembering something too difficult to believe. "Well, you'll just have to see it when we get there."

They rolled on, awed into silence by the vast space around and above. Johnny found himself glancing back at times with more than one eye, wondering which ghost he was trying to see.

If you can't find us out here, you panzer . . .

They passed a long gouge in the plain, dark and jagged, hundreds of metres wide. If this whole place was a metaphor, then Johnny didn't want to know what that represented. To take his mind off it, he said, "You know what else I don't understand? You said to fix the Skidsphere we had to get inside it. So why are we going to the Core? Is the Skidsphere in the Core?" If the Thread was really as big as the space around them seemed to suggest, then that seemed a pretty ridiculous coincidence.

"Physics are a little wacky here," Betty explained. "The Core is the centre, but it's also everywhere at once. So we're going to the Core to enter the Skidsphere at its heart which is nowhere near the Core."

"We seem to be approaching that area of discourse where my skull hurts again," Torg drawled. "Any idea what we'll see, darling?"

"Not a clue," Betty replied, grinning. "But it will

probably hurt everyone's skull."

Gradually, the glow on the horizon got bigger. At some point, Johnny expected it to solidify into something he could understand: a tower, a fortress, some kind of symbol. But it remained a glowing light, reaching into the sky, growing brighter and brighter until it filled the space in front of them. A great, glowing pillar of light.

"Aw, snakes," Torg said suddenly. He looked at Johnny. "I just figured out what the Core is."

Johnny might have asked him what he meant, but at that moment, they ran out of plain.

"Ladies and gentlemen," Betty said. "Welcome to the Core."

CHAPTER TWENTY-FIVE

The Core didn't rise up. It went *down*.

Light spilled from the edge. It took Johnny a few seconds to realize that the cliff descending into the glow was concave: the space before them a perfect circle, several kilometers across. And below . . .

Johnny was surprised to see so much black; he expected a sea of gold. Instead, most of the space below was the same deep darkness that made up the Thread, stretching down, seemingly forever. The brilliance that rose into the sky came from familiar golden lines threading through the dark, burning a thousand times brighter than any they'd seen before.

He found it impossible to look at them directly. It wasn't just the intensity—he couldn't get a fix. The nearest might have been a few feet below the edge; it might have been kilometers away. It was easier to look into the darkness, beyond those first layers of gold, down to where . . .

"What's going on down there?" Far, far below, shadows

danced across the threads and flashes of white sparkled in the black.

"A war," Betty said grimly.

"It's the Hole," Torg whispered, his eyes fixed on the shadows.

"What?"

Torg's trail-eye gaped at Johnny even as his other two stared into the abyss. "Look at it, Johnny," he said, his voice tight with fear. "It's the vaping Hole. It exists." His eye closed. "Oh, snakes, we're going in there."

Johnny suppressed a shudder as he glanced over the edge. He tried to remember the last time he'd seen Torg frightened. Torg was the calm one, the skid with the casual remark that soothed everyone's nerves and stopped bar fights in the pit. Now, he sounded terrified.

"Hey." Extending an arm, he patted Torg's stripes. "That isn't the Hole. And even if it was, I'm the one going in. With Betty." He forced a laugh. "You get to stay here, you old panzer."

"No, I don't," he said immediately.

"No, he doesn't," Bian agreed softly.

Johnny blinked. "I beg your pardon?"

Near the lip of the Core, glimmering in the glow, Betty sat and watched, one eye on Bian and another on Torg. With the third, she glanced over the edge and said: "Why don't we back up a bit? I'm not expecting SecCore to notice us right away, but let's not take any chances."

They rolled back from the edge, stopping thirty metres away.

"So . . ." Betty said, her voice deceptively bright. "This is a good spot. We could fortify it, set up a bunker for you guys to hold until we return. The Antis probably wouldn't find you; they'll be fixated on Johnny, Wobble and me. Even if you did get attacked, it's a good place to take a stand—you'd have first shot at anything coming out of the Core." She paused. "That was the plan." She paused again. "Why do I get the feeling we're not doing that anymore?"

"Because we're not doing that anymore," Bian said, looking to Shabaz and Torg. Shabaz bobbed an eye in support. Torg didn't move. "We're coming with you."

"You're . . ." Johnny started to protest, then realized two things. One, he didn't know where to start. Two, he wasn't sure he wanted to.

"We're coming," Bian said evenly. "Whatever plan you had isn't going to be the plan anymore. Do you see Albert anywhere?" She looked at Betty. "You needed him, right?"

"That was the plan," Betty agreed, pursing her lips. If Johnny had been a betting skid, he'd have said she looked amused.

"Well, he isn't here," Bian continued. "And that's . . . that's my fault." She raised a hand to stop Johnny before he could protest. "Don't. I know it isn't all my responsibility. Albert . . . Albert has his own demons. But I didn't help." She sighed a long ragged sigh. "And I'm tired of not helping."

"But how . . . ?" He stopped before he got any further. *How are you going to help? Really?* If he said that he was a grade-A jackhole.

Shabaz must have sensed where he was going anyway. "We don't know exactly what we can do," she said, rolling up beside Bian. "But we talked about this, all three of us. We're tired of being baggage. We're skids—you're going to save the Skidsphere. So we're coming." Looking at Betty, she asked: "You said we need to go inside the Skidsphere to save it. Like Albert and Johnny did with me. Right?"

Betty bobbed an eye.

"Right," Shabaz said. "Well, when they did that . . . I think I was part of it. I mean, I helped." She glanced at Johnny. "I did, didn't I?"

That was it. That's what had bothered him when Betty had laid all the praise on him and Albert alone. Shabaz *had* been part of saving her own life: she'd fought for it. From the inside. "Yeah," he said. "Yeah, you did."

Shabaz hesitated, her stripes quivering as if she hadn't known whether or not he would confirm her belief. Then her gaze tightened and she settled into her treads like she could no longer be swayed. "Then maybe I can help here, too. Bian said it: Albert isn't here. Maybe we can't make up for that, but we mean to try."

A feeling trickled along Johnny's skin, so alien that it took him a second to recognize it. It was pride: pride in another skid. His mind flashed back to the Combine, his surprise at how good helping another skid had felt.

"Huh," he said, swinging an eye towards Torg. "And you're in on this?"

Torg took a deep breath. "Didn't get to Nine by sitting out the race, son. Besides . . ." He hefted the rifle in his arms. "Someone's got to watch your back. Recently, you can't seem to remember what a trail-eye is for."

"This . . ." Betty said slowly, as if she were running calculations in her head, ". . . is not a bad idea. It lets Wobble and me focus on forward." She grimaced. "Which is going to be bad enough." Her eyes swept the group, stopping on each of them, holding the look, then moving on. "All right," she said finally. "We all go. You've earned the right to make your own decisions. Who knows? It's not like I really have any idea how this is going to go down."

She rolled over to the edge. "I go first. Wobble next:

he'll stay close to you, keep you supplied. Shabaz, you ride directly in front of Johnny in case Wobble gets overwhelmed." That thought made them all flinch. "Johnny, you're in behind Shabaz. Bian and Torg, you make sure nothing takes us from above."

Johnny grinned at Torg. "Look who's baggage now."

"Just because we're shielding you, doesn't mean you're not getting any action," Betty said grimly. "I don't know exactly what's going on down there, but it's bad. And I don't know how long we're going to have to fall and fight."

"What's the Skidsphere going to look like?" Johnny asked. "What do we aim for?" Betty looked back at him, her lips pressed tightly together. "Right," he sighed. "You don't know that, either."

"I'm almost certain we'll get a reading on it when we're close," Betty said, "but be ready to move quick. Any last questions?"

"Just one thing," Torg said. "Wobble? If I may?"

The machine opened his side compartment. Reaching inside, Torg exchanged his rifle for the massive weapon he'd first admired back in the jungle.

"It's all down from here," he said, hefting a barrel almost the size of Wobble. "Weight don't matter, damage does." He winked at the machine. "How's that saying go? We bring the end?"

A broken grin split Wobble's face. "Like black holes and gravity," he whirred. "Wobble."

"Like black holes and gravity," Betty agreed. "All right, skids. Let's go save the world." She dropped over the edge.

Johnny looked back across the plain a final time. *Any time, jackhole*, he thought. *Now would be better.* But the flatland was empty as, one by one, the skids followed Betty Crisp into the darkness and the light.

CHAPTER TWENTY-SIX

The first thing that struck Johnny was the absence of light.

Nearly a minute passed before the first glimmering thread flashed by, zipping past at unbelievable speed. Before that, it was as if they fell through space, without any idea how far from the walls they were. The only gauge was a circular slice of dome, high above the plain, its already distant glow getting more distant by the second.

Below them, beneath lines that rose up with increasing density, the war between the shadows and the slivers of white raged on.

"Stay tight," Betty said over the com. "We'll start to hit strays any minute now." As if on cue, a shadow peeled out from the darkness to their left. It was torn apart by three separate rounds of rifle fire.

"Keep focused on your area!" Betty snapped. "Don't waste ammo. If Wobble and I need help, we'll tell you."

"Sorry," Bian and Torg muttered together.

Slowly, Johnny began to make out the walls: some threads running vertically and at the same distance, gaining in frequency.

Another shadow and Betty's gun barked again. Then an Anti, clear as day, emerging from the walls and met by one of Wobble's fire-wheels. "Eyes open," Betty said. "You might start getting trouble from above."

"Got one," Torg said calmly. "Hold this," he said to Johnny, handing him the huge gun like they were passing sugar on the top of the Pipe. Reaching into his treads, he removed a small pistol and lined the barrel up with a shadow that was almost invisible against the background above.

"Where'd you get that?" Johnny asked, as Torg shot the Vie.

"Figured I needed something for any one-on-ones. Stole the storing trick when I saw Betty whip out her BFG. May I?" Torg took the huge gun back and slung it under one arm, holding the pistol in the other. "Amazing how light this thing seems when you're falling this fast."

The walls gained definition and the number of attacks increased. Another Anti appeared; Wobble dispatched it with a pinwheel. Shabaz took out a Vie on the other side. Down below, Betty was encountering the first serious pocket of trouble, her BFG barking destruction to clear a path.

And below that . . .

Look at that, Johnny thought, staring into a world of black, white and gold. The Core writhed as if it were a living thing, as wave after wave of Vies attacked the walls and lines of gold, with wave after wave of Antis counter-attacking in return. For a moment, Johnny's senses were overwhelmed and he lost any sense of individual forms:

the inner Core became a single entity—alive and at war with itself.

And they were going into it.

"Uh, Wobble?" Johnny said nervously, staring at the shifting mass. "Maybe you better give me a gun. Make it a big one."

His timing was good. Even as a rifle drifted up to Johnny, a threshold was passed. The walls became clear and distinct: the nearest a hundred metres away, curving around with layer upon layer of lines, tightly bunched. The attacks increased and increased again; they were all firing constantly now. Vies and Antis came from every conceivable angle.

"I really wish these squids would pick a side," Torg grunted, as an Anti disintegrated at the end of his gun.

Johnny kept his eyes in constant motion, holding his fire unless something got through, usually from his immediate side. Bian and Torg each took half the Core above—Bian hurling curses at her targets along with her fire. Johnny didn't remember her acting like that back in the Skidsphere, but whatever worked for her was good with him—the tip of her barrel was a blur, sweeping her half with chaos. Torg's huge gun spat out projectiles that flew a short distance then burst, taking out dozens of Vies at a time.

Just beneath Johnny, Shabaz fell—her eyes and Hasty-Arms split, a gun in each hand—picking off anything that got past Wobble. Meanwhile, the former Anti spun like a miniature version of the scene below: it seemed like every part of him was moving as he swept across the Core. A deluge of weapons streamed from his front, back and sides: wheels of fire, spikes, rockets, pulses of energy, clusters of plasma. At one point, Johnny swore he saw Wobble hit an Anti with a giant hammer.

But Betty outshone them all.

Maybe it was because she was one of them: a skid. Maybe that's why she amazed Johnny even more than Wobble. As Johnny watched her clear a path through a maze of destruction dense enough that it seemed a wall, he got the sense he was watching a skid play every game at once. The Slope, the Pipe, the Skates, Tilt: they were all there. Plus a gun. Okay, half a dozen guns.

Half a dozen Big-Vaping-Guns.

What truly amazed him wasn't the firepower, overwhelming though it was. It was what Betty did with her body. Johnny had pushed the boundaries of what a skid could do; he'd done things during the Drop he was pretty sure no one had done inside the Skidsphere in a long, long time.

But they were outside the Skidsphere now and Betty Crisp—black, pink, and fierce with fifty-five years—was doing things that no skid had even dreamed.

You couldn't even call her round anymore. Her body was a fluid mass, shifting constantly as her stripe blazed like a comet. Jets popping in and out of her torso; she seemed to grow arms at need. She flattened into a knife and sliced through a wave of Vies. An Anti appeared out of nowhere and—unable to bring a weapon around in time—Betty snapped into a donut-shape, the Anti passing through the hole.

Need to remember that one. Be good for mass points on the—

"Johnny!"

The Anti came from the side, fast and lean. Desperately, Johnny began to swing the rifle in his hands—a part of him tried the donut trick he'd just witnessed and failed miserably. Instinctively, he pulled his cells inward, packing them together. The Anti's point gleamed . . .

Bian plowed into the Anti, knocking it off target. Sliding under Johnny, the Anti turned to reacquire, but Shabaz took it out.

"How did you do that?" Johnny breathed, staring at Bian. She'd come out of nowhere, hitting the Anti like a tank.

"Bounced off another Anti," Torg said. "Damndest thing I ever . . . Bian? You all right, sweetheart?"

The red-yellow Seven's face was pale. Grimacing in pain, she stabbed an eye up and off to their right. Still clutching the rifle in its hand, Bian's Hasty-Arm floated about ten metres away, drifting farther behind as they fell.

"Oh, snakes," Johnny breathed. "Can you grow another?" He remembered what Betty had said about Albert's scar.

"I'm trying," Bian said through clenched teeth. "I don't think it works that way. I think I may owe Albert another apology. Crisp Betty, that hurt."

"Everything all right up there?" Betty said over the com, sounds of combat in the background.

"We're fine," Bian growled. She levelled an eye at Johnny and said, "I think we're even now. Try and keep at least one eye on the fight, maybe?"

"Right," Johnny said, appalled.

"Need help on your side?" Torg asked.

"Nope," Bian said firmly. "Just another gun. Wobble?"

They continued to fall and the onslaught continued to get worse. The group tightened up and, like a giant rolling snake, they blazed through the seething mass of black and white. Arms a-blur, Shabaz muttered, "You know, knowing where we're going sometime soon might be nice."

That's when Johnny saw the first hole. On the far side of the Core, an opening appeared in the wall. Inside, he glimpsed a waterfall of light and billions of box-shaped mems darting to and fro. Then another appeared off to their left, this one empty save for a glowing red dot, far in the distance. Then another, open for a second before closing again.

"Be ready," Betty said. "The Skidsphere's going to be in one of those. Don't know what it'll look like, but hopefully we'll get a signal. We'll have to move fast."

Wobble fell tight against Shabaz, screaming destruction. Bian, one-armed and filled with fury, downed wave after wave of Antis and Vies. The air around them was a blur.

How long has it been like this? Johnny thought. If the Out There really was gone—maybe even for thousands of years—then no wonder SecCore had an attitude. Johnny had been here for less than an hour and already his gears were twisted.

"Warning!" Wobble chimed. "Gumballs and James Caan at four o'clock."

"Got it!" Betty said. "Okay folks, I see the Skidsphere, follow me. Right on my tail, this could get nasty."

"I SEE YOU, LITTLE SKID," a familiar voice boomed.

"Well, at least he's got timing," Betty muttered as she dropped back towards the group, even as she cut towards one of the walls.

"I KNOW WHAT YOU ARE DOING, BETTY CRISP."

"I'm fixing your mistakes, jackhole. Care to get out of my way?"

"YOU WILL NOT BE ALLOWED TO DAMAGE THE THREAD, LITTLE SKID."

"I'm not going to damage anything. As for what I'm allowed to do . . . come get me."

They sliced through a whirling clot of black and white. Even though the Antis terrified Johnny more than the Vies, he found himself rooting for them. SecCore was mad, but that didn't mean it wasn't defending something worth defending.

Then the storm parted, and through a hole in the wall Johnny saw what he knew was his home.

"Grab Wobble, we need speed!" Betty commanded, bursting ahead, clearing as much space as possible. Behind her, Shabaz and Johnny latched onto Wobble with one hand and Bian and Torg with the other. Two jets emerged from the machine's body and fired, yanking them forward with a colossal jolt. Like a rocket, they roared past Betty, then down and through the hole.

Inside a glowing blue space, a flickering sphere with platforms scattered all around. Wobble threw them towards one of the platforms. They all swung an eye to watch Betty follow them in.

Except she didn't follow.

Stopping in the centre in the hole, she focused all three eyes on Johnny. "Don't screw this up."

"Wait!" Johnny yelled, "What are you . . . ?"

"They'll come through. We can't fight and do what we need to do. I'll seal the door, keep them busy." Then she reached out, her Hasty-Arms spreading impossibly wide. Behind her, a hurricane of Antis and Vies.

"Wait, Betty, wait—"

"Run the race you're running, Johnny Drop. Save the sphere. Torg, you're kind of cute."

Then she pulled her arms together and sealed them in.

CHAPTER TWENTY-SEVEN

They stared at the wall. Surely, any moment it would open and Betty would . . .

"She's not going to," Torg said harshly.

"Going to what?" Johnny said, staring at the wall. Surely. . . .

"Come back," Torg said, his voice like a bruise. "She'll hold the line. Make sure nothing interferes with us. As long as she can."

"That's probably pretty long," Shabaz said, her body heaving as she sucked in air, slick with sweat. "Did you see her out there?"

"Yeah," Johnny said. He couldn't tear his eyes away from the spot where Betty had disappeared. "But she's alone now . . ."

"Her call," Torg snapped. "Let's get whatever we're going to do done so we can help."

"Maybe one of us—"

"*And how are we going to do that?*" Torg roared. "You

know how to open one of those things? Didn't think so. We're here. We do what she wanted." He took a deep breath and in a voice more resembling his usual patter he drawled, "It's your show, Johnny. What are we going to do?"

That's a real good question. He glanced at Bian. "How are you?"

"My arm's somewhere on the other side of that," she said, pointing her rifle at the wall. "Other than that, I'm sugar. Torg's right: what's next?"

"Working on it," Johnny murmured. He rolled over to the lip of the platform and got his first good look at his world from the outside.

A planet of hollas. A million shots of life, all at once. It was like every highlight ever run bundled together, strung side-by-side-by-side and rounded into a massive ball. The Skidsphere was a sparkling orb of shifting colours and light; every race, every game, every skid radiating from its core.

"Now that's a sight to see," Torg said softly, his eyes shining with the reflected brilliance of their home.

In orbit, ring upon ring of small machines spun around the sphere, zooming in on the hollas. "Cameras," Johnny murmured. "Someone's watching."

"Or was," Bian whispered.

Suddenly, Torg chuckled. "Someone is: us." He chuckled again. "Right now, we're the Out There."

A wave of emotion swelled inside Johnny. Down below, someone was getting popped on the Slope. Another pounded off the paddles in Tilt; another survived the madness of Tag Box. A skid got vaped in a sugarbar. Panzers and squids were learning how to survive in the Combine. Panzers and squids were getting vaped.

These were his people. This was his home.

And it was dying. With his eyes overwhelmed by the flashing stream of images, it took him a moment before he saw it: a huge sprawl of black across the bottom hemisphere. Spikes and razor teeth sawed around its edges, devouring the hollas surrounding it. Johnny noticed a smaller sprawl around the sphere's equator. Then another, near the upper pole. Then another and another; the entire sphere covered in sprawls of darkness, spreading . . .

"Crisp Betty," he swore softly. "It's like Brolin."

"It's like me," Shabaz said firmly. "And I'm still here. Treat it like you treated me."

But it's so big. He didn't say the words out loud. Doubt wasn't going to do anyone much good now. *Run the race you're in,* he thought with ragged determination. Looking to Wobble, he said, "Are you coming with us?"

"Negatory," the machine grinned. "I-We will hold the station, in case Betty fails." A dozen weapons sprouted from hidden compartments until Wobble resembled a demented tree. "You-We will not be bothered. Wobble."

"Guess we won't," Johnny said. He eyed the others. "Last chance to bail."

They all exchanged a look. Bian's stripes tilted. "It's a nice view, Johnny. Bet it's even better up close."

"Let's find out." He tossed the rifle he carried to the ground. "Won't need this."

The others followed suit, Torg gazing at his huge gun with affection. "Can you imagine how many Slopes you could win with one of these?"

"Maybe GameCorps will come up with a new game." Johnny took a deep breath. Another. "Okay, don't know if it will help, but everyone grab hands."

"Guess that means I'm on the end," Bian said dryly.

"Oh, yeah," Johnny said, wondering if her injury

would make her vulnerable. Too late to worry about it now. If she wanted out, she'd have gotten out. "Guess no circle."

"I'll take the other end," Shabaz said calmly.

They strung out. "We aim for the black," Johnny said, squeezing Torg and Bian's hands. "Hit it with names and colour. After that . . . Albert and I got in each other's way with Brolin. Don't know how that could happen in something the size of the sphere, but try to cover my back until I find the core." He looked at Shabaz. "That's how we saved you. That's where we start."

As they edged towards the lip, perched over the sphere of glimmering hollas, they heard a familiar voice.

"I SEE YOU, LITTLE SKIDS."

"Think it starts every conversation that way?" Shabaz mused.

"We must be doing something right if we're getting its attention," Bian said.

"YOU WILL NOT BE ALLOWED TO INTERFERE, LITTLE SKIDS."

"We're trying to help, you panzer," Johnny muttered, trying to judge how far they had to fall. *Snakes, that's a big scar.*

"WE DO NOT NEED HELP, JOHNNY DROP."

"No?" Suddenly, any fear Johnny had evaporated, replaced by anger. "That's not what it looks like outside. You're barely holding your own. And you're wasting energy trying to vape your own allies."

"WE DO NOT NEED—"

"*I don't care!*" Johnny yelled. Somewhere, Betty Crisp was fighting in a sea of black and white. "You don't need help: fine. You want to stop us: *fine.* Then get to it. But if you aren't going to—or you can't—then shut up. We've got work to do." He glanced at the others. "Ready?"

"Drop Johnny Drop," Torg said.

"Right on," Johnny said. And dropped.

Immediately, he started having second thoughts. Not about what they were doing, but how they were doing it. The surface of flashing hollas began to grow: hundreds, thousands, millions of images filling his eyes. *Maybe we should be aiming for that. Get a feel for what's healthy, what isn't broken.*

"Snakes," Shabaz swore softly. Her eyes were wide with awe, glittering as they reflected the sphere.

Maybe not, Johnny thought grimly. *If we're this overwhelmed up here . . .*

Not that the sprawl below wasn't overwhelming. They'd fallen through the broken Thread enough times that its existence alone didn't terrify him. They'd survived the black.

But snakes that sprawl was big.

As it grew, they could make out the edges. They looked fuzzy, but only because every knife and saw and row of teeth was lined with rows of knives and saws and teeth. Which were lined with rows . . .

It doesn't end, Johnny thought, a shiver passing around his stripes. *It never . . .*

Out of the corner of his eye, he caught a single image: a squid in the Combine, white with red stripes, working on greasing her treads . . .

The shiver in his stripes hardened into a bar of rage. *It does end,* he thought. *It ends right here.* Thinking of Wobble, a vicious grin split his face. "Hold tight," he said over the wind. "The first shock will be the nastiest. Remember your name." The black rose to greet them and they dove in: Johnny, Torg, Shabaz, and Bian.

Instantly, Johnny was back in those first terrifying moments on the Pipe: his mind splintering and shattering into a hundred fragments. *This isn't . . .* he tried to think. *This isn't . . .*

The last time they'd gone into the black, Betty and Wobble had been there, leading the way. But Betty and Wobble weren't here: Wobble was guarding their back and Betty . . . Betty might be . . .

I can't . . .

Of course he'd gone into Shabaz. He'd saved Shabaz. But this wasn't some little Vie attacking a skid. This was the Skidsphere. And this black was so deep and sharp and hungry it was a wonder he hadn't been vaped on contact. Inside the dark: faint fragments of gold, but they were broken, broken, broke—

Johnny!

Peg?

His hand throbbed with pain even as he heard the following thought: *Crisp Betty, you know how to make a girl feel special.*

Bian. His hand squeezed again and reflexively he squeezed his other and felt it squeeze in return. Bian was here. And Torg. And . . .

Like I didn't get enough of this already. Shabaz's thought came through clear and fierce.

They were all here. Of course. After all, they'd survived this before. The feeling of being eaten assailed them from every side, but they could feel each other now, solid and strong. If they could find the centre fast enough, maybe they could pull it off.

We need to find the core, he thought at the others. *When we healed Shabaz, we fought from the core.* Centring his own mind, he aimed for what he felt was the middle of the black.

And found nothing. Deeper and deeper he went, but still the darkness went on without end. The broken black ate at their thoughts, biting and cutting and scraping them away. *Johnny,* Bian thought. *Soon would be good.*

But there was nothing. No signs, no images of light . . . no centre.

There had to be. Shabaz had been a ball of black by the time Albert and Johnny had dived into her, and even then there'd been a core of health. Not nearly that much of the sphere was gone; they'd seen that from the outside. Where the hole was the heart? Why couldn't they find the core?

Because there isn't one, a voice came floating out of the darkness. With it, a smear of silver and white.

Jackhole.

CHAPTER
TWENTY-EIGHT

The Skidsphere doesn't have a heart.

Albert?!

And friends, chirped a strained voice.

And Torres? *Where the hole did you come from?*

Out There, Albert said, his thoughts dripping sarcasm. *I see you've brought the gang.*

I didn't bring them, Johnny snapped, stunned and angry and confused. *They brought themselves. Where the hole were you?*

Think we could save Q&A for after the show? Torg's thoughts came, blithe and strained at the same time.

There's an idea, Bian said. He became aware of how hard she was squeezing his hand and remembered where they were: big trouble.

Amazing the effect Albert could have, as Johnny again felt a thousand buzzsaws chewing his skin, his stripes, his mind. This was not something he should've been able to ignore.

What do you mean there's no heart? Johnny asked, dropping everything else.

Isn't it obvious? This isn't a skid—it's the Skidsphere. It's everything. Even if it was just the skids, there'd be a thousand hearts. Seventy thousand. And then the rest of the sphere. Anyone looking at it from the outside should've been able to figure it out.

Well, there were four of us and Wobble, Bian thought angrily, *and none of us did. Anything else you want to explain to the idiots?*

Not the place, people, Shabaz thought.

Shabaz's right, Johnny agreed. *All right Albert, you figured it out. What do we do?*

This time there was a clear rim of guilt surrounding the thought that came out of the darkness: *I don't know.*

WELL, SOMEONE . . . FIGURE SOMETHING . . . OUT . . . Bian screamed raggedly.

They couldn't stay here, they were getting vaped, cell-by-cell. If they didn't find someplace safe and fast . . .

Two ideas came on top of each other: his last thought before they plunged into the black, thinking they should aim for the healthy hollas instead of the broken dark; and the Spike, the oldest place in the Skidsphere. It might not be the heart, but it was the closest thing the sphere had to one, a place where every skid went to find some peace.

Which would be nice right about now.

With the thought, a spar of light flared in the darkness. *Let's go, people. Albert, Torres, grab hold if you can.*

Way ahead of you. A second later Johnny felt a connection, even as they roared towards the light.

He had no idea how they arrived: if they fell from the sky, rose from the earth, tumbled out of the woods—hole, they might have come through the Spike itself. All

Johnny knew was that the light grew into a star; he felt a twisting sensation as they crossed the threshold . . . and then they were there, in the clearing centred by the Spike.

Except it wasn't.

Johnny realized it immediately on some instinctive level, even before he saw the signs. There was no clear path away from the clearing: nowhere to go, only trees, stretching back in every direction. Plus the sky was . . . well, it just wasn't there.

Nor was a stone, etched with a name . . .

Still better then where we were. Which was good, because they were in bad shape. They all looked like Brolin before he died. Black splotches covered their skin. Torg's arm hung at an odd angle; Shabaz's stripes looked like a test pattern.

And Bian . . . Bian looked old.

Her skin hung loose around her body as if it were two sizes too big. She leaned awkwardly, trying to balance, her remaining arm hanging withered at her side. Most of her body was black.

"Snakes, Bian," Johnny whispered. "We need to get you—"

"We need to solve the problem," Bian whispered harshly. "This isn't real. We're still out there, getting eaten. We don't have much time."

As if spoken by a prophet, the first Vies began to emerge from the woods.

"Right," Bian said, shifting on her treads, centring her weight. "Betty always said it was up to you and Albert. So I suggest you two geniuses figure something out while we hold down the fort."

"With what?" Torg said, staring at the Vies coming from every direction. There were hundreds of them.

He glanced at Johnny. "Guess we should have kept the guns."

"Silly boys," Bian drawled in a voice that sounded remarkably like Torg's. "Didn't you listen to Aunt Betty?" Her withered arm snapped up and down—*Cha-Chack!*—and a double-barrelled rifle appeared in her hand. "We are the program," she growled, her grin feral as her skin smoothed a little and the rifle boomed. The first Vie exploded, replaced by another. "Ladies?" she said, looking at Shabaz and Torres as she tread for the woods. "Shall we?"

"Damn straight," Shabaz growled as a rifle appeared in her hands. Torres hesitated, glancing from Albert to Johnny and back.

"Go on, Torres," Albert assured her. "We'll make it work."

Torres held his gaze, then her eyes bobbed once and she turned to face the trees.

"I'll go put on the dress," Torg grinned, following the ladies.

Albert swung a second eye towards Johnny. "Well? You brought us here. What's the plan, squid?"

"We are the program," Johnny whispered.

He wasn't really looking at Albert. He wasn't even watching the fight that was breaking out at all points, explosions beginning to rock the imaginary Spike.

Because it *was* imaginary: this wasn't really the Spike, they weren't really here—they were still somewhere in the black, clutching hands while their skin was vaped.

Of course, if Betty was right, the real Spike wasn't really there, either. The entire Skidsphere was just part of the Thread—all information, created by something out there that probably wasn't there anymore.

"We are the program," Johnny whispered again, the

world around him a blur of darkness and light.

He couldn't cure the Skidsphere like he cured Shabaz—*like* we *cured Shabaz; don't be a jackhole.* The Skidsphere was too big and, more importantly, it had no heart. It had seventy thousand hearts—he wouldn't know where to begin. And the sphere wasn't just sick, parts of it were broken down, the same way the entire Thread was breaking down . . . "We are the program," Johnny whispered a third time.

"You know," Albert growled, "I may need a little more than that."

Johnny's vision snapped back into focus. To his right, the woods were on fire, Torg laying round after round into the trees. Behind him, Bian was roaring like a bear. Swinging a second eye towards Albert, he said: "Wait here a minute."

Albert's eyes flared with contempt. "Crisp Betty, don't you ever learn? We—"

"I'm not going solo," Johnny spat, unable to keep the old resentment completely from his voice. Snakes, he was a pain. "I need something here to tie me to the group, jackhole."

Albert glared at him, then bobbed his eyes. "All right. What am I doing?"

"Don't know yet," Johnny admitted. "But hopefully you'll figure it out when I need you to." Before Albert could make a snide reply, Johnny gathered himself and moved . . . up.

Instantly, he was back above the Skidsphere, floating in space above a sea of highlights. Not far away, Wobble was battling wave after wave of Vies and Antis, pouring through a reopened gap into the Core. Johnny tried not to think about what that meant about Betty.

He considered helping Wobble—the machine seemed

in constant danger of being overwhelmed—but then again, there was plenty of constant danger going around. Somewhere, Johnny heard the sound of gunfire; somewhere else, his skin was being eaten . . .

The race you're in, Johnny thought, turning from Wobble and looking down on his home.

From the inside, he couldn't imagine healing it, he wasn't big enough. But from up here, looking down on his world flickering like a jewel in the night . . . here, he could take it all in, see the entire sphere, love every holla, every skid.

Here, he could imagine it whole.

He didn't try to wipe out the black—he didn't even think about the black. Instead, he concentrated on the light, the images filling his soul. He knew the Skidsphere like the back of his treads. He could picture the whole thing . . .

For a moment, he thought he was doing just that. In his mind, the Rainbow Road unfurled like a wave, every centimetre of track, every line of colour—the exact spot where Betty had started the Leap, the exact spot where she landed. The Slope dropped two hundred dusty kilometers across his vision and Johnny plotted each pebble, popper, and tree with mathematical precision. He knew how far the final ledges lay beneath the finish line down to the millimetre; he knew how far below them lay the eviscerating sea. He knew the popper shaped like a cone of sugar two-thirds of the way down that was death for even the most accomplished skid.

He could see every one: The Pipe; Tilt; The Spinners; Up and Down; Tunnel; The Skates . . .

And that's when he realized he couldn't see every one after all. Because he might have thought he knew the Skidsphere like the back of his stripes, but the truth was no skid could. Each seasoned skid might have played every game a hundred times, but they didn't love every game. Hole, Johnny usually went out of his way to get vaped early in The Spinners—he hated that game. And while he might have been the king of the Slope, it was Albert who was murder on the Skates.

Then why don't you let me do this one, a sardonic voice said. *I get it: good plan. Jackhole.*

Immediately, the image of the Skates grew clearer in Johnny's head: a layer of fragile blue, deep within the ice that he had never realized was there; the violence of the collisions and the elegance of a collision avoided; the nick in one corner on which you could grind a squid.

Nice, Johnny thought, rolling his eyes.

Not everyone could skate like Peg. A surge of anger spun through Johnny before he caught the reverence in Albert's thought. Of course, this was his game; he would admire anyone who played it with grace.

No, Johnny thought, picturing Peg. *No, they couldn't.*

Bit by bit, Albert filled in Johnny's vision: the way the flags furled on the Rainbow Road; the way the pits in Up and Down were crenulated at the edges. The way the bumpers in Tilt got slick, a ring on the Pipe Johnny had forgotten . . .

We don't have it, Albert thought abruptly. *We've got a lot but we don't know nearly enough. Neither of us was ever that great at the Pipe.*

Good thing someone was, Torg drawled and a fresh new wave of sights, sounds and smells washed over Johnny and Albert. *This ain't bad gentlemen, but you forgot a few things . . .*

A few seconds later, even as the sugarbars gained a clarity that he'd rarely experienced inside their confines, Shabaz joined them. Remarkably, she'd spent almost as much time near the Spike as Johnny. Then Torres chimed in and the Combine exploded with detail: the sheer number of squids and panzers; the overwhelming sound of grunts and curses and flesh on plastic, wood, and stone; the fear, the fear, the fear.

Whatever you're doing, came a strained thought, *keep it up, I think it's working.*

Bian? Johnny thought. *Where the hole are you?*

She stayed behind to cover. Like Wobble did. Shabaz's thought was tinged with guilt, even as she painted the saw-blades in Tunnel.

Stayed behind? Johnny's concentration wavered. In his mind, his eyes swung towards the woods, imagining the flood of Vies pouring out from the trees. *We've got to help—*

Somewhere, something squeezed his hand so hard the pain shot through his eyes and a voice roared: *RUN THE VAPING RACE YOU'RE IN OR BY CRISP I'LL RIP THE GREASE-SUCKING STRIPES FROM YOUR SKIN!*

Which focused the concentration quite nicely. Although Johnny did drop a thought Torg's way: *Where'd she find that voice?*

Same place she found the gun.

Together, Johnny, Albert, Torg, Shabaz and Torres envisioned the Skidsphere, piece-by-piece, until . . .

It's still not enough, Johnny thought. *I can't—we can't hold it all.*

We all could, Albert thought.

No, we can't. Even with Torg, Shabaz and—

No, Albert thought, hard and clear. *I mean: we all could. All of us. All the skids.*

How . . . ? Johnny thought even as a jolt went through his stripes. He could almost hear Albert's stripes tilt. *We're here. They're all here somewhere.*

258

Uh . . . Bian's thoughts, rimmed with pain, came crawling through the ether. *Remember when I said it was getting better?*

Time's up, Johnny thought. Either do it or don't. He reached out for the skids, trying to touch every one that still lived and breathed and played somewhere in the Skidsphere.

He failed.

Not like that, Albert thought. *Don't be so specific. You've got to feel it. Like this.* And an image came to Johnny of Albert: his Hasty-Arms spread wide, spread so much wider than they should've been able to go.

At least this time the silver skid had the grace not to call him a panzer. You've got to feel it—hadn't Johnny said that somewhere in the last week?

Seriously, gentlemen, Bian cried, *whatever the vape you're going to do . . .*

Looking down on the sphere he called his home, Johnny reached out his arms.

A thousand, two thousand, seventy thousand minds and memories hit him like a hammer. He might have faltered, but Albert was there—somewhere—helping to guide the storm, then Torg, then Shabaz . . . then Torres. Seventy thousand minds, from the newest panzer, staring off the edge of the Slope as if he could already feel the eviscerating sea far below, to the seasoned Fives and Sixes and Sevens that made up the meat of the games, with all their knowledge and love of the sphere. Every single millimetre of space; the taste of every single grain of sugar; the feel of each pica of dust, ice and rain; the feel, the feel, *the feel* of the world in which they played.

Then Johnny added a final image to the chorus: a clearing, a spike and some woods, free from Vies, the leaves on each tree shimmering in the sun as it looked on the hollas. In a small hollow near the edge of the glade: a stone polished on one side, rough on the other—three letters etched onto its surface as crisp and clean as when they'd first appeared not so long ago.

The last shred of black vanished and the Skidsphere returned to its original state: a million shots of life, living fast, glittering in a sea of blue.

CHAPTER TWENTY-NINE

They reappeared on the platform in orbit, the unflawed Skidsphere glimmering below. Wobble stood nearby, the gap behind him closed once more. Listing to one side, with dozens of metal teeth missing from his smile, the machine appeared as battered as ever. Although, as ever, he was healing.

The same couldn't be said for Bian.

"Oh, snakes," Johnny breathed, rushing to where she lay collapsed. Her skin was black. No sign of her stripes. Pressed flat against the platform, one of her eyes hung over the edge. Johnny thought of the Drop, holding on to his molecules . . .

"She took it all," Shabaz whispered. "All of it."

"Hold on, Bian," Johnny said. The Skidsphere flashed below without a trace of the black that covered Bian's side as it rose in short, weak heaves. "Just stay with us, we'll fix you up."

"Yeah, right," she croaked and the eye hanging over

the edge pulled itself up. "Not this time."

"Shut up, we can do this," Johnny said, trying to pull himself together. After all they'd just done, his mind felt like mush. Even his skin felt exhausted.

"You shut up," she wheezed. "I haven't got long and I think I'll hold the spotlight while I can, Johnny Drop." She had a point. Swinging the only eye she could, she said: "Albert?"

"Right here," Albert said, holding her hand in his own, all three eyes on her. "Right here, Sticks."

"You haven't called me that in a bit," Bian murmured. "I've missed it. I'm sorry—"

"Don't," Albert said. "I knew the rules going in. You don't have to—"

"Anyone else want to interrupt the dying chick?" Bian snapped, and for just a second the ghost of her yellow stripes shone through the black. "You're as bad as he is." Albert sent a guilty glance at Johnny, then squeezed her hand and didn't say anything else. "Better," Bian murmured. "Where was I? Oh yes, I was apologizing for treating you like grease." She chuckled. "It's a wonder what you ever saw—"

"I saw a star," Albert interrupted, his voice tight with grief and pride.

She studied him for a heartbeat. "Okay, that one was sweet. See Johnny, I told you he could be sweet."

Johnny didn't say anything. He wouldn't dare.

"Now I know even a dying girl's last wish isn't going to make you two play nice—you're both too '*boys*' to do that—so how about this: remember what you did here together. I don't care how you feel, what you did to each other in the past; you remember what you and Shabaz and Torres and Torg and . . . oh snakes . . . Betty!" Her eye went wide. "I treated her like crap—snakes, I can be a bitch when I'm nervous."

"I'm pretty sure she liked you," Torg said, his voice as tight as Albert's.

"I'm pretty sure she liked *you*, Torg," Bian said, and again her stripes flickered beneath the black. Then the stripes were buried once more and she fell silent, nothing but the agonizing rise of her breath. "Maybe I would have been better after this," she whispered, her voice barely audible now. "We shouldn't have to die so young. We're just figuring it out. We should have a chance to . . ."

Then her side went still and her eye dropped back over the edge. *Oh*, Johnny thought, unable to think of anything more. He started to reach forward . . .

Bian's body evaporated.

Albert sat like he'd been carved there, staring at the space in his hand where Bian's had disappeared. "See you later, Sticks," he whispered.

An urge to know why he called her that surged through Johnny so strongly that he had to fight it down. Beside him, Shabaz, Torg, and Torres hung their eyes, their stripes dim with grief. Trying to think of something to say, Johnny opened his mouth to speak.

"No one will remember this," Albert whispered harshly.

Johnny blinked. "What?"

Albert was still staring at his hands as if by keeping them open they might fill again. "No one will remember this."

Johnny had a lot of experience with Albert's anger. Albert had a lot of experience with Johnny's own rage. But Johnny had never heard that tone before. "Wait, what are you talking about? Of course she'll be remembered."

"Really?" Albert's eyes swung up and the hurt and venom in them was so vivid Johnny backed up a tread.

"Just what do you think happens now, Johnny Drop?"

"Now?" Johnny said, the word sounding idiotic even as it emerged from his mouth. He was exhausted: Bian was dead; Albert was so pissed it vibrated the air. "What are you—?"

"There's two possibilities," Albert began.

"Look, would you just slow down for a—"

"There are two possibilities," Albert spat. "One: you go back in there," he stabbed a finger at the Skidsphere, "and they pick a hero to celebrate saving the world. Who do you think they'll pick, Johnny Drop? Think it'll be the girl who hopped from skid to skid or the jackhole with two names?"

"Snakes, Albert, I won't let that—"

"The second possibility," Albert said, his voice a hammer, "is the one I'd bet on. That the sphere we just recreated was based on the Skidsphere we knew before we got out here. Which means none of what happened out here happened. And the skids that . . . the skids that died—Brolin, Aaliyah, Bian, all the others—couldn't have died out here because this . . . didn't . . . *happen*. And what's the easiest way for history to justify that?"

"Do you want an answer?" Johnny snapped. "Do I get to say something?"

"The next time the great Johnny Drop doesn't have something to say will be the first."

"Oh would you just back the—"

"You know," Torg drawled, "I'm pretty sure Bian said something about wishing the two of you would get along. Pretty sure I heard that. Course, probably wasn't important." His voice took on a rare hardness. "Being her dying words, and all."

That stopped Johnny. And Torg may as well have slapped Albert. His entire body went still momentarily, then his eyes dropped. "Yeah," he said softly. "She did say something like that."

Beneath them, the Skidsphere dappled like leaves shot with sunlight in the breeze. The only sound was the soft creak and whir of Wobble pulling himself back into shape.

"Albert," Johnny said. "Al," he added, and it was the first time in a long time he'd called Albert that. "Maybe those things happen. I can't stop seventy thousand skids from celebrating . . . from doing whatever the hole they want to do. But we don't have to let them forget Bian or anybody else. Hole, you won't—"

"I'm not going back."

Johnny started to snap something about not interrupting again but he caught himself, glancing at Torg who—having said his piece—now sat silently, watching them with a sombre expression. Behind him, Shabaz and Torres did the same, both overwhelmed by the speed and emotion of the events. They weren't the only ones.

"What do you mean, you're not going back?"

Albert took his time. When he finally spoke, it was like he was choosing each word. "I can't. I can't go back to playing the game. I can't go back to . . . to playing Albert to your Johnny. Like nothing happened." One eye dropped to his hands. "Even if Bian was there . . . I couldn't do that. I can't. I won't." He took a deep breath and sighed. "Go be the star, Johnny. It's what you always wanted." He chuckled. "Hole, it's what we all wanted. Live fast, die fast. Play the games. But not me. Not after this."

Johnny got it. Had their positions been reversed, he'd probably have felt the same. For the first time he put himself in Albert's treads, imagining what it would've been like to be good, even great . . . but not quite great enough. He shuddered. Yeah, that would have full on sucked.

"So . . . uh . . . what are you going to do?"

Albert swung an eye towards Wobble. "Betty didn't make it through." A statement, not a question.

"Affirmative," the machine whirred. "They had-had the entire Antaran army out there, sir."

"Is she dead?"

"Unconfirmed. There was a loss of signal."

Albert appeared to consider this. Then . . . "Want to go see if we can find it?"

Wobble's entire body stopped in mid-whir. "Yes, sir," the machine replied. "Yes, sir, I would."

"Then I guess that's what I'm going to do," Albert said, swinging his second eye back to Johnny.

"That's what *we're* going to do," Torres said firmly, rolling forward.

"Right," Albert said, smiling a rare smile. "That's what we're going to do." Pursing his lips, he looked at Torg. "How about it, squid: want in?"

I'm pretty sure she liked you, Torg.

Torg stared at Albert, his eyes tight and searching. His trail-eye drifted and looked over the edge, down at the Skidsphere. The reflected images popped and flashed in the eye for a minute, then the lid slowly closed.

"Yeah," he said to Albert. Glancing at Wobble, he grinned. "Yes, sir, panzer-sir, I would."

Johnny half-expected Albert to make the same offer to Shabaz. He didn't expect one for himself. "So you think you're going to find Betty?"

"Someone should find out what happened to her. Don't you think she earned that?"

"That's the least she earned." Johnny tried to imagine fighting his way through that storm in the Core alone.

He couldn't do it. He'd just been a part of something pretty amazing himself, but he couldn't imagine taking on that hurricane of black and white by himself. Then he pictured Betty: twisting, turning, doing things most skids wouldn't have even thought to do. If anyone could have survived . . .

Swinging an eye towards Torg, he sighed. "Who's gonna keep me clean at the pits?"

"Johnny, ain't nobody ever kept you clean." A smirk crept across Torg's face. "You'll manage. Got to grow up sometime, squid." His expression sobered. "You get it, right?"

And that . . . that almost broke Johnny. Snakes, he'd miss Torg. "Yeah, you old panzer, I get it." He paused, and then added, "I hope you find her."

They held the gaze, then Johnny swung an eye. "Speaking of panzers . . ." he said, looking at Torres. "You did all right."

Torres cast a guilty glance at Albert, who—lips twitching with amusement—took the moment to go examine the far side of the platform. *He's got some tact after all,* Johnny thought, as Torres rolled right up and leaned in.

"You did too," the young skid whispered. Her expression was so sincere that Johnny almost laughed. "Really."

"Thanks, Torres," Johnny said, fighting down the urge to pat her on the stripe. In a slightly louder voice he added: "Take care of Torg for me, would you? He's crazy old."

"So's your game," Torg grinned.

Shabaz met Albert as he rolled back to the group. "Thanks for everything, Albert," she said. "I mean it, I . . . thanks."

"My pleasure," Albert murmured.

Johnny turned to the machine humming nearby. "You're amazing, Wobble. I don't know what happened to Betty, but I saw you defending us when we were in there. Whatever happened to Betty, she'd have been proud of you."

Gears whirred and the lids over Wobble's lenses tilted. "That-that's my boy and mama's getting it framed. Thank you Johnny Drop Johnny Drop." Two of his arms still hung at a weird angle and one of his teeth was forever gone, but you could still see the Anti that Wobble had been once.

It hurts, he'd said. More than once. Johnny leaned in and whispered: "Keep at it, Wobble. You're making it better."

The lids tilted even more and Johnny half expected tears to appear in the lenses. "Thank you," Wobble said without stuttering. "Thank you."

Johnny bobbed an eye and looked at Albert. "I'm pretty sure all Shabaz and I need to do is jump back into the sphere. How are you getting out of here?"

"Same way Torres and I got in." Albert's stripes tilted. "With Torg and Wobble along, it'll be like popping a squid."

The fact that he didn't actually answer the question just made Johnny chuckle. *Always the gearbox.* Aloud, he said: "Well, don't let us keep you."

That at least drew a smirk. Albert looked at Torg. "You ready?"

"Are we going to need the guns?" Torg said, trying not to sound too eager. Albert glanced at Johnny. "Not at first," he said, still smirking.

Torg swung an eye towards Johnny and tilted his stripes. "I tried. All right, Albert, let's tread."

"Good. Torres?"

"All set, boss."

"Wobble?"

"Affirmative."

Crisp Betty, Johnny thought. *I'd follow the jackhole.* He grimaced. *A little.*

"Get tight," Albert said, rolling over to the edge. As the others joined him, he bunched up.

Johnny rolled his eyes. *Show off.* Before they could leap or launch or whatever the hole they were going to do, Johnny called out, "Hey, Al?"

An eye swung.

"Thanks for coming back. Really."

The eye hesitated, then bobbed once. Then they all disappeared.

Johnny stared at the now empty platform. "Okay. That was cool." He glanced at Shabaz. "Now I want to know how the jackhole did it."

Shabaz chuckled. "He was probably cheating." She peered over the edge. "You sure we just have to dive into that? Seems we had a far longer road to get here."

"I'm not sure of anything," Johnny said. "But Betty said we are the program and this is the only thing I can think of. Unless you got any other ideas."

"Me? I'm just along for the ride."

Johnny stopped. He focused all three eyes on Shabaz. "No. You weren't."

Shabaz held the gaze. "No," she said. "No, I guess I wasn't." She sniffed. "Do you think . . . do you think if Albert was right and it's all just a reset . . . do you think we'll remember Bian and the others?"

That was a good question. "I hope so," Johnny said softly.

"Yeah," Shabaz said. "Me too." An eye wandered

towards the wall separating them from the Core. "Think they'll find Betty?"

"He's got Torg, Torres, and Wobble with him. That's a pretty sweet crew." His stripes twitched. "So yeah, if anyone can do it . . . it's Albert." He chuckled. "I can't believe those words just came out of my mouth."

They lined up along the lip of the platform. "That was a nice thing you said to Albert," Shabaz said, snapping a thinlid into place. "Right at the end. That was good."

"Yeah," Johnny said, looking down on the glimmering sphere below. "Well, Bian was right. We did something here. Together. We should remember that." He glanced at her. "Shall we?"

She smiled back. "Let's go home."

Johnny and Shabaz dived over the edge, heading for home.

CHAPTER THIRTY

Of course, Albert had to be right.

In one heartbeat, Johnny and Shabaz were hitting the flashing sphere, an image of the Slope expanding to fill Johnny's view; in the next, he was sitting at the top of the Pipe.

Beneath him the snow shone pristine and white. Not one shred of black to be seen. The race right after he'd broken Betty's record. This time, he ran it slower than before, pulling a couple of tricks to make it legit. Mainly, he was watching, waiting for the black to appear. By halfway down, he knew it wouldn't.

That wasn't the only difference.

No Albert to cut him off at the start. No Dingo, squeaking from a near miss on the rings. No sign of Torg, no sign of Torres.

No Bian.

About two-thirds of the way down, he caught sight of Shabaz on the far side, running like he was: slow and watchful. Their gaze met. They passed by each other twice, then crossed the finish line at the same time coming from opposite sides, dead last.

"You see anything?" Johnny said, even as he heard dozens of skids murmuring in surprise. After all, Johnny didn't finish last too often in anything.

"Not a thing," Shabaz said. "I don't think they're here."

"Let's check the boards."

They got to the leader boards and stared at them in silence. "Huh," Shabaz said at last. "Looks like there's a Level Ten."

"Looks like someone else is a Level Eight."

"Never even got to taste Seven," Shabaz murmured. Around them, hundreds of skids came and went, checking the boards, exchanging trash-talk, living their lives. Living them fast.

"Couple of weeks back," Shabaz said, "if you'd asked me, I'd have said that if I made Eight before I died, I'd die happy. But now . . . hole, I could make Nine easy."

"Or you're a Nine already," Johnny said softly. "Maybe better."

Shabaz nodded. "They don't mean anything, do they?"

It's a good question, Johnny thought two days later.

He was at the Spike. The real one—there was a stone near his treads, etched with a name. The sun shone down as it always seemed to here, dappling the leaves in the trees, creating shadows and light on the wood.

"At least you're here," he said to the stone, gazing at Peg's name.

No one remembered any of the skids that had gone into the black. Johnny and Shabaz confirmed it the first night back, quietly dropping names at a sugarbar and drawing blank looks. They spent the next day piecing together the new history: Johnny had been awarded Level Ten after breaking Betty Crisp's records; Shabaz was an Eight on the verge of Nine, one of the hottest skids since, well, since Johnny. There were only four Level Nines, none named Torg. There was no Bian, Brolin, or Daytona. No Albert.

How could you have a Johnny without an Albert? He just couldn't wrap his mind around it. "It's like me without you," he said to the stone. Snakes, it was worse than that.

Staring at Peg's name, he wasn't sure how he felt. Part of him believed what Betty had said: Peg was gone, all the things he'd seen and heard were just ghosts. It made sense, except . . .

I miss you too.

Of course it was just another type of ghost: sight didn't have to be the only sense fooled; he'd heard her voice before, in the ether. It was just a ghost. Except . . .

"I miss you too," he said to the stone. "I guess I'll just have to make peace with that."

He was going to have to make peace with a few things. He was a Ten, something he'd dreamed of his entire life. The youngest Ten ever.

Except that might not be true. Betty had said there'd been Level Tens before her—hundreds of skids with two names, maybe more. With their record wiped every ten or fifteen generations. When Betty had first explained it, Johnny hadn't understood how that could possibly happen, but he understood it now. Shabaz and he were in the middle of it: two skids knowing a history that no one else shared.

There must've been other skids like them in the past and they'd probably done what Shabaz and Johnny were doing now: they kept their mouths shut. Run the race they were running.

Not that Johnny had done much of that since they'd returned. Shabaz had—"I gotta vapin' do something," she'd muttered in the Skates pit—but Johnny had skipped the three events on his schedule. That got noticed, especially because it was him. Still, it probably wouldn't matter after he competed in the Slope later today. He couldn't skip it, he still had a record to extend, and besides . . . he was Johnny. He couldn't skip the Slope.

But he did wonder if it mattered. All his life he'd played that game, won at that game, and then looked up and out, wondering who was watching. Now he knew that there was a pretty decent chance that no one was watching at all. No one to remember the name Johnny Drop.

Just like no one remembered Bian.

It was strange, but that bothered him more than losing his own legacy. Albert had been right: she should be remembered. He was beginning to understand just how angry Albert had been that moment after she died. It was *insane* that no one knew who she was, that no one knew her name.

"They should remember all of them," Johnny said to the stone. "Even Albert." He grimaced. "Yeah, I know, shut up."

He couldn't bring them back. He couldn't rewrite the history that had been rewritten. But not long ago in both histories, something had created a stone, a memorial for a skid that had not been forgotten. The only memorial of its kind. Who knows why; probably because it made for good watching—a story within the story of the best skid alive—and because somewhere in the Thread something was still worried about the watching, even if no one was on the other end. Whatever the reason, the stone had been made. Skids born after Peg would know her name, even if they had no idea who she'd been.

"We are the program," Johnny whispered, staring at

the stone near his treads. Then he swung all three of his eyes and focused on a spot beside the stone.

He thought of Bian. He thought her in the sugarbars, flirting with any skid nearby. He thought of her with Albert; he thought of her coming here, to this very spot, to ask Johnny to back off. He thought of her with Daytona and Brolin and Shabaz, trying to offer what little comfort she could. He thought of her bitching at Betty, of her being a bitch to Albert. He thought of the moment she'd kissed him on the cheek. He thought of her in a clearing like and not like this one: a double-barrelled rifle in her hands as she snarled, "Ladies?"

He thought of her dying, asking Johnny and Albert to remember what they'd done.

Together.

A second stone appeared by the first. Johnny stared at the name on it for a long time. "I'll miss you too," he whispered. One of his eyes swung, up and out. "That's the best I can do. I know it's not enough . . . but it's all I could think of."

Sunlight and shadow dappled the surface, fluttering across Bian's name just as it did on Peg's. Maybe no one other than he and Shabaz would know who the second stone was for, but that didn't matter.

"Torg deserves one," he murmured. "Hole, they all do." He pursed his lips and checked the time. Creating the stone had taken longer than he'd thought; he had a game to get to. "Maybe I'll come back tomorrow." Really, every skid that went into the black deserved some kind of memorial.

Even Albert? The thought came and Johnny snorted. "Well," he said to the empty woods. "Maybe I'll do his last." Turning on his treads, he looked a final time at the stone he'd created. "See you later, Sticks," he said, wondering what it meant.

He paused by the Combine on the way to the Slope. He could already hear skids filling the stands not far away; the Skidsphere's most popular game built near the Combine, so all the panzers and squids could hear the roars of adulation they dreamed one day would be theirs. Johnny may have broken Betty's record, but the novelty wouldn't wear off for a while: every skid not in the race would be in the stands today.

Maybe not every skid, Johnny thought as a Two darted down the ramp, glancing back towards the Slope as he slipped inside. Johnny didn't blame him; not getting eviscerated was good motivation to practice. Before he realized what he was doing, Johnny followed him inside.

Settling into the same nook by the entrance, he leaned on the wall as hundreds of squids and panzers milled about. As before, no one noticed him there. He could hear the Slope through the opening in the roof; it wouldn't be long before he'd have to go.

He looked towards the grease-pit. Several skids were working at greasing their treads with various levels of success. Not the skid he was looking for, however. Disappointed, he looked away. *Hey, the squid can't be here every . . .*

He stopped. "Well, what do you know?" he murmured, bumping off the wall.

He remembered the first time, watching the Ones and Twos collide with a wall designed to teach them how to absorb energy. *They might as well be tickling it,* he remembered thinking.

This time, one particular skid was doing a little more than that.

WHAM! The sound boomed as the squid slammed into the wall. She picked herself up, shook her stripes, then reset with a grim determination, geared up and did it again. *WHAM!* The other squids and panzers, moving at half her speed, kept glancing in her direction.

Johnny watched the wall absorb some of her energy. But not all. The Two's body flattened slightly, then snapped back into place. *She's learning*, he thought with a grin. It had only been five days.

She'd learned to trail an eye as well. As he approached, she noticed him and stopped. The other Ones and Twos, glancing at her, followed her gaze.

A small section of the Combine went dead quiet.

"Uh . . . hey." Unblemished red stripes on clear white skin widened in surprise. "You came back."

"I did." Around them, skids began to whisper. "What happened to the dragon?"

The stripes flushed. "I got rid of it." Her gaze grew shy. "You don't wear any glam. I . . . I thought that was kind of cool."

"Really?" he said, genuinely pleased. "Well, I think that's pretty cool." He glanced at the wall. "Hitting that pretty hard," he observed.

She winced. "Yeah, it's starting to hurt. Did you know you can change the safety settings?"

He smiled. She *was* learning. "You can turn them off, too." More skids, noticing the lack of activity, began to gather.

"Yeah." Her stripes tilted. "I haven't had the guts to try that yet. You were right though, thinking of colour really helps. If I had a name . . . I'd try that to." He could hear the yearning in her voice.

Johnny studied the two red stripes. It suddenly occurred to him that even if the numbers might not mean as much to him anymore, they did matter. They meant something to seventy thousand skids—they meant life and death. The difference between Two and Three. About not having a name or . . .

Not long ago, he'd suggested a name to a squid named Aaliyah. About the same time, Albert had let a panzer name herself.

He decided he liked Albert's way better.

"If you could have a name, any name . . . got one in mind?" The stripes flushed and he laughed. "Why don't you tell me?"

She hesitated, suddenly still. Then . . . "Onna. I keep . . . thinking it. All the time."

"Okay. How about you focus on that for a while?"

"But what if GameCorps gives me a different name?"

She's already assuming she's going to make Three. Crisp, I like this kid. Aloud, he said, "If that happens, then you'll switch to the new one." Johnny was pretty sure she wouldn't need to switch.

He rolled over to the wall. Switched off the safeties. "You don't have to hit it at full gas the first time, but don't go soft. Try three-quarter speed. Think of your colours. Think of the name Onna."

Another hesitation. Then her stripes went stock-still and a look of determination hardened across her face. She took a deep breath. Geared up.

WHAM!

Her body compressed, started to shake . . . then snapped back into place. She hissed through her teeth.

"That was great," Johnny said. "Now do it again. Harder."

"Uh, excuse me?"

A silver skid with green stripes tread forward. He pointed at Onna. "Do you . . . could you teach me how to do that?"

Silver, Johnny thought, suppressing a smile. Watching

Onna with his trail eye, he looked over the crowd that was growing by the minute. *Snakes, they're young.* Bian had been right, he realized—her and Betty both. They were all so young.

Maybe they didn't have to stay that way.

Every skid, even if they got their name, still died after five years. That was another number that mattered—the hardest number. But one skid had lived longer than that, more than ten times that long. And if she could do it . . .

Somewhere, Johnny's friends were looking for that skid; a skid with a single bright pink stripe. He couldn't help them . . . but there were other skids in the universe.

Through the gap in the roof, the cheering from the Slope rose. Soon, they'd gather at the starting gates, preparing to line up. Not long now. Not long at all.

The silver skid glanced up, towards the sound. "We could do it later, if you want." He flushed, as if he suddenly realized what he was asking, who he was asking it from. "I mean, we don't have to, I just—"

"No," Johnny said. "It's okay. We can do it now."

Behind him, a white skid with two red stripes stopped what she was doing. "Don't you have a game to get to?" she asked.

Johnny listened to the noise coming through the ceiling. It was loud, though not so loud as the skids around him, coming and going, desperate to learn. Living fast . . .

"Nah," he said, smiling at the skid. Her name was Onna, even if she didn't know it yet.

"I'm good here."

CONTINUE READING FOR A PREVIEW OF

THE THREAD WAR

THE NEXT CHAPTER IN THE JOHNNY DROP SAGA

SLAM!

"Again."

SLAM!

"Again."

SLAM!

"Again," Johnny Drop said, watching the pile of panzers and squids moan their way back onto their treads. The Level Ones and Twos rolled back to the starting line. The safeties were still set on the crash pads, but at least the group was hitting them with some authority now. The beige-yellow Level One on the end had a lot of potential. She'd get her second stripe soon.

Letting an eye drift, Johnny took in the entire Combine. Slide-rock filled the massive centre bowl, pounding off the walls. Everywhere, One and Two level skids practiced the skills they needed in the game, desperate to learn how to control their molecules and survive being evaporated. Skids on spin mats spun, skids on treadmills tread, skids on weave-drills weaved.

Next to the crash pads, skids bounced back and forth between bang bars, learning to take a hit. Nothing like what they'd face on Tilt or the Spinners, Johnny thought with a grin, but it was a start. On the pressure pads, huge blocks not-so-gently squeezed skids between them, getting the panzers ready for the more deadly versions in Tunnel. Skids were violently rotated on gyroscopes or thrown about in wave pools. Some worked in the empty spaces just absorbing and popping their Hasty arms, one of the skills that took a skid from level One to Two.

Dozens of skids worked the row of crash pads, many of them glancing nervously at the group working with Johnny. Despite his willingness to help and their desperation to get better, the majority of the Ones and Two still wouldn't seek his help.

He didn't blame them: it *was* weird.

"Again," he barked, keeping one eye on his trainees even as he let the other two wander. It wasn't because he wasn't focused; it was a subtle reminder to any skid watching that they needed to split their vision and focus on multiple things at once. He grinned—the panzer trying the gyroscopes for the first time was still looking at everything with all three of her eyes. She'd be puking sugar in five minutes tops.

He'd been in the Combine every day since they'd returned from the Thread to find a world reset to the moment they'd left. Reset except for no Albert, Torg, Bian, or the others who'd fallen from the Pipe with them that day two months ago. Reset with Johnny a Level Ten and Shabaz a Nine.

But even those numbers might not be right. For the

first few weeks, Johnny had at least *tried* to play the games, only coming to the Combine in his down time. But it had become clear very quickly that Johnny and Shabaz were far beyond anything the Skidsphere had experienced in Johnny's lifetime. He remembered the day they'd destroyed Tag Box: Johnny and Shabaz in the centre of the carnage, every other skid vaped, with half the time left on the timer. They'd looked at each other and left the game. Johnny hadn't been back since.

Shabaz had, but not in the same way.

Tag Box had also made Johnny realize he'd moved beyond the games in other ways, too: he couldn't vape skids any more. He didn't even like doing it with skids over Level Three who he knew would come back. But the first time he vaped a Two after he'd returned . . . he'd gone out to the woods for a day and broken down, crying the entire time.

Since that day, Johnny had been in the Combine continuously, helping any skid who asked. And the amazing thing was . . . he wasn't the only one.

"Crisp Betty, Akash," a snarl came from nearby, "stop tickling it and hit the damn thing."

Suppressing a smile, Johnny let one eye drift towards the far side of the crash pads, where a solitary white skid with four red stripes was helping a solitary mint-green skid with two lemon stripes. Although, the word, "*helping*" might be highly dependant on your point-of-view.

"I *am* hitting it, Onna," the squid protested, visibly exhausted. "Gimme some credit, the safeties are off."

The senior skid rolled over and bumped the squid's treads, harder than Johnny would have. "They've been off for two hours. And you've hit it with the same gas the last six attempts. I said: *hit it full*."

"If I do, I could die."

Onna swung a second eye. Somehow, she made it loom over the other skid; Johnny was going to have to learn how she did that. "Or . . . you might never die again." She grinned. "At least 'til you're five."

The squid they'd started calling Akash let his eyes retract. "Easy for you to say," he grumbled. "You've got your name. Mine's just pretend."

Onna's eyes narrowed. Then she sniffed and swung her whole body, rolling away. "Keep hitting the pad that soft and it'll stay pretend." She didn't even bother trailing an eye.

Ouch, Johnny thought, suppressing another smile as a horrified expression spread across the squid's face. It was obvious he had a crush on Onna. It was equally obvious that the squid called Akash was on the verge of Level Three and had potential to do a lot more, otherwise Onna wouldn't have bothered to give him so much time one-on-one.

Well, maybe that last part's not so obvious, Johnny thought, watching the squid's face. For a second, Johnny thought Onna had gone too far—the poor kid looked crushed.

Then another expression settled into the Two's stripes. He rolled back to the start, slowly but with purpose. Sat there a minute, staring at the pad. Flicked an eye in Onna's direction.

Then he geared up and tread.

SLAM!!!!

Everyone on the pads turned and looked as the impact echoed through the combine. The mint body compressed and the two stripes appeared to shatter. For a second, Johnny thought it was done; the squid really had hit too hard.

Then the stripes reformed and the mint body returned to something resembling round. Almost round. The poor kid looked like he might throw up.

"Crisp Betty," one of the panzers working with Johnny breathed.

"About vaping time," Onna's voice cut through the chatter of the Combine. Johnny was going to have to figure out how she did that too. When a shaky eye swung in her direction, she added, "Nice work, squid." What might have been a smile.

Slowly, the mint green body settled into its three lemon stripes. "I'm not a squid. I'm Akash." He grinned.

Onna sniffed and rolled away. "We'll see, squid." This time, there was definitely a smile.

Of the many amazing things that had happened since their return, Onna was possibly the most amazing of all. She was the first skid Johnny had ever helped—he smiled at the memory of her freaking out the day she'd realized who was talking to her in the Combine. He'd been thrilled when she'd made Three, relieved that she would at least survive until her fifth birthday. He'd expected her to do well.

What he had not expected was for her to return to the Combine one week after she'd left.

He'd been helping a group on the pressure blocks when she'd rolled down the ramp, obviously nervous. He watched her sit at the bottom of the ramp, staring at the Combine like it was a foreign country. Then her stripes had flared once and she'd rolled over to the grease pads and started barking orders.

She was a lot more tough love and manipulation than Johnny was, which wasn't a bad thing—they actually complemented each other. She sometimes got results when Johnny didn't. And she was only a Level Four, moving up rapidly from Three. She remembered even more than he did what it was like to be a squid.

And she wasn't the only one. Nigel, the first skid who'd ever asked Johnny for assistance had shown up a week ago, his eyes bowed as he asked Johnny where he was needed. Right now, he was across the centre court, trying to teach the panzers at the tracking station to split their eyes and follow multiple targets.

There were only three of them so far, but they were getting results. Since Johnny had begun training skids in the Combine, more and more Ones had made it to Two, and more and more Twos had made it to Three. A record number of Threes and Fours played the games now; Johnny and Shabaz had begun tracking the data and there were already seven hundred skids over Three. Given that historically there had rarely been more than five hundred, it was an amazing increase.

Shabaz told him they were doing better in the games too, a large percentage of the recent Combine grads jumping from Three to Four in less than two months.

Of course, not everything was sugar. In one of the hollas, he caught a squid he recognized getting shredded on a spike pit in Tunnel. A pain shot through his stripe and he swallowed the grief.

This was the worst aspect of helping at the Combine: he cared. Everyday, he helped dozens if not hundreds of panzers and squids, and every day most of them didn't make it back to the Combine. He hated watching the highlights now, not because he was no longer in them, but because he'd see some One or Two he recognized getting vaped.

Constantly.

Most of the time it was only a vague feeling of recognition—like he'd passed them on the ramp—but even that was horrible. It was like every squid and panzer in the Combine had become as important as Shabaz.

At least that one made it, Johnny thought, watching the newest Three make his way out of the Combine. Akash was Shabaz's to work on now. That had been her solution to their situation: she worked on the skids in the games. It was a good system, she took over where Johnny left off—spotting the skids who might have real potential to advance and working on them in the games, the sugar bars, and more. Johnny had a feeling she was the reason why Onna and Trist had returned to the Combine.

And maybe there's more help on the way, Johnny thought, as Akash passed a group of skids huddled at the bottom of the ramp, staring into the combine. Most of them were Fives and Sixes from the look of things, although the yellow-black skid in front was a Seven.

Or maybe not help, Johnny thought, catching the expression on the Seven's face. He did not look happy. Trist—the skid's name was Trist.

The skid briefly made eye-contact with Johnny. Yeah, definitely not pleased. He muttered something to the teal-plum Six beside him, who bobbed an angry eye in agreement. Then the whole group turned and rolled back up the ramp.

Wonder what that's about.

Johnny didn't have time to follow the thought, as the ground beneath his treads began to rumble.

ABOUT THE AUTHOR

Ian Donald Keeling is an odd, loud little man who acts a little, writes a little, and occasionally grows a beard. His short fiction and poetry have previously appeared in *Realms of Fantasy*, *On Spec*, and *Grain*. He's on the faculty for sketch and improv at Second City in Toronto and likes all forms of tag and cheese. *The Skids* is his first novel.

ACKNOWLEDGEMENTS

Welcome to the acknowledgements section! Please don't stop reading now, you made it this far. *The Skids* is my first novel, so bear with me because I have many people to thank for helping this weird little dream come true.

In 1982, I read a little book called *This Can't Be Happening At MacDonald Hall*, written by a young Canadian writer named Gordon Korman. I was eleven at the time and when I read that Korman was twelve when he wrote his novel, I thought: I can do this! And off I went.

Now I'm forty-five years old and here I am. It's a cliché, but it really has been a long, strange trip.

So many people kept me going over the years. Simon Donner has been one of my closest friends and supporters since high school. David and Reagan White did the same, including a wild night in Philadelphia when I first got my agent (More on her later). Mary Haynes gave me work and libations, two essential supplements to any writing career. Al Smith and Cary West have been both my business partners and close friends.

I have to thank all the organizations that have

supported me over the years, if for no other reason than they allowed me to eat, another one of those essential supplements. I have the privilege of working at The Second City in Toronto, and I'm grateful to everyone there, in particular Kevin Frank, Erin Conway and all the people in the administrative offices that put up with the weird little man prowling their classrooms and theatres. Mysteriously Yours, Theatresports Toronto, and The Bad Dog Theatre have all employed me at various times and have been wonderful places to work.

For a long while, I wandered in the woods when it came to my writing peers, but in 2009 I attended the Ad Astra conference in T.O. for the first time and found my kin. Adrienne Kress and Lesley Livingstone were kind enough to the weird little man following them around—sense a pattern?—and have been kind ever since. Derek Molata and I traded sad stories and beer, a fine combination. Later that year, Suzanne Church and Doug Smith personally took me around Anticipation World Con in Montreal and introduced me to about half the science fiction and fantasy community, for which I am grateful to this day.

It was also at Anticipation that I met Leah Bobet, who has published my short stories, introduced me to my writer's group, and been a great friend. She was also one of the two major beta readers for *The Skids*, and the novel is so much better for her input.

The other reader is Chris Szego, who in addition to managing Bakka Books and offering sound and profound notes on *The Skids*, also deals with the weird little man who keeps barging into her store and demanding coffee. I cannot begin to overstate her importance to the genre community in Toronto, nor how important her support has been to me. Thanks to all the staff at Bakka for their support and patience.

I mentioned writer's groups and I'm fortunate enough to be associated with two. The TorKidLit group that meets once a month at the Bedford Arms has been a great solace to me. And The Stop Watch Gang, my critical writers group, which includes the aforementioned Suzanne Church, but also Richard Baldwin, Brad Carson, Karen Danylak, Costi Gurgu, Stephen Kotowych, Tony Pi, Mike Rimar, Pippa Wysong. All are exceptional writers and all have exceptional patience for dealing with . . . well, you know.

Special thanks must go out to my agent, Miriam Kriss of the Irene Goodman Agency. She was one of the first professionals to show faith in my work and has worked tirelessly for me ever since our hooking up in 2009. Plus, she introduced me to sour beers, which is grand.

Thanks go out to the members of the ChiZine family—and though it is a press, it is a family too. To Sandra and Brett and the incredible effort they bring to the Canadian genre community. To Sam for helping get the final draft in shape. To Erik for a simply outstanding cover—I saw it and thought: oh, that's what they look like. And to all the ChiZine authors, in particular Michael Rowe, who bought me my first beer as a professional author, which is the best damn beer I ever tasted.

And finally to my family: my mother and my father, my brother David and sister-in-law Kat. I've been a weird little man for a long time and they've put up with me for the longest. Thank you for everything.

And finally-finally . . . if you're reading this, thank you. So much. This is my first published novel, and it doesn't exist without you. I hope you liked it. I hope I write you a better one in the future. Thank you all.

UNLEASH YOUR WEIRD

DID YOU ENJOY THIS BOOK? CHECK OUT OUR OTHER CHITEEN TITLES!

PARASITE LIFE
VICTORIA DALPE

Life in small town America is hard for Jane. On top of the usual teenage troubles with peers and homework and boredom, Jane lives alone in a strange old house with her invalid mother. Her mother has been near catatonic for years, afflicted by some strange wasting disease. It's only Jane who keeps her alive, day in and day out. Day in and day out. Day in and Day out.

But then one day everything changes. A new girl shows up in school. Her name is Sabrina and she sees something in Jane that she doesn't even see in herself. Their friendship will push Jane to unearth the mysteries of her mother's past and the dark history of her missing father. Forced to face a monstrous lineage, Jane will have to make decisions about just who and what she wants to be.

AVAILABLE OCTOBER 2016
978-1-77148-397-1

CHITEEN.COM

FLOATING BOY AND THE GIRL WHO COULDN'T FLY

P.T. JONES

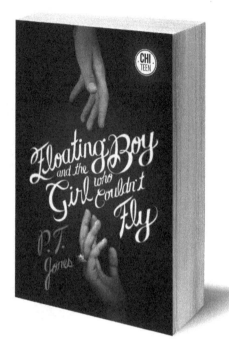

This is the story of a girl who sees a boy float away one fine day. This is the story of the girl who reaches up for that boy with her hand and with her heart. This is the story of a girl who takes on the army to save a town, who goes toe-to-toe with a mad scientist, who has to fight a plague to save her family. This is the story of a girl who would give anything to get to babysit her baby brother one more time. If she could just find him.

AVAILABLE NOW
978-1-77148-173-1

ALSO AVAILABLE FROM CHITEEN

THE DOOR IN THE MOUNTAIN
CAITLIN SWEET

Lost in time, shrouded in dark myths of blood and magic, *The Door in the Mountain* leads to the world of ancient Crete: a place where a beautiful, bitter young princess named Ariadne schemes to imprison her godmarked half-brother deep in the heart of a mountain maze . . .

. . . where a boy named Icarus tries, and fails, to fly . . .

. . . and where a slave girl changes the paths of all their lives forever.

AVAILABLE NOW
978-1-77148-191-5

The Flame in the Maze picks up the thread of the tale begun in *The Door in the Mountain*. The Princess Ariadne is scheming to bring her hated half-brother Asterion to ultimate ruin; Asterion himself, part human, part bull, is grappling with madness and pain in the labyrinth that lies within a sacred mountain; Chara, his childhood friend, is trying desperately to find him. In a different prison, Icarus, the bird-boy who cannot fly, plans his escape with his father, Daedalus— and plots revenge upon the princess he once loved. All of their paths come together at last, drawn by fire, hatred, love and hope—and all of them are changed.

THE FLAME IN THE MAZE
CAITLIN SWEET

AVAILABLE NOW
978-1-77148-326-1

ALSO AVAILABLE FROM CHITEEN